RELICS OF THE WOLF

MAGNETIC MAGIC
BOOK 2

LINDSAY BUROKER

1

FOUR AIR PURIFIERS WHIRRED, THE DUCTMASTER 5000 RUMBLED, and my XTreme Power steam cleaner roared across the carpet like a Ford Mustang on the final lap of a NASCAR race.

A few days ago, I'd heeded the moon's call and turned into a powerful and noble wolf, hunting magnificent prey with my pack. Now, I was attempting to eradicate the smell of cigarette smoke from an apartment. As my sons had been quick to point out before they'd left home, my life wasn't the most glamorous. Or *bussin*. That had been their word.

"Hi, Luna," came a call over the noisy equipment. Bolin, my twenty-three-year-old intern, leaned into the entrance of the apartment. "Should you have the door open with your back to it when there are known muggers in the area?"

"Don't worry. I'm armed." I patted the machine I was wielding with two parts efficiency and one part irritation. We had a no-smoking-indoors rule that was highlighted no fewer than four times in the lease, but Mrs. Chang had desecrated the unit with her two-packs-a-day Marlboro habit. There was no way I would refund her damage deposit.

"With... a vacuum cleaner?"

"It's a one-hundred-and-seventy PSI commercial-grade carpet cleaner that heats the water tank to two-hundred-and-ten degrees Fahrenheit." I hefted the steam wand. "I could flay every skin cell off your body from here."

Bolin wrinkled his nose. "Flaying involves peeling skin away. You'd be scalding someone with that."

"What's the origin of the word flay? Are you *sure* it's not appropriate? Did you ever get any words that simple in your fancy collegiate spelling bees?"

"I did not, no. But it's from the Old English flēan, which came from the Old Norse word flā meaning *to peel*."

"Wow, you even know roots that aren't Latin or Greek?"

"English words have antecedents from all over the world. The more you learn about where something originates, the more you'll know about it as a whole."

When my intern had first shown up without warning, I hadn't wanted him, especially since he was the son of my wealthy employers, the Sylvans, who owned this complex and many others. But, with a mixed heritage that included a grandfather who'd been a real druid out of Ireland, Bolin had turned out to be unexpectedly helpful, even employing magic to eradicate mold in one of the units. Doing something useful for the complex was the quickest way to my heart. That and high-quality dark chocolate.

"You probably didn't want to know all that," Bolin admitted sheepishly.

"I did ask."

Bolin tilted his head, as if I were a curiosity. Or maybe a *rarity*. "You did, didn't you?"

I turned off the steam cleaner so we wouldn't have to yell over the noise, though I left the air purifiers running. It would take a lot to get this apartment rentable again. I had a vinegar solution with vapors potent enough to kill flies—and possibly small mammals —waiting so I could spray all the window screens.

"You're useful, Bolin. I hope your parents are paying you well for this gig."

The next nose wrinkle was so intense that it showed me all the hair in his nostrils. "They're not paying me at all for it. As I think I told you before, I'm earning real-world experience and proving my worth before they hand me the reins to a *real* job with their company."

"The one that involves traveling to their apartments in exotic places?" I recalled he'd mentioned Saint Lucia and Singapore, among others.

"Yes." Bolin sighed wistfully as he looked toward the drizzle pattering on the fallen leaves that had coated the lawn since my last pass with the backpack blower.

When I'd been a teenage girl turning into a wolf and hunting with my pack, I'd never envisioned the collection of power tools and cleaning equipment that I would one day wield.

"They must at least pay you an allowance. You spend fifteen dollars on coffee drinks before the workday even begins." I hadn't seen my caffeine-powered intern arrive at the complex in the mornings with fewer than two espresso-stand beverages clutched in his hands. "And I'm positive gas for your Mercedes G-Wagon costs a pretty penny. What's that get? Three, four miles per gallon?"

"Ha ha."

"I *know* it's not more than twenty."

"It's thirteen. Fifteen if I will magical power into it when I park it at night."

"Are you allowed to use druid *nature* magic to enhance gas-powered monstrosities?" I asked. "That seems like it should be against the rules. In fact, I'm surprised your blood doesn't compel you to wreck that SUV against a tree. Or maybe a boulder. You wouldn't want to damage a tree."

Bolin squinted at me. "Your truck isn't an eco-blessing either."

"It's a small truck, gets okay gas mileage, and I use it to haul supplies and equipment for work. The only thing I've seen you use your SUV for is to tote you and your coffee cups."

Bolin took a pointed sip from his beverage. "I don't think one of your duties as my mentor is to insult me."

"Oh, it definitely is. It's at the top of the list, falling under the category of *building character*. Your parents are paying me big money for that."

"They are?"

"No. I'm not being paid any more than you are." Less, most likely. I wasn't horribly paid, and my rent was included, but I had a feeling his *allowance* was more than my salary. "I didn't even agree to take you on. You just showed up."

"But I *have* been helpful to you." His expression had been confident, but it grew a touch hesitant. "I have been, right? I'm sorry I lost your case."

The *case* was a magical ivory artifact with a wolf carved into the lid, but it wasn't really mine. I hadn't known it existed until someone—a nomadic werewolf named Duncan—had used a magic detector in my apartment to find it. Since I'd only had it in my possession briefly—apparently, my ex-husband had stashed it in the heat duct under the floor—I couldn't pretend to be devastated by its loss, but I did regret it. Mostly because of a hunch that the artifact could be important to my kind. It had a *wolf* on the lid, after all.

"It's okay. I'm sorry I asked you to bring it here." I was glad to see his black eye had healed, but the stitches above it couldn't hide the scar tissue forming; he would probably have a mark forever. "It was safer in your dad's vault."

Bolin nodded and looked around the apartment complex, the

older but well-maintained buildings occupying several grassy acres near a greenbelt. "My parents live in a *good* neighborhood."

"They're only three miles from here."

As the property manager, as well as handywoman, I always bristled at insults to the apartment complex, even if I couldn't do anything about the neighborhood. It wasn't *bad*, other than the freeway being on the other side of the greenbelt and close enough that we heard the traffic, but this part of Shoreline experienced more crime these days than there once had been.

"In a gated neighborhood where the houses overlook Puget Sound and the snow-capped Olympic Mountains." Bolin lifted a hand. "I didn't mean to pick a fight, Luna. I came because I found out my dad did drawings and took rubbings of the case." He opened the leather Stefano Ricci bag that was dainty and decorative enough that I'd been thinking of it as a *man purse,* and withdrew some folded sheets of paper. "Remember that writing I mentioned being on the bottom? That was hard to read? My dad magnified it and copied it. Turns out it's Ancient Greek."

"That's not a language I would have expected on a druidic wolf case."

"Yeah, my dad and I were surprised. You'd think Gaelic for something of druidic origins, but when I poked around, I learned that there *is* evidence that druids were in Ancient Greece as early as 200 BCE. Anyway, we borrowed some books and were able to translate the writing." Bolin unfolded a number of precise drawings and a couple of rubbings.

The familiar wolf portrait was on one page, its head tilted upward, as if to howl, but it was instead displaying its rows of sharp teeth. Bolin shuffled through the papers and held out one showing the bottom of the case. Someone with a tidy hand had translated: *Straight from the source lies within protection from venom, poison, and the bite of the werewolf.*

The bite of the werewolf. My mother had brought that up when I'd visited her.

She'd spoken of how our kind were slowly dying because the breeding pool had grown limited and we had, as a species, lost the ability to make more of our kind by biting humans and passing along our werewolf magic to them. Since our people had been hunted for eons, and our own ferocious live-by-the-fang-die-by-the-fang ways caused fighting and killing within our packs, we'd always struggled to keep our numbers up. Because the bite magic had been lost, fading from the world like so many other paranormal elements, we'd been dying off. That had seemed to distress my mom even more than her own impending death from cancer.

"I remembered your interest in werewolves and thought you'd be curious," Bolin said after I'd perused the papers.

"Yes." I didn't mention that I would be more interested in something that fostered the transition of werewolf magic rather than offering protection against it, but I had no problem understanding why normal humans would have feared those bites and wanted nothing to do with them. Those from respectable packs had never inflicted their fang magic on an innocent, bringing only those who wished to become werewolves and who were deemed worthy into the pack, but history told us that others had preyed on humans, claiming mates and slaves whether they'd been willing or not.

The case might not hold any answers to our lost bite, but the fact that it mentioned it made me wonder. Bolin's earlier words came to mind. *The more you learn about where something originates, the more you'll know about it as a whole.*

Was it possible that whatever was in the case, if not the case itself, could offer clues about that lost magic?

Unaware of my meandering thoughts, Bolin continued, "My dad and I assume that whatever is or *was* stored inside offers protection, not the case itself, but we don't know for certain. We never did figure out how to open it. I'm upset that I let a thug beat me up and take it. I described him to the police, but they were as unhelpful as I expected."

"I don't doubt it. Didn't you say the guy who attacked you was big and strong and seemed... supernatural?" I didn't want to suggest he'd been a werewolf, since my intern claimed werewolves didn't exist, but Bolin's description had made *me* think that was a possibility.

The thug might have been working for my surly cousin Augustus. He'd been trying to kill me to keep me from inheriting a magical medallion from my mom, so it seemed plausible he would have his paws on another artifact.

"He was extremely strong. I don't tend to win physical battles with other men, or even sturdy and aggressive women—" For some reason, Bolin eyed *me* when he said that, as if my five-foot-three inches and one-hundred-ten pounds would put me in contention for an Olympic shot-put medal. "But this guy threw me against a post like I was a toddler. My feet left the ground completely."

I nodded. A werewolf, even in human form, had greater-than-typical strength.

"I admit that I'm invested in your case now. Last night, it occurred to me that the assault and theft might have been recorded." Bolin waved toward the parking lot and the main walkway where security cameras were mounted here and there.

Not a week earlier, I'd checked some of the footage, wanting to see how Duncan had not only defeated a couple of big biker men but also ripped pieces off their motorcycles. The cameras hadn't been mounted in good locations to catch much of his battle, but I had glimpsed enough to believe he'd done it with his bare hands. Speaking of greater than typical strength... Even for a werewolf, Duncan was a beast in human form.

"We can check them," I offered.

"If nothing else, I can give the police a photo instead of my vague description."

"Your description was vague? You know all the words in the dictionary. How could vagueness have been involved?"

"It being dark and him hurling me against posts was the reason for vagueness, not a lack of vocabulary on my part." Bolin rubbed the side of his head.

"Ah, understandable." I pointed toward the leasing office, indicating that we could go check the security cameras from there, but Bolin held up a hand.

"Whether we get a good look at the man or not, my dad said he would offer some reward money if we want to put word out to the paranormal community. Curiosity aside, he feels bad that I lost your case."

"It's not your fault. Or anything he needs to pay for."

Bolin shrugged. "You've been my parents' employee for a long time. Even if they usually run everything through Mr. Kuznetsov, they appreciate that you've worked for them and kept the place running smoothly. And that you've taken me under your wing and are suitably building my character." Bolin cocked an eyebrow, and I trusted he was quoting me rather than his father. "Dad also wants to know what's in the case."

"Don't we all?"

"Do you think the European guy with the metal detector could find it?"

"No," I said promptly, even if Duncan might have been able to help. My ex-husband had hired him to steal that case from me. Duncan was the last person I would ask for help finding it. For all I knew, *he,* not my cousin, had hired that thug.

"No? I looked up the name on his van. It's a YouTube channel, and there are a bunch of videos of him finding things. All *kinds* of things."

From his emphasis on that word, I assumed Bolin had seen the videos of Duncan with his magic detector, sauntering through cemeteries at night on the quest for ghosts or who knew what paranormal magics lingered around tombs.

"I know, but he's..." I didn't want to explain my ex or how Duncan had betrayed me. "He left."

"Oh? I thought you two might be..." Bolin turned his palm skyward.

What, dating?

"We're not," I said firmly.

"Too bad. He seems like just the guy to find a missing magical case."

Or he was the one who'd *stolen* my missing magical case.

I scratched my jaw, realizing I *should* check to see if Duncan was in the area. If he was, and if he had the case, maybe I could get it back. Probably not by beating him up—alas—since that footage showed him being much stronger than I—than anyone. But he *had* sent me a gift. Maybe he felt conflicted about his betrayal.

"He *should*," I muttered.

Bolin arched his eyebrows again.

"I'll see if I can find him." I grabbed the carpet cleaner to fire it up again. If Duncan had my case, I would flay and/or scald him until he gave it back.

"Maybe we could contact him through his YouTube page?" Bolin pulled out his phone and had the app open in an instant.

I shot him an exasperated look. I hadn't intended to seek Duncan out that second.

Reluctantly, I admitted that if he did have the case, trying to catch him before he left the area would be best. It might already be too late.

"All right. Send him a note."

"Should I include a photo of my mugger?"

I almost snapped that Duncan probably already knew the

mugger, but that would be jumping to conclusions. It was possible that thug had been working alone, and Duncan was also still looking for the case.

"Let's see if we have one." Leaving the air purifiers running, I led Bolin to the leasing office where we pulled up the footage from the security cameras. It was a good thing I hadn't waited longer since our data-storage plan started deleting old recordings after a week.

"I think it was about nine p.m." Bolin leaned over my shoulder as I skimmed through hours of uneventful footage of people going to and from the parking lot. Then his shiny blue G-wagon rolled in. "That's me."

"You sure that's not a tenant with a six-figure SUV?"

"I'm sure." Ignoring my sarcasm, Bolin frowned and leaned closer to the screen. "There. That guy isn't a tenant." He pointed to a hulking figure leaning out from behind a lamppost as the video version of himself got out of the SUV and walked toward the office, carrying something in his hands. The case. "He's the one who grabbed me," Bolin added.

In the video, the scene played out for us. With long blond hair and a black leather jacket decorated with metal studs, the guy looked like a Northern European metal drummer from an eighties band.

He charged up so quickly that Bolin didn't recognize the danger in time. The thug gripped him by the arms and, shoulder muscles bunching under the jacket, threw Bolin ten feet into a lamppost.

I winced in sympathy when he hit it hard, crumpling to the ground. He'd dropped the case, and the thug bent to grab it. Despite the blow, Bolin reached into his pocket and threw something at the guy—another of his vials? It bounced off his attacker's chest, landed on the cement walkway, and shattered. Vapors wafted up, and the man jerked back, waving at the air in front of his face.

On hands and knees, Bolin scrambled in and tried to grab the case. But the man recovered, grabbed him, hoisted him up, and punched him in the face. That accounted for the black eye and stitches.

After that, the man threw Bolin aside again. Stunned and probably groaning in pain, Bolin hadn't continued to fight. I was surprised he'd had the gumption to do as much as he had.

When the thug picked up the case, he glanced toward the parking lot, giving the camera a good view of his face.

Bolin leaned in, pressed pause, and used his phone to take a photo before letting the footage finish playing. After that, the thief jogged through the parking lot. He didn't get into a car but headed into the street, then disappeared from the camera's range of vision. We didn't know if he'd gotten into a vehicle out there, been picked up by someone, or had gone for an evening stroll to bask in his victory. I did know that there'd been no sign of Duncan in the video.

"You've got some gumption, kid," I said, though Bolin was fiddling with his phone.

"What I've got is a date for you." He smiled brightly and held it up. "He already replied."

"Duncan?"

"Presumably. Whoever mans his channel and answers messages."

"I doubt he has staff. He lives out of a *van,* after all."

Bolin glanced out the window at the complex, but he didn't point out that I lived in the same modest apartment I'd had for twenty years, so I wasn't the epitome of financial success. It was, however, a valid point, so I shouldn't have insulted Duncan for his lifestyle choices. In truth, I was more upset that his lifestyle had led him to be a nomadic treasure hunter who'd taken a gig from my ex-husband.

"Well, whoever replied said he would love to help you, and you can find him at the Ballard Locks this afternoon."

"Okay. Which tool should I take to pound him with if it turns out he hired that guy?"

Bolin opened his mouth but paused, his brow creasing.

I hadn't told him about Duncan's betrayal, so it wasn't surprising that he didn't suspect a link.

Finally, he replied with, "Interns aren't versed on that kind of thing. Do you want me to ask him?"

I snorted. "Yeah."

Bolin typed in the message. It only took a few seconds for a reply.

"He says he'd prefer to be pounded by a bar of chocolate but, if you must, the big wrench is flattering in your hand. *Flattering*?" Bolin lifted his upper lip. "Are you *sure* you two aren't, uhm?"

"Positive."

2

THE TWENTY-YEAR-OLD CLERK WATCHED IN BEMUSEMENT, OR possibly condescension, as I counted bills out of my GAS envelope and laid them on the counter. I was used to it. It wasn't that I didn't know *how* to use plastic or the various online payment processors, but sticking with cash had helped me get my budget locked in and pay off my debt. Given all the extra driving I'd been doing this month, not to mention buying gift boxes of salami and smoked salmon for werewolf bribes, my budget needed all the help it could get.

"Sixty on nine." I waved toward the pump where my beat-up truck waited.

"Anything else?" The kid flicked a finger at an assortment of cheap candies, gum, and bottled vitamin boosters that promised to give me the energy of a puppy on amphetamines.

My gaze trailed over a chocolate bar, and I sneered almost as much as Bolin did every time he talked about the *neighborhood* of the apartment complex. It wasn't my fault gas stations sold inferior chocolate.

"No, thanks." I had already picked up a couple of quality almond-and-sea-salt dark-chocolate bars.

Depending on how this meeting with Duncan went, and what I was able to sus out about his involvement with the missing case, I would either bribe him with the sweets or torment him by enthusiastically eating them in front of him.

I never minded having to nosh on fine chocolate and practiced doing so regularly. Such treats were non-negotiable in my budget. More than once, I'd put back cauliflower or broccoli to pay for desserts. It wasn't as if werewolves needed that many veggies anyway, right? I'd mostly purchased such things for my boys when they'd lived at home. Given all the other crap they'd eaten, I'd figured cruciferous vegetables played an important role in scouring out their innards. Like a Brillo pad.

After filling up, I drove to the Ballard Locks and cruised through the nearby parking lots until I spotted Duncan's blue-and-white Roadtrek, the vehicle modified for off-roading. At the least, it had atypically large tires. They'd been helpful when I'd needed to ram into a belligerent werewolf.

I would have expected Duncan to have wandered through the botanical gardens to the walkway, where he could toss his magnets on ropes over the railing and into the ship canal, but the side door was cracked open. Maybe he was inside, taking a nap. Or waiting for me?

A curious silver cylinder in the shape of a bullet—or maybe a rocket—squatted on the pavement next to the open door. And there was a satellite dish mounted to the van that I hadn't noticed before. Maybe the rocket was a gift from his mother ship.

I snorted at the idea that Duncan might be an alien. No, he was a werewolf—I'd hunted with him in wolf form the week before. He was just oddly strong for one.

Maybe it had to do with his old-world origins. My pack had originated in Italy, but they'd been in the New World for generations, hunting in the Pacific Northwest since Seattle had been a logging town and launch-off destination for prospectors heading up to mine in the Yukon.

When I parked and opened the door of my truck, a scintillating scent of cooking beef wafted to me. Brisket? Oh, was the bullet-shaped object a *smoker*?

My nostrils and salivary glands drew me for a closer investigation.

"Greetings, my lady!" Duncan said with enthusiasm as the door slid farther open and he hopped out of his van.

Halfway to the smoker, I paused with one foot in the air. Why did I feel like a cartoon rabbit led toward a box trap by a carrot lying innocuously underneath?

I put my foot down, reminding myself that I'd reached out to Duncan. Okay, technically, Bolin had. But, either way, Duncan hadn't *lured* me here.

"I'm delighted to see you." Smiling, he stuck his arm out, as if sweeping a cloak wide, and bowed as deeply as a medieval knight. A briny breeze wafting in from Puget Sound tossed his wavy salt-and-pepper hair and stirred the scents of the meat, the scintillating smoke tempting me closer. "I didn't know if I would encounter you ever again."

"My intern thought I should ask you about something." I eyed Duncan, trying to tell from his expression if he was scheming or had deception in mind. Also if he had my case.

But if he had hired that thug and stashed the artifact in his van, would he be lingering in the Seattle area? Where I—or my large werewolf family—might find him?

"You mean you weren't pining achingly and deeply for my company?" Duncan peered past me toward the truck. "Did you bring your big wrench?"

"Do you *want* to be pounded by it?"

"No, but you're appealingly fierce when you wield it." He winked.

"Don't you think you should be more respectful and less irreverent, given that you accepted a gig to break into my apartment and steal from me?"

"I did leave you an apology gift."

"So, all should be forgiven?"

"Perhaps not." His expression grew more sober, and he bowed again. "I do apologize for allowing my craving for adventure to entice me into rummaging in your apartment and deceiving you."

"Apology not accepted." If someone besides my cheating ex-husband had hired him, maybe I could have gotten over it, but Chad was an ass who'd slept all around the world on me. Worse, and even more unforgivable in my eyes, he'd stolen the kids' college funds before the divorce had been finalized.

"Not even if it's accompanied by brisket?" Duncan lifted the lid on the smoker, revealing a perfectly cooked haunch of meat dripping with juices and allowing out an even more intense aroma of delicious, mouthwatering seasoned beef.

"No," I said, though I couldn't help but lean closer and inhale.

My primal werewolf side wanted me to spring upon the brisket, rip it from its mount, and drag it off into the forest to enjoy. Not that there were many forests remaining around the Locks in Ballard. Maybe the bare-branched trees in the botanical garden would do.

"It was your intern's idea to reach out to me, you say?" Duncan asked, though he'd fielded Bolin's messages and knew.

"Yeah. We're searching for something." I tore my gaze from the brisket so I could study him.

He merely lifted his eyebrows.

"Did you hire the guy who mugged Bolin and stole the case?" I watched his eyes for a reaction.

He blinked a couple of times. "The little magical wolf case that I came looking for?"

"Yes. I assume you still want it. That your *employer* still wants it."

Duncan had the grace to wince. "He's not my employer. I was just... doing work for him."

"We can check the dictionary later, but I'm pretty sure that makes you an employee."

"More of an independent contractor. There aren't any benefits. As to the rest, yes, I'm sure he still wants it, but I told him I wouldn't get it for him."

"Is that so," I said in a flat tone.

A part of me wanted to believe Duncan, but a part of me wanted to punch him in the nose. I didn't even know if I could blame my savage werewolf instincts. Wouldn't any woman feel this way about someone who worked for—*independent contracted* for—her loathsome ex?

"It is. I thought about putting that in my note, but I didn't know if you would even read it." Duncan scratched his jaw. "Uhm, did you?"

Was that a hopeful look in his eyes?

I was tempted to quash that hope out of a desire for retribution, but I reminded myself why I'd come. Bolin thought Duncan could help. And maybe he could. On the chance that case was pertinent to werewolves, I wanted to get it and show it to my mother. And maybe Bolin and his father could learn more about it —and what it had to do with wolf bites—if they had more time to study it.

"I read it. And I got the potion vials." Maybe I should have said thanks, but I couldn't dredge the words from my soul. With my body still tight from the feeling of betrayal, I... couldn't be that big of a person. Besides, I didn't know if he'd *truly* stopped working for Chad or if that was a lie and he was trying to get back on my good side in the hope of getting a second chance at the case. Asking him for help was probably dumb.

"But you haven't consumed one of the potions," Duncan said in a curious tone. "I can tell from the feral way you looked at my meat that the wolf still lurks close to the surface in you."

"Your meat, huh."

Duncan grinned. "I refer, naturally, to the brisket."

"Naturally."

I didn't doubt that he could tell I hadn't taken the potion. A werewolf, even when in human form, had keener senses than normal people, so he would be able to sense and smell what I was. What I, if strong emotions or the full moon roused me, could become.

Since I didn't want to discuss my decision not to take another werewolf-sublimation potion, I pulled out my phone instead. "Do you know this guy?"

I showed him the photo that Bolin had shared with me and the footage of the thug beating up my poor intern.

"I already told your assistant, but I haven't seen that man before." Brow furrowed, Duncan leaned closer to my phone. "Will you play that video again?"

Hoping he'd decided he *did* recognize the guy, I did so without question.

"He's strong," Duncan said. "Abnormally so."

"Yes. Bolin commented on that after the guy hurled him into a lamppost. He's lucky that he didn't need a cast for broken bones to go with his stitches."

"Quite," Duncan murmured thoughtfully, his gaze locked on the video. "I don't think he's a werewolf though."

That caught me by surprise. "You don't? What else would he be?"

"I'm... not sure, but he doesn't move like an animal. Like *we* do."

I twitched a skeptical eyebrow. Though I didn't deny that wild instincts guided me at times, I didn't think I moved like an animal, not when I was in human form.

"If I could smell him," Duncan said, "I would have a better idea of what he is."

"Sorry, we haven't upgraded to security cameras with scent receptors."

"That's unfortunate."

"If you want to sniff this guy up, you'll have to help me find him."

"Is that what brought you here?"

"I'm more interested in locating the case than the thief, but they might be together. Bolin pointed out that your supposed expertise is finding things."

"*Supposed*. Really, Luna. I located all sorts of interesting things in your bedroom." Duncan might have decided that sounded odd —my mind went to the tube of estradiol cream he'd shrieked over—because he added a finger point upward, no doubt to remind me of the magical hidden cameras we'd uncovered in the ceiling.

"It's almost as if you knew paranormal items would be there to find."

"I... did possibly have that information. About the wolf case, though, not anything else."

"Maybe Chad thought it would be skeezy and creepy to admit he put cameras in the bedroom of his ex-wife to spy on her." I didn't have verification that he'd been the one to do that, but, given that he'd placed the case, it seemed likely. "Next time you chat with him, let him know he's a douche, will you?"

"I wasn't planning to *chat* with him again. As I said, I told him I wouldn't take further actions against you or send him that case, should it reappear."

"Okay. Good."

Duncan's handsome face, his jaw outlined by his carefully cultivated three days' beard growth, held an earnest expression.

A little twinge in my gut, or maybe my *soul*, made me want to believe him, but too many years of life being hard and people lying to me made me wary. If I had a nickel for every time a tenant had told me the rent wouldn't be late again or the check was in the mail, I could have bought my own apartment complex by now. At the least, I wouldn't be carefully divvying up my paychecks under the guidance of a strict budget to make sure there was money left to eat at the end of the month.

"Do you think it's possible your lovely cousins could be associated with that fellow?" Duncan pointed to the paused video on my phone.

"It is possible. I asked Augustus if he was responsible, but it was after I shoulder-butted him off a train trestle and into a raging river. He wasn't cheerfully inclined toward me at that moment."

"He did seem the sort to hold a grudge."

"Absolutely." I eyed the blond guy in the video. "I wouldn't be surprised in the least if Augustus lied to me, but... it's also not very werewolfy to go outside of the pack for help. Assuming things haven't changed since I was a kid, Mom wouldn't even call a handyman to fix a leak in the roof. She expected Uncle Carlo to handle all the maintenance."

"Was he who taught you how to wield your big wrench?" Duncan leaned into his van and pulled out a carving fork and knife.

"I did assist him numerous times."

"I could ask Rue, the alchemist who made your potions, if she knows of anything that could give a regular human greater than typical strength. And I can poke around the paranormal pawn shops and check if anyone has seen your case."

"If you get any leads, I'd like to come along."

"Because you don't trust me not to take off with the case if I find it by myself?" Duncan sliced off a piece of the brisket, more juices dribbling out and making my stomach growl.

"I don't trust you, no. You keep bad company."

"I met him randomly, chatting about treasure hunting on a dock on an island in Costa Rica. We didn't keep *company* for an extended period of time."

I wanted to snap that Chad's evilness and sleaziness should have oozed off him and informed Duncan about what a loser he was, but that was silly. Chad could be quite charming and cordial. After all, *I'd* fallen in love with and married him. It hadn't been until years later that I'd learned about the deceitful, double-timing, thieving side of him.

"Okay." I lifted a hand, as much of an apology as I could muster. "It's not personal. I just... after being..." I couldn't bring myself to use *duped* to describe myself, at least not out loud. "After he did me wrong, I'm not quick to trust anyone. Like I said, it's not personal."

"I can accept that." With a smile and a flourish, Duncan extended a piece of meat toward me. "Please accept this small token as a further apology for my poor behavior."

"It's almost as if you knew a werewolf would visit you today." I plucked the brisket off his knife, my rumbling stomach demanding that I accept his offering.

"I'm ever hopeful. I've felt bereft without having someone to show my day's finds to." He pointed to a box of grime- and seaweed-covered metal whats-its, proof that he *had* been magnet fishing earlier.

"Don't you record yourself and share all that with your YouTube followers?"

"It's not quite the same as sharing with a real person. I—" Duncan paused, cocking his head to listen to something.

Once he stopped talking, I heard it too. Night hadn't come, but the howl of a wolf floated across the ship canal toward us.

It sounded like it originated out on the point in the largely wooded Discovery Park. Since the area was surrounded by busy neighborhoods, it would be an unlikely place for a *normal* wolf to show up. I had a feeling my family was still keeping an eye on me.

"Did you ever find out why your cousin was trying to kill you?" Duncan gazed in the direction of the howl.

"My mom is dying and planning to leave a family heirloom to me." I almost described the magical medallion, and how it had glowed when I'd touched it, apparently a sign that I was a proper heir for it, but that wasn't information that I could trust Duncan with. Maybe he was telling the truth that he was done hunting for treasures located under my nose—or my bed—but he might be lying to me. I dared not let myself be fooled twice.

"And he's irked because he's not in the will?"

"Sort of. It's magical and I guess attuned to women." Maybe I should have asked Mom more about the medallion. "My cousin believes it should go to his wife. He also doesn't think I'm worthy to inherit it because I walked away from the pack all those years ago." Worse, in his eyes, I'd taken that potion that had kept me from feeling the call of the wolf and changing into our true form.

"I'd imagine that would be for your mother to decide. More meat?"

I blinked, hardly realizing I'd wolfed down the first piece. It had been so tender I'd scarcely had to chew or pause my speech. "Yes."

"I thought so." His eyes gleamed.

The image of a rabbit lured in by a carrot came to mind again, and I looked frankly at him. "Are you trying to win my trust with food?"

"A certain amiability, perhaps. You've explained why trust might be difficult to earn, and I understand. I *did* originally come to you with deceit in mind." Duncan bowed again. Apologetically. Then he sliced off another piece of brisket. "I was making this for myself since there's nothing like returning from a hard day's work to a perfectly smoked haunch of meat, but I'm most pleased to share it with you."

"I was skeptical from the beginning that there was any treasure in the greenbelt by the freeway."

"Oh, there were all *sorts* of fascinating things lost in there. I found not one or two but *three* antique hubcaps." He extended the slice of meat on his fork. "But you're correct that it wasn't my treasure-hunting research that led me to that particular patch of woodlands. Does it even have a name?"

"Smoker Woods is what the teenagers who lurk back there against their parents' wishes call it." I pantomimed tagging a puff from a cigarette. The recently vacated apartment wasn't the first smoke-tainted unit I'd cleaned over the years. Not by far.

"Catchy."

"I can't say that it's a tourist hot spot."

As Duncan and I ate, sharing the delicious brisket, another howl sounded. Was it closer? It was hard to believe a werewolf would cross the Ballard Bridge and attack us in a public area during daylight hours, but night wasn't that far away.

"Perhaps we should vacate the premises. I doubt it's my brisket that's prompting that wolf to howl." Duncan absently rubbed his side, the place where he'd been gouged in the fight with my cousins. Since werewolves had magical regenerative powers, the wounds should have healed, but the memory would doubtless linger. His gaze shifted toward my phone. The screen had gone dark, but maybe he was thinking of the mugger. "The alchemist who made your potions was full of knowledge, not only about alchemy but about the paranormal scene in Seattle. Why don't we visit her first and ask about magical ways in which a man's strength might be enhanced?"

"There are plain *chemical* ways that can be achieved."

"I don't think that bloke was a victim of 'roid rage," Duncan said dryly.

Maybe not. His face had been calm as he'd hurled Bolin into the post. Even the punch after the vial throwing hadn't been accompanied by much expression. Maybe that was what made Duncan believe the guy wasn't a werewolf. When our wild savagery surfaced, *calm* wasn't an appropriate descriptor.

Duncan disassembled his smoker and placed it beside the van's tiny sink for cleaning later, then sliced up the rest of the meat, storing it in a compact, counter-high refrigerator. He laid three slices of brisket on a post in front of the van.

"In case the wolf comes to investigate," he said.

"Are you trying to win his amiability too?"

"It's more likely the seagulls and crows will find the meat first, but you never know." Duncan looked wistful as he opened the passenger door. "May I offer you a ride to the alchemist?"

I hesitated. Nothing bad had happened when I'd ridden with him before, but...

"There's not much parking down there." Duncan waved in the direction of the Space Needle and downtown. "Oddly, alchemists don't have reserved spots for clients."

"That *is* odd."

"The package-shipping place under her second-floor apartment has *three* dedicated spots for customers."

"The power of being part of a large corporate chain." Though I didn't know if it was wise, I locked my truck, grabbed the chocolate bars I'd brought, and climbed into Duncan's passenger seat.

Whether I should trust him even this much, I didn't know, but the odds of finding the case would be better with his help and expertise. If we *did* find it, I would have to make sure to get to it first.

3

"DID CHAD SAY WHAT THE CASE IS FOR?" I ASKED AS DUNCAN DROVE past the Space Needle on his way to wherever the alchemist lived. "How he got it? Or why he wanted it?"

I was reticent to bring up my ex, not wanting to discuss him in any capacity, or even think about him, but the need to know more about the wolf case overrode my distaste for the topic.

At first, Duncan didn't answer, and I thought he might claim there was some confidential employer-employee relationship that treasure hunters and those who paid for their services claimed. But maybe he was simply trying to remember their encounter because he did eventually answer.

"He didn't tell me anything about it or its purpose or provenance. What led to him wishing to hire me was a discussion about werewolves. He saw me in a brawl with riffraff on the dock in Costa Rica that I mentioned—they wanted to steal some of my pricy locating equipment—and he recognized that my attributes couldn't be entirely human."

"You *are* strong. Even for a werewolf." I eyed him. "I dug up the footage of you gleefully ripping pieces off motorcycles."

"Yes, I've found that it's more acceptable to the authorities in this and other lands if you rip pieces off property instead of people. When someone swings a tire iron at me or someone in my company, I'm more inclined toward the latter, but as I've grown older and more silvered, I've learned to rein in my instincts some."

That had been a lot of words to not answer my implied question.

"Do *you* take an alchemical substance to enhance your abilities further?" I asked more bluntly.

"I do not. I work out, and I eat sardines."

"Uh, sardines?"

"Their health benefits are great, and they're shelf stable, thus easy to store in a van. In addition to being good for your bones and muscles, they help make your coat lush and glossy."

"So, if I open that cabinet back there, I'll find stacks of sardine tins?" I waved toward an upper door above a rack of SCUBA equipment.

"The drawer by the mini fridge, actually. There are anchovies too. Feel free to help yourself." Duncan glanced at the chocolate bars in my lap. "I understand the antioxidants in cacao beans are also health promoting."

"Is that your way of saying you'd like a couple of squares?"

"Quite. Had you brought the kind with bacon pieces in the chocolate, I might already have leaped upon you, unable to restrain my inner wolf."

"You have urges to be that juvenile? Despite your silvering pelt?"

He'd called it that before, and I glanced at his salt-and-pepper hair. It *was* lush and glossy.

"Maturity can't *entirely* subdue one's base instincts. I like almonds also. And salt."

"As we all do." I opened the bar, broke off a couple of squares, and held them up to entice him. "After Chad saw you fight, what did he say?"

"Ah, those are bribe bars? Not amiability-earning bars?"

"You're already amiable. It's the information you like to withhold that I'm after."

"Hm."

Duncan looked at a brick building on a corner with retail on the bottom—there was the package-delivery service he'd mentioned—and apartments above, metal balconies attached to some of them. His window was down, and a hint of incense wafted to me over the smells of gasoline, the nearby fish market, and sea air drifting in from Puget Sound. Duncan drove around the building, looking for parking. Numerous bars and restaurants in the area ensured the lack he'd promised.

"Your ex-husband asked if I was indeed a werewolf and then spoke excitedly about research he'd done on our kind. His questions seemed innocuous enough, and I even thought... Well, I've encountered fanatics before."

"Werewolf fanatics?"

"Those a touch obsessed with the lore. Sometimes, they have even known actual werewolves, though I don't have to tell you that we're a dying breed."

"No."

"Your ex said he'd been studying werewolves for ages," Duncan continued, "and that he'd picked up numerous trinkets on business trips around the world."

"In between sleeping with women in exotic locales, no doubt."

Duncan looked over at me. His expression was sympathetic, but I felt immature since I'd mentioned Chad's betrayal to him multiple times already—I'd mentioned it to a *lot* of people. As one of my friends had pointed out, Chad still lived rent-free in my head.

I longed to rise above it all and put him out of my mind, and

I'd been making progress... until this. His return, however obliquely, to my life had stirred up all the old emotions. There was a part of me that wondered if I should have just handed the case to Duncan and let Chad have it, but it seemed pertinent to me and my kind, not a human *fanatic*.

"I'm sorry," I said. "I'm working on getting over my bitterness, but being mature is an ongoing challenge."

"You lack the silver in your pelt to convey the needed peace and wisdom." Duncan smiled, glancing at my hair before wedging his van into a parking spot a Toyota half its size had vacated. It was a good thing the Roadtrek had a sliding door in the back, as there wouldn't be room to open the passenger door.

"I use hair dye. My pelt *is* silvering. Trust me."

"Oh? Your fur was a beautiful raven black as a wolf."

"Was it?" I knew it had been in my youth, but I hadn't caught my reflection at any point during the last two changes. I'd assumed my fur was as hoary as Duncan's, who'd been a similar salt-and-pepper color as a wolf. "You're not lying to me to flatter me, are you?"

"You're shrewd, being highly aware that I'm salivating over the chocolate you're waving about, but I am not lying to you about your raven lushness. It was quite striking with your blue eyes."

I squinted at him. He appeared sincere, but I would verify my lushness with one of my werewolf relatives later. Maybe my niece, Jasmine, who seemed to be on my side and should have no reason to flatter me.

In the meantime, I handed Duncan two squares of chocolate, more to keep him talking than as a response to his praise. Even if a part of me craved such attention from a man. I didn't want to need it, but it had been a long time and was nice to hear.

"*Thank* you, my lady." He popped the chocolate in his mouth. "Your ex said the case was a trinket he'd picked up at a street market in Bangkok."

I scoffed. "I know that's a lie just from the research Bolin and his dad did on it. It's of druidic origins, and there's Ancient Greek writing on the bottom. There's no way it came from the Far East." I slid a square of chocolate into my own mouth. The mixture of salt and sweet, with crunch from the almond pieces, soothed me slightly.

"I did sense that its magic was nature-touched, not born of witches, sorcerers, alchemists, or necromancers. But Greek? I didn't know druids lived in that part of the Old World."

"Apparently, they got around back in the day. But not to Thailand." I gave Duncan another piece of chocolate, feeling like a dog owner handing out treats for good behavior. Bribes, indeed.

"Items do move from country to country, especially in this day and age, but it's possible he lied to me. Now that I've heard your side of what he said about your relationship and you... I believe he lied to me about many things."

"He did," I said, then admitted, "but I guess there's no reason you should, as an outsider, believe me over him."

"Sure there is." Duncan pointed to the chocolate bar. "*He* didn't give me food. He didn't even give me a deposit. If not for the uniqueness of the item and promise of adventure in this land I hadn't visited before, I would have been far less enticed."

I didn't want to be touched that he said he believed me over Chad, but it was hard not to feel mollified. "Do treasure hunters usually get a deposit?"

"Established ones being requested to find a specific item do. I generally require twenty or thirty percent of the agreed-upon fee, depending on how many flights and train rides I'll have to take. If I have to hire sherpas and trek into the Himalayas, it's fifty percent."

"You've done that?"

"Visited the Himalayas, yes. But I shifted into wolf form and trekked myself. Our kind are hearty, even at high altitudes."

"You've led an interesting life."

"I strive to do so. Traveling the world is far preferable to the alternative." Duncan slid a square of chocolate into his mouth before climbing into the back of the van.

"Staying at home and having a steady job?" I unbuckled my seat belt to follow him.

"That was never my alternative." He gave me a wistful look as he slid open the side door so we could ease out that way.

Something about his words and look made me wonder if he'd been running from something when he first left home. A fight with his pack? He'd once said he'd never *had* a pack, but there must have been at least a mother and siblings at some point, surely.

I thought about asking, but voices sounded nearby, couples and groups walking past on the sidewalk. To follow Duncan, I had to squeeze past a driver-side mirror jutting out and almost clipped my chest on it.

"This is why I don't go downtown often," I muttered.

"Difficult parking conditions?" Duncan led me past shops and a sushi restaurant, then around a corner toward an entrance in the building, presumably for the upstairs apartments.

"An overabundance of people."

"Your wolf side makes you crave the vast solitude of the wilderness? I understand completely."

"Yes. Also not having my boob mashed against oversized vehicles."

"It may be your *female* side that makes you crave that. I understand that less."

"I'm sure you don't like having your male parts mashed either."

"Indeed not." Duncan paused outside the glass doors and looked up.

The smell of incense had grown stronger, and I followed his gaze toward a slight figure standing on a second-floor balcony and looking down at us. A woman? It was hard to tell, except by the size. She had a hood up, and I couldn't make out her face, but the incense scent seemed to waft out of her open door. Further, twists of dried herbs and strings of roots and bulbs dangled from the railing.

Duncan lifted a hand but didn't call up to the woman, only opening the door. "She might have sensed us coming. She has power of her own."

"Alchemists usually do, I think. It's not just the ingredients but the addition of a person's magic that makes their potions potent, right?"

"I believe that's correct." Duncan led me inside and to carpeted stairs instead of an elevator. "Wolves don't mix up concoctions, so I wouldn't know."

"I don't mix more than cake and brownie batters, so I'm not an expert either."

"What is a brownie?"

"Kind of like a big chewy chocolate cookie but thicker. You make them in a pan and cut them into squares. You haven't encountered them on your world travels?"

"It's possible they're called something else in other countries, but chocolate, you say?" Duncan glanced over his shoulder at me as we climbed.

"Yup. I have a recipe for bacon-caramel brownies that are amazing."

"I'm salivating again. I didn't know I was such a fan of chocolate until I met you."

"You must not have had the right kind."

"The kind with salted meat cubed up in it is new to me."

"You were missing out before."

"Clearly."

The second-floor hallway was empty, but something raised my hackles as we headed toward a door near the end. I thought of the wolf howl we'd heard, but it wasn't an approaching enemy that had my instincts bristling. This was an unease prompted by the proximity of magic.

I stopped before reaching the door Duncan waved to. It was covered in graffiti, and notes and signs stuck around the frame held messages such as *witches aren't allowed, demon worshipper,* and *devil-spawn be gone.*

I eyed them, wondering what the alchemist did besides burning incense. Maybe her magic stirred up other people's hackles as well. When it came to detecting paranormal influence, humans didn't have senses nearly as strong as werewolves, but many did have *some* sensitivity.

"Are you sure this is the right place?" I asked.

"I am." Unfazed by the graffiti, Duncan knocked on the door.

He'd been here before to get my potions, so the alchemist presumably didn't greet visitors with guns—or wands. That reassured me slightly until I remembered, with a jolt, that I hadn't *taken* her potions. Would she be offended? If she had power, she would sense that my werewolfness wasn't being subdued.

"Is she going to be—" The door opened, and I didn't finish with *upset I haven't used her potions.* Instead, I turned the sentence into, "—okay about seeing us without an appointment?"

"We'll find out."

4

DUNCAN BOWED TO THE WOMAN WHO'D OPENED THE DOOR, HER hood back, revealing white hair, a wizened face, and almond-shaped eyes. Almost a head shorter than Duncan, she squinted up at him, the light from the hallway bright compared to her dim apartment lit by oil lamps and candles. What was the woman's name? Rue. That had been it.

"Greetings, my lady alchemist. Your radiant beauty and superb skills in your profession have brought me to seek advice from you again."

Her suspicious squint changed into a shy smile, though she grew wary when she glanced at me. "I sell potions, not advice, but you are welcome inside." She didn't look anything like Beatrice, the retired nurse alchemist who'd lived in my apartment complex, but she had a familiar vibe, and I could sense the paranormal about her. I didn't doubt that she could imbue her potions with magic. "And you..." She pointed her finger at me. "Who are you?" Her eyes widened with enlightenment before I could answer. "Oh, you are his mate. The confused werewolf. Yes, you may also enter."

"*Mate?*" I mouthed, but Rue had already turned to go inside.

"I didn't tell her that," Duncan whispered. "I told her you were a female friend who I was doing a favor for. That's it."

"Men who are only *friends* with women don't go to great lengths and collect ingredients from dangerous locales to buy them potions to further their identity delusions," Rue said without looking back. Her age didn't make her hard of hearing.

I didn't have a *delusion* about my identity, but I kept my mouth shut since we wanted information from her. I also glanced at Duncan, surprised to learn he might have had to ingredient hunt for me. He'd gone through more work than I would have guessed to have my potions made.

In the beginning of that quest, he might have thought to use them to get on my good side—or get into my apartment to search it—but after I'd caught him, he had to have known that I wouldn't let him have the case, no matter how many potions he plied me with.

"I may not have mentioned that she's blunt." Duncan shrugged apologetically at me before following Rue into the apartment. He didn't respond to the woman's comment about ingredients.

"As long as she can make what people need."

Before following him in, I glanced again at the *witch* and *demon* graffiti on the door. She probably didn't deserve that, assuming she wasn't using her power to do anything harmful to people. Since she'd made *me* a potion to help, I was inclined to believe she didn't regularly put hexes on the neighbors or turn kids into toads.

"Those who know what to ask for, yes," Rue said, waving us to cushions and mats on the floor and surrounded on all sides by stacks of hardback books with yellowed pages and tattered bindings. A square of glass rested on one of the stacks, turning it into a table with two oil lamps and a cup of tea on it. "Shoes off, please. You may relax, as I have sent my familiar off to hunt in the alleys."

"A cat," Duncan told me, then shook his hand as if it had been bitten. Maybe it *had*. Cats did not care for our kind.

I removed my shoes, and more scents than incense inundated me as I followed Duncan to the mats. Smoke coalesced near the ceiling, and what had once been white paint was dingy gray. Countless hooks had been drilled into the drywall to support hanging plants and baskets of who knew what. The handywoman in me cringed, and I wondered if half the notes on the door had been placed by an aggrieved property manager.

"My sophisticated werewolf abatement elixir did not work?" Rue settled on a cushion near her tea mug. "You reek of lupine power and barely restrained chaotic energy."

"Well, we were just talking about my ex-husband." I sat on a cushion next to hers and pulled out my phone, intending to show her Bolin's mugger on the off-chance she'd seen him before.

"That accounts for the latter," Duncan said, plopping down on another cushion, black-and-tan checkered socks on display.

"You account for it some too," I informed him.

He splayed a hand over his chest. "*Moi?*"

"He also vexed me during his visits," Rue told me. "But he also flirted with me, as if I'm a youthful beauty, so I did not inflict upon him genital warts. As you doubtless observed during your coital times."

"There haven't been *coital* times." I glared at Duncan.

He was still hand-splaying and looking innocent.

"No?" Rue asked. "He is quite virile for a werewolf of his years."

"So he tells me," I murmured.

"I asked him what talisman he wears or elixir he consumes to give him superior power to a normal one of his kind, but he would not tell me."

"He hasn't told me either." I eyed Duncan, glad to have my hunch about him confirmed.

"I'm all natural, ladies. The virility is in my blood."

"I have a talisman that allows me to sense when clients are lying to me," Rue stated.

"Blunt," Duncan whispered to me.

I waited to see if he would say more. I was curious about his extra power too.

"Ms. Rue," Duncan said, "Luna's intern was attacked by a man I don't think is a werewolf but who has greater than human strength." He pointed to my phone. "We thought you might know if *he* has a talisman or potion that could account for such."

"There are many magical items and elixirs that can grant supernatural strength to a person," Rue said. "Most have side effects. A trade-off, if you will, for the power that is shared. That is particularly true of the elixirs. Sometimes, the items do not cause physical unpleasantness, but your muscles, relying upon the magic from an external source, may atrophy over time." She looked at Duncan again. Still wondering about his virility?

"Nothing is atrophying here, thank you," he said. "Luna can attest to that. She's seen me naked."

Rue looked archly at me, as if the statement confirmed her suspicion that we were mates.

"Only when he changed forms," I said. "We hunted together."

"And you did not mate afterward? From what I've read—" Rue waved toward books on a shelf rather than in a stack, "—a bonded wolf pair will often feel amorous after a successful hunt, especially after feasting on fresh prey."

"*I* felt amorous." Duncan smiled.

"Which is no doubt why I woke up with your hand on my boob," I muttered.

Rue squinted at me. "You are *certain* you did not notice his lack of genital warts?"

My cheeks heated. Duncan's smile only widened.

"This is the guy." Eager to change the subject, I held my phone out to her, the video pulled up again. "He took something important that my intern was bringing to me."

Rue watched the footage. "Your intern is lucky this man didn't take his life."

"I know."

"I recognize him."

I leaned forward. That I hadn't expected. "You do?"

"Yes. Assuming he found an alchemist willing to make such a foul elixir for him, he likely imbibes a Tiger Blood potion regularly. It is one of the most potent strength enhancers that we can make, but the ingredients are dangerous to acquire. And immoral, some say. I refused to make it for him, even when he, and the others with him, brought the vials of tiger blood and freshly harvested human livers that are required. I am not squeamish about extracts of ox bile and dried porcine organs, but I must draw the line at certain ingredients."

"Did you say *human* livers?" I stared.

"Those from fertile females, yes. They are high in iron and other minerals that are required for the strength-enhancing potion, and they have the aura of the recently sacrificed."

I drew back, horrified. Women had to *die* for this elixir to be crafted? Die and have their livers harvested?

"I do have the formula in a very dark grimoire, but, as I said, I would not make an elixir requiring such ingredients. I told them so. They sought to force me to do their bidding, but that was not wise." Rue's eyelids drooped. She had to be close to seventy and weigh a hundred pounds, if that, but somehow I didn't doubt that she'd threatened the men convincingly.

"So, they found someone else willing to make the elixir?" Duncan asked.

"Based on that one's strength, it appears so." Rue waved to the phone. "Other powers granted by the Tiger Blood potion are a strong immune system, regeneration equal to or even greater than that of a werewolf, and the ability to see apparitions, though some consider that a side effect rather than a desired attribute. Other deleterious effects of the potion are an upset stomach, the runs, shortened lifespan, infertility, and a propensity to develop toenail fungus."

"People find that trade-off worth it?" I wondered.

"Some do. Often it is the *employers* of such persons who do. In this case, I believe the men knew about the side effects of what they requested, but it is possible they'd had enough that it didn't matter. The Tiger Blood potion is, like so many elixirs, addictive. You are fortunate that the werewolf sublimation elixir is not. Especially since you do not seem to have taken it." Rue's eyebrows rose.

"Not yet. My life has grown dangerous of late, and I thought I might need my heritage." I *had* needed it to survive my cousin's attempts on my life.

"I am relieved it was not a failing on my part that caused the elixir to be ineffective. It is always displeasing to the ego to fail in one's career."

"And to have to refund the money one charged to one's client?" Duncan asked dryly.

"Quite. The expenses of living in the city are great, especially since the landlord of this facility charges *me* for the cost of painting over the graffiti that the ignorant denizens leave on my door. Twice, he's had to replace the door altogether. Why he does not charge *them* for the vandalism, I do not know. I have provided him security-camera footage of the cowards leaving their marks."

"Maybe you should try Shoreline," I suggested. "We have a vacancy. My alchemist moved out, and she had a quiet spot in the back of the complex."

Duncan smirked. Amused that I had turned into a leasing agent during our foray into Seattle? It wasn't as if my property-management gig had set hours. Besides, I was responsible for keeping the units at Sylvan Serenity rented.

"The denizens up there are too busy going to work and making a living to notice witchiness going on in the buildings," I added. "Though you might need to cut back on the incense." I didn't recall that Beatrice's apartment had ever smelled from the outside. Inside was another matter, but she probably hadn't invited the neighbors over for coffee that often.

Rue gazed at me. "What *did* happen to Beatrice? Mr. Calderwood assured me that you were not responsible for her disappearance."

"Not directly, I wasn't, but I eventually learned that my niece scared her into leaving the apartment. Apparently, she knew of the danger that would find me and didn't want me to be able to get more potions."

"Scared her into leaving? And this is the apartment you believe I should move to?"

"I'm just mentioning it as an option. Besides, I doubt you'd be scared away by a mid-twenties werewolf with a perky ponytail." If the blond thug and a bunch of his buddies hadn't fazed Rue, there was no way my niece would, not even if she changed into a wolf on the doorstep and showed off her fangs. Rue would probably grab a rolled-up newspaper and bop her on the snout.

"I will keep it in mind. I do enjoy the conveniences of the city, but the tenants in this facility are foolish and tedious."

"You could also try living in a van," Duncan said. "It's quite freeing. Though it can be a challenge to find a parking spot where nobody is threatening to have you towed." He gave me a sidelong look.

I stuck my tongue out at him.

Rue looked back and forth between us. "Not mates? You are certain?"

"*Yes,*" I said firmly, then stood, afraid that if we lingered, she would bring up warts again.

Duncan lifted a hand. "Rue, do you know what other

alchemist in the area might have supplied those men? Or where we might find them? They didn't mention an employer to you, did they?"

"They did not. They grew hostile when I said I would not make their elixir. Fortunately, I have ways to defend myself. As to other alchemists in the area, no. Even those that I would consider as having few scruples would be hesitant to make a potion using what could only be the stolen organs of dead, possibly murdered, women. In this city, one must worry not only about staying on the right side of the law but not drawing the ire of the paranormal watchers that patrol the area."

Duncan nodded. I'd not heard of *paranormal watchers* and would have to ask him about that later.

"As to locating the men, you might ask around at El Gato Mágico, a bar in the industrial part of the waterfront that attracts quirky individuals affiliated with the paranormal. It's known to be a place where those with particular needs can go to hire and be hired. You can also get an excellent margarita there." Rue winked. "With a kick."

"We'll check." Duncan stood, took her hand, and brushed his lips on her skin before releasing her.

"You're a ridiculous flirt, Mr. Calderwood." Rue managed to look pleased and stern at the same time.

"I am merely a werewolf who knows the importance of staying in an alchemist's good graces." Duncan bowed before heading out.

I left without kissing anything of Rue's, though I did give her the name of our apartment complex. The smells and smoke-stained ceiling suggested she wouldn't be an ideal tenant, but it had been convenient having a potion maker a few doors away. Given how fraught my life had grown of late, it might be even *more* convenient going forward.

5

"IT'S ONLY A FEW BLOCKS TO THE WATERFRONT," I TOLD DUNCAN after looking up El Gato Mágico in my Maps app. "It might be easier to leave your van here instead of trying to find another parking spot."

The chilly late November air, punctuated with spats of rain, should have kept people home, but weather couldn't keep humans from wanting to eat and drink out. Further, Christmas lights already adorned store windows and the bare-branched trees lining the streets. Lots of pedestrians clutched shopping bags as they hurried between shops.

"Leave it here?" Duncan looked blankly at me. "When we're going to the waterfront?"

"Yes..." I pointed west. "The bar is right down there."

"But out on a pier, yes?" Duncan leaned over to consider my map, then pointed. "One of *many* piers thrusting out into the water. They're huge. And with all those shops and restaurants on them, imagine the amount of foot traffic passing near those railings."

The reason for his objection finally clicked.

"You need to park closer so that your magnetic fishing gear is at hand?" I asked dryly.

"Of *course*. And my SCUBA gear. I found a number of antique logging tools when I dove around the Edmonds waterfront. Did you know that started out as a timber town?"

"Yes, most of this area did. I think the term *skid road* comes from Seattle. They used to grease slats and slide the logs down the hill to the mills on the waterfront." As we climbed into the van, I added, "What kind of logging tools could survive a century in salt-water? A saw would corrode away in that time, wouldn't it?"

"Oh, yes. Nothing was in good shape, with little left but barnacle-covered saw handles, but it was a fascinating find."

"A valuable find?"

"I donated the tools to the Edmonds Museum."

"So no value."

"They were of historical interest." Duncan backed his van out, a zippy electric vehicle immediately pouncing on our vacated spot, and drove toward the waterfront.

"I'm beginning to think you're as delighted finding rusty forks as real treasures."

"It's possible there's a reason I live in my van." He smirked at me.

"You can't be that impoverished. The gas money I tried to give you last week is still on the dash." I pointed to six dollars pinned down by a bobblehead fisherman holding a giant salmon. It looked like it had been hand painted, or at least touched up after damage, so something told me *that* had come out of the water too.

"I wasn't sure if I'd see you again. I was keeping it as a memento."

"Nothing evokes the nostalgia of an old acquaintance like US currency." That reminded me that I needed to chip in again since he was driving us around tonight, so I opened my purse to find my

GAS envelope and grimaced at its depleted state. At least pay day wasn't far off.

"Well, you didn't leave me any other keepsakes." Duncan glanced over while circling the block to find a vacant spot. "Do you still have that locket we found together?"

"I do. It came in useful when I faced off against my family—the part of my family that believes I'm a heretic who should be dead."

"You should avoid that part of your family."

"Tell me about it." I pulled out three dollars, making a guess on an appropriate amount for the evening's drive. This wasn't as long of a trek as when we'd gone to the mountains to hunt, and I could tell Duncan didn't care if I gave him money or not, but I hated to feel in debt to anyone. I tucked the bills under the bobblehead with the others.

"Since you've deigned to speak with me again, I won't ask you for a more personal keepsake," Duncan said.

"You think I'm going to be a regular part of your life now?"

"At least until we find your case." He saluted toward me, then pulled into a spot.

"It's not really my case. I just don't think it's my ex-husband's case either. Knowing him, he probably stole it. If we find it, I'd like to show it to my mom and also get Bolin's dad to research it more and see if it holds any clues for my people—*our* people. We haven't seen what's inside yet. After they're done researching, his family can figure out who it should go to. Maybe there's a museum for druidic artifacts. They have to be at least as educational and interesting as rusty logging tools."

"I should think so. What link to werewolves do you think the case has? Besides the obvious wolf on the lid?"

As we climbed out of the van, the salty air heavy with mist, I debated again whether to tell him about the writing. It wasn't as if the words had hinted of a tremendous secret, and the information shouldn't make Duncan more eager to snatch the case for Chad. If anything, Duncan might feel some loyalty toward our kind and *not* want to hand the artifact over to a mere human *fanatic*. My lip curled at that description for Chad. I didn't doubt that werewolves were an obsession for him—overhearing that conversation had given me more evidence of something I'd suspected for years, that he'd only been interested in *me* because of my lupine heritage. But something told me there was more than a fan's curiosity behind his desire to get the case back. He'd known it was valuable when he'd gone through all the effort to hide it in the apartment. And install those cameras. The memory of finding those made my lip curl again.

When Duncan looked over, doubtless waiting for an answer to his question, I said, "The writing on the bottom that I mentioned. Bolin and his dad translated it. *Straight from the source lies within protection from venom, poison, and the bite of the werewolf.*"

"So whatever clunked inside might be a powerful artifact, more than the case itself."

"I wondered if it might give us clues about the lost magic of the werewolf bite. My mother was recently lamenting about that, about how our people are slowly dying without the ability to create werewolves through means other than procreation, and inbreeding has been on the rise as a result these past centuries. Maybe that's why Augustus turned into such a turd."

"You think genetic insufficiencies could account for that?" Duncan asked.

"A *lot* of insufficiencies. He probably licked glowing toadstools as a kid and wandered through radioactive ponds."

Duncan chuckled as we headed out onto a pier with walkways on either side and restaurants and shops in the middle. They all looked like normal human destinations. Would we truly find a paranormal bar among them? Maybe it would also look normal but have a back room for warlocks and clairvoyants to swill beer and throw darts under the guidance of their powers.

As I searched for a sign, Duncan peered over the railing into the dark water lapping at the pilings. Fog was drifting in, so I doubted he could see much.

The hazy weather reminded me of the night we'd been attacked by wolves and stray dogs with glowing eyes. I hoped the wolf—presumably the *werewolf*—we'd heard howling hadn't followed us and didn't have similar plans. Unfortunately, my face-off with Augustus hadn't led to anything conclusive, like a promise that he would leave me alone. My mom and her mate, Lorenzo, had threatened to kick Augustus's ass if he tried to kill me again, but we were a long way from the pack's hunting grounds. My cousin might think he could get away with offing me if it happened in the city. Who would know? It wasn't as if the pack would trust or even listen to a report from the lone wolf Duncan if he survived and I died.

"I'll only stop if I sense something magical, but I'll wager there's all kinds of good stuff down there." Duncan's voice was full of longing. He had no idea I was mulling over my death.

"Even better than the barnacle-covered wooden handles of saws from the 1800s?" I put aside my grim thoughts about murdering cousins. Ahead, a sandwich-board read El Gato Mágico in chalked cursive writing and had a round flask on it, blue liquid bubbling inside. An arrow pointed to a narrow alley between buildings.

"Most assuredly." After another longing look at the water, Duncan followed me into the alley. "I can come back later when I'm not on an important mission."

"I won't stop you if you want to look."

"And leave you to enter a den of paranormal danger on your own? I am certain you're capable of dealing with such places, but a gentleman doesn't abandon a lady to possible plight."

"That means you didn't sense anything magical under the pier, right?"

"Not in the spot we just walked over, no." Duncan smiled, stepped forward, and held the door open for me.

Pop music with a Latino flair floated out, not what I would have expected from a bar where witches and warlocks hung out. Before I could step in, a gangly man who looked like a forty-year-old version of Harry Potter stumbled out. He had a lean face, beaky nose, wore glasses, and clutched a cape against the cold as he peered blearily around like he might be trying to remember where he'd parked.

"Is that a pencil tucked behind his ear? Or a wand?" I murmured as he shambled past us.

As far as I knew, real magic wands didn't exist, wood being a poor conductor for power of any kind, but that didn't keep hucksters from selling such things.

"I don't know," Duncan said, "but I think this is the right place."

"Probably so."

The scents of grilled onions, hamburgers, and beer wafted out the open door—all normal bar-and-grill odors. But I also caught a few whiffs of essential oils and dried flowers that reminded me of the alchemist's apartment. As we walked in, I glanced toward the rafters for dangling bunches of herbs.

More caped and cloaked people sat at tables in the front, playing board games as they nursed mugs of ale, glasses of wine, and cocktails in glasses, more than a few of the beverages throwing colorful vapors into the air. I didn't sense actual magic in the drinks, so maybe the owner employed molecular gastronomy to give his visitors what they expected from the establishment.

In the back, past a bar along the side wall, people stood, waiting their turns at pool tables. Beyond them, a couple of big men threw axes at targets. The occasional *thunks* of the projectiles landing mingled with the music.

Here and there, a few men and women danced, but the board-game playing was most popular. A Dungeons and Dragons box caught my eye. Even more grown Harry Potters sat at that table.

Based on sight alone, I might have dismissed the place as catering to those into fantasy novels and games, but my nerves tingled as we took a few steps inside, a hint of magic floating in the air. The drinks might not be enchanted, but some of these people had power.

"This might be a more promising place to magnet fish," I said to Duncan over the music, an axe *thunk* punctuating my sentence. "Or *magic* fish."

He had that detector, after all.

"Yes, but people get upset when your magnets attach themselves to their pockets. Also when your magic detector beeps at them." Duncan lowered his voice and added in a warning tone, "Watch the bartender."

The bartender was watching *us*.

A brown-skinned man of average height and build, he had short gray hair and wouldn't have looked intimidating, but he had a feral aspect, and my senses pricked further as our eyes met. He was a werewolf. Or something similar? My brow furrowed as I considered what my senses told me about him. After so many years dulling them with my potions, I was out of practice at reading signs.

"*Lobisomem*," Duncan said. "Our South American kin. I met one in Brazil during my travels. They're even scarcer than we are."

The bartender might have had sharp ears, or maybe he didn't like the way we looked at him, because he finished making a couple of drinks and walked around his patrons and toward us.

Duncan lowered into a crouch with his arms loose. Expecting

a fight? Maybe his meeting with the Brazilian *lobisomem* hadn't gone well.

But the bartender raised his arms in a conciliatory gesture as he approached, glancing between us before stopping a couple of paces away. He gave Duncan a long look, but his gaze settled on me.

"I already paid my taxes to the Savagers this month," he said, naming my pack. "I don't want any trouble, and I set up my bar outside of what I was *told* was their territory so they would leave me alone. I run a respectable business and don't bother anyone. I'll have the fee again next month, but I won't be *extorted* for more." He glared at Duncan.

I glanced at Duncan, to see if he'd heard about this, but it didn't sound like something that had anything to do with him. I was surprised the guy had recognized me as one of the Snohomish Savagers. Other than the recent hunt, I hadn't interacted with my family in decades, but I supposed he, being lupine himself, could smell or sense that I shared their blood.

"That's not why we came," I said. "We're here for—"

"Beer and camaraderie." Maybe Duncan didn't think it was a good idea to announce what we were really after. "And to hire people. *Strong* people. Do you get any regulars like that who might need work?"

He looked toward big guys at one of the pool tables and also a man caressing his axe between throws.

"Yeah, maybe. You can put a card on the community board. Job listings get posted there." The bartender waved toward a short hallway that looked more like it led to bathrooms than employment opportunities. "I'm Francisco. You're *sure* you didn't come to extort me?" He squinted suspiciously at me.

"Nope. I don't even think..." I paused, not knowing much about the pack dynamics and where they extended their influence these days. When I'd been a girl, it had only been Snohomish

County and a few miles across the border into King County. Raoul's pack, the Cascade Crushers, had ruled the rural and suburban parts of east King County. Everyone had mostly ignored Seattle itself, the urban density making it unappealing for werewolves. But maybe all that had changed when the Crushers had departed. Even if my pack didn't claim two full counties as their territory, that didn't mean they would let lone wolves linger in close proximity to what they *did* claim. That was probably what this guy was. "Who's extorting you?"

"A big *hombre* who's always in a black leather jacket with slicked-back black hair. Last time he came by, some of my clients tried to help me get out of paying his supposed taxes, but he had buddies with him, and it didn't go well for me *or* my establishment." Francisco glanced toward three deep claw marks in the surface of the polished wooden bar.

"Sounds like your cousin," Duncan said, "unless that's a style favored by lots of males in your family. Lots of males stuck in the 1960s. I wonder if they had white T-shirts with packs of cigarettes rolled up in the sleeve too."

"Werewolves set their own styles," I said.

"True enough."

"We're not here looking for trouble," I told Francisco. "Or taxes."

I was tempted to apologize for Augustus's behavior, but I didn't know anything about the agreement this guy had with the pack.

"No? Then please enjoy the offerings here. The cook is happy to make all-meat meals, and we have some potent drinks. I can make a delicious margarita that allows you to see into the spiritual realm. It's popular with my ghost-hunter clientele." Francisco pointed toward a table of young men and women who hunched around a machine and a backpack instead of a board game. Maybe they were heading out to a graveyard later.

"I have equipment for that, no alcohol needed," Duncan said.

"*Equipment* won't fortify you with bravery while enhancing your senses," Francisco said, "but maybe your kind don't need enhancements. You seem especially..." He squinted thoughtfully at Duncan.

"Well fortified naturally, yes." Duncan winked, then pointed toward the hallway. "We'll check the job board. Thanks."

"What about you, *señorita*? A margarita?"

"No, thanks."

Francisco rested a hand on my arm and raised a finger. I bristled at the presumptuous touch, but a wariness in his eyes as he glanced again at Duncan, who was walking toward the hallway, made me pause without complaint to see what he wanted.

"Your *señor*... He does not work for the Savagers?"

"No. They want him dead. Or at least for him to leave their territory."

"He is a lone wolf." It was a statement, not a question.

"As far as I know, yes."

"From... the Old World?"

"I think so." I lowered my arm, hoping to walk away without answering more questions about Duncan. If the bartender wanted information, he could talk to Duncan directly.

"He is very strong, yes?"

I thought of the motorcycles that Duncan had torn apart. "Yeah."

"I am relieved he does not work for the *lobo* who comes to extort me. This one is..." Francisco drew his hand back from me and groped in the air. "Like us but greater. The same but different. More dangerous. You sense this, yes?"

If I hadn't seen Duncan fight, it would have been hard for me to think of him as *dangerous*, but even when he was simply standing in his human form, his affable smile didn't entirely hide his feral power.

"You wouldn't want to pick a fight with him, no." I didn't

mention how many times I'd threatened to have his van towed. It wasn't as if I was great about following my own advice.

"No," Francisco whispered, the word barely audible over the music and nearby conversations. "He reminds me of the very old *lobisomem*. Those who came from the mountains and into the villages along the river, to *my* village in my youth. Those who could take the bipedfuris form and whose bite spread the magic of the wolf." He turned his head and pointed to his neck, to faint scars near his carotid artery, an old pair of puncture wounds. Fang marks.

An uneasy chill of knowing went through me. Even though I *was* a werewolf, it was because I'd been born one to my mother, not because someone had bitten me. As I'd been discussing with Duncan, that magic had supposedly faded from the world long ago. I hadn't realized it had existed as recently as in this guy's lifetime. Fifty years ago? Sixty? Nor had I realized our kind had been able to take the in-between form and walk furred and deadly on two legs that recently.

"I don't think he has that power." I looked in the direction Duncan had gone. He'd disappeared into that hallway.

I admitted I didn't know the extent of Duncan's powers. Just because I hadn't *seen* him change into that form didn't mean he couldn't, did it?

As if my thought had summoned him, he leaned around the corner and into view, eyebrows raised as he looked at Francisco and me standing side by side. He tilted his head toward the hallway—had he found that job board and something promising on it?—and crooked a finger at me in invitation.

Nodding, I stepped in that direction, but Francisco touched my arm, his grip tighter this time, as if in warning.

"Please, *señorita*, encourage him *not* to work for your pack. They have power enough. Those like me, those who wish only to do business for the paranormal... we do not bother anyone. It is not right that we should have to pay so much to werewolves who believe they are like the mafia. Some of us fled from countries with systems like that to work in a fairer place."

"He's not going to work for them," I said, disturbed that Augustus and who knew how many other family members were acting like thugs. "I doubt he'll even be in the area long. He's a traveler."

Saying those words aloud sent a twinge of sadness through me. I was still conflicted about Duncan, because of his association with Chad, but he was here with me once again, being helpful and pleasant company. Something I'd been without for a long time.

"Good." Francisco released me, relief on his face and in his voice. "Good."

As I headed toward the hall, I wondered if I would one day learn there was more that was disturbing about Duncan than that he'd taken a gig from my ex-husband. Maybe I *shouldn't* think of him as pleasant company.

6

When I joined Duncan in the bar's short hall, he was studying a cork board with mostly normal and innocuous things on it, though there were a few atypical items. A voodoo doll pinned to one corner, a tuft of fur with a phone number stuck to another, and paper promising free samples of Tooth and Tongue Tonic. A couple of business cards also glowed slightly.

"Did you know that other magical beings get a weird vibe from you?" I asked.

Duncan, who gripped his chin as he read the cards and notes, merely raised an eyebrow. "*I'm* not the one the bartender thought was going to beat him up if he didn't pay *taxes*. Your cousin is a real gem of a werewolf."

"Werewolves in general don't have a history of being *gems*. As I'm sure I don't have to tell you, we're driven by animal instincts and savage magic even when we're in human form." That was one of the reasons I'd taken that potion for so long. Not only had I deeply regretted losing myself to the savagery of the wolf and killing my first love in a fight, but I hadn't wanted to lose my temper—my *humanity*—with my children. Chad's normal human genes had ensured they didn't have any magic themselves, no great strength or power to heal from wounds quickly, so they had only average human means of defending themselves and recovering from injuries.

"They don't? Huh." Duncan had avoided answering my question.

I didn't miss it, but I didn't press him. He was here helping me; it wasn't as if he owed me any answers.

"Looking to hire *strong* men for seasonal work." Duncan pointed at a card in the middle with those words and a number, then shrugged and pulled out his phone.

"Seasonal work, as in mugging people for their invaluable magical artifacts?"

"A druidic wolf case could make someone a lovely Christmas present." Duncan dialed the number.

"Now that you mention it, I see things like that on the end caps at Walmart every winter."

I perused the board further as Duncan spoke to someone who answered. He promised that he was vigorous, strong, and had a hobby of howling at the moon. Between the people speaking in the bar, laughter and cheers over pool shots, and thuds of axes landing, I couldn't hear the other side of the conversation, but he did a lot of, "Uh-huh," and, "I see," finishing with, "Saturday? Okay."

"I'm guessing that wasn't the person who hired thugs to steal the case," I said when he hung up.

"No, but if I want to unload a special cargo of cauldrons and other witch paraphernalia at the Port of Tacoma this weekend, the pay is $20 an hour. Having a hearty constitution is a plus. I'm guessing some of that paraphernalia might zap people handling the crates."

"$20 an hour? You could get more than that moving boxes around in an Amazon warehouse. Zap-free boxes."

"I'm not sure the cauldron-import business is that lucrative." Duncan returned to reading the board. Presumably the guy on the other end of his call hadn't sounded like he also stole and exported magical artifacts.

"This may have been a waste of time," I reluctantly admitted after not seeing any more promising cards.

"Spending time with you, my lady, is never a waste of time."

"I'd be flattered, but I think you are, even now, fantasizing about getting your fishing magnets and dropping them over the pier."

"Naturally, but you're *with* me in the fishing fantasies. Holding my pole."

"You don't use a pole." Numerous times, I'd seen him toss his heavy cylindrical mega magnets into the water. They were attached by a rope that he used to drag them along, then haul them up with whatever the magnets attracted.

"Not for the fishing part, no." He smiled.

"I should have known there would be flirting tonight."

"Of *course*. You fed me chocolate. It's an aphrodisiac." Duncan opened his mouth to continue but looked past me, and his eyes widened.

A big blond man ambled into the hallway, a hand on his belt, already unfastening the clasp on the way to the bathroom. I gaped. It was the guy from the video.

He glanced indifferently at Duncan but spotted me, and his eyes widened with recognition. Other than in the video footage, I'd never seen him before, but he sure knew me.

Duncan sprang past me and toward him.

The guy cursed and ran around the corner toward the pool tables. Duncan would have caught him, but two servers with empty trays were heading toward the kitchen, and he crashed into them. I squeezed past and lunged into the main room first. Recovering, Duncan leaped out right behind me.

"Wolves!" the blond guy barked as he ran past the pool tables and toward a back door.

Instead of getting out of the way at the warning, burly men with cue sticks and throwing axes stepped *into* the way. They faced us, and when Duncan passed me, charging after the blond man, they deliberately blocked him. One lifted a pool stick like a baseball bat and swung.

"Look out," I warned.

A faint tingle ran through my veins. The full moon was past, but, as I knew from the old days, danger and fury could rouse the wolf almost as well as its magical silvery beams. This wasn't the place to change, to turn into a wild animal and possibly hurt—or *kill*—innocent people.

Not slowing, Duncan ducked the blow of the man swinging the pool stick. It smashed into the wall where his head had been and broke. Another guy surged into his way, blocking him like a football fullback.

Duncan roared and rammed a shoulder into the man, sending him flying. So powerful was the blow that the guy's feet left the floor and he landed on his back on the pool table. Its stout legs shuddered under the weight.

These were big guys, and, as I crept closer, not sure how to help but wanting to, I sensed that some of them had magic about them. They weren't werewolves, but could these be more imbibers of the Tiger Blood potion?

With one man out of the way, Duncan tried to get by again, to chase the blond guy, but the big brutes continued to block him. One did more than that; he hurled an axe at Duncan's chest.

I cried an alarmed warning and raced in, grabbing a pool stick off a rack on the wall.

Duncan blurred as he dodged, moving so quickly that the axe didn't even brush him. It struck the wall instead, bounced off, and landed on the floor. Another man with a pool stick in hand lifted it, aiming for Duncan's back. With my new weapon, I surged forward and cracked him on the head.

The man staggered as the wood snapped. They did *not* make pool cues stout enough to handle paranormal strength.

Unfortunately, my target didn't drop. He snarled and turned toward me, swinging his own stick. I managed to duck but felt the wind of its passing over my head.

"You dare attack a lady!" Duncan snarled and sprang onto the man's back, his arm snaking around the guy's neck.

"Don't kill him!" I blurted in fear, glimpsing the utter savagery in Duncan's brown eyes.

He had to be close to changing, but this wasn't the wilderness where the authorities would shrug off a death caused by a wolf attack as a force of nature. That was especially true in this bar where at least half the people knew exactly what we were.

I expected Duncan, his instincts ruling him, to ignore me—or not even hear my cry—but he glanced at me. Instead of choking the man or breaking his neck, he drove a knee into the back of the guy's thigh and hurled him sideways. Our foe smashed into the wall, then pitched to the floor, dazed.

"You okay?" Duncan asked me.

"Yes, but— Look out!" I warned again.

A man who could have tried out for the role of the Incredible Hulk shoved the pool table across the floor, demonstrating much greater than human strength as the thick legs skidded across the floorboards. That table had to weigh hundreds of pounds.

The hulk caught Duncan off-guard and managed to pin him between the table and the wall as his buddy crawled away, barely avoiding being crushed himself.

Duncan grunted as the table rammed him in the waist. The guy kept pushing at it, as if he could smash a werewolf like a bug.

Grabbing another pool cue, I moved toward him, but a couple more men crouched in the way, eyeing me with axes or fists raised.

They glanced toward the back of the bar. The blond man had disappeared through the door. They seemed to be checking to make sure he'd gotten away. Damn it, he might have had the case with him. We had to finish this so we could try to catch up with him.

His back against the wall, Duncan gripped the edge of the pool table and pushed back. The tendons in his neck stood out as he growled and shoved it away, overriding the strength of the hulk. When he had space, he sprang atop the table, landing in a crouch and dodging dangling light fixtures hanging from the ceiling. Not hesitating, Duncan kicked his adversary in the face. The man spun away, not able to maintain his footing, and tumbled to the floor.

I growled, the noise far more lupine than human, and advanced with the pool cue. The two men who'd been blocking me considered me anew and decided to back away. Duncan jumped down, ready to attack further, but the hulk was crawling away on hands and knees. The rest of the men backed farther, dropping their weapons and raising their hands.

Crouched with his fingers curled, Duncan looked like he wanted to keep fighting—like the savage *wolf* in him wanted to keep fighting.

"The blond guy," I reminded him.

I jogged toward the back door, keeping the pool stick in case one of the men changed his mind about letting us go. But they'd accomplished their goal of buying time for their buddy to get away. They didn't impede us as we ran out the back door.

On the walkway, the foot traffic had dwindled, the fog thickening and muting the city lights. The mist had turned to drizzle, and the blond man wasn't anywhere in sight.

Duncan thrust his nose upward, inhaled deeply, then ran toward the waterfront street. I couldn't smell our enemy but would have guessed he'd gone that way, regardless. It was either that or hiding out on the pier—or jumping into the water.

I jogged after Duncan, glancing left and right, half-expecting the guy to leap out of an alcove or doorway and attack us. But all we saw were shoppers and diners meandering along the walkway. Duncan paused when we reached the street, again testing the air.

"Can you smell his trail?" I wouldn't have doubted he had that power as a wolf—I would have also—but, even though our senses were keener than typical in human form, we lost the anatomy necessary to rival bloodhounds.

"He smelled of crushed lavender. It was noticeable." Duncan took off along the sidewalk of the waterfront street.

I hadn't caught a floral whiff from the guy, but Duncan had gotten closer to him than I had.

"Maybe the soap in the men's room has that scent," I said before remembering the man hadn't gotten to go in. Still, I couldn't imagine that thug carrying lavender sachets around for kicks.

"That's possible." Duncan slowed when he reached his parking spot.

His van had a puzzling slump to it, but it wasn't until he cursed and crouched by a front tire that I realized why. It was flat. They were *all* flat.

"He let the air out?" I asked.

"The tire is slashed." Duncan hurried around the van to check the others and groaned. "They *all* are."

Alarm flashed in his eyes, and he lunged for the side door. Had he locked it when we left? I couldn't remember and grimaced, imagining all of his fancy—and probably expensive—treasure-hunting equipment stolen or maimed.

The door was locked, and he jammed his hand into his pocket for his keys. The van was old enough to have manual locks, and it took him a moment to get in and look around.

"Nobody has been inside. That's a relief anyway." Duncan hopped back out and slumped against the side of the van. "What a bastard. You don't attack someone's woman, and you *certainly* don't attack their automobile."

"Or beat up their intern to steal their case." I rubbed my face. "How did he even know about your van? I'm the one he recognized, and he was surprised to see me. I'm sure of it. It's not like he was lying in wait for us."

"No," Duncan agreed, then returned to the sidewalk, sniffing again. But he shook his head. "I've lost the scent. The rain, I think. Unless..." He slipped between his van and the next car, sniffing toward the street. "Ah. I think he got a ride."

"For a surly thug, he has a lot of buddies."

"Indeed. Maybe we should ask *them* where he went."

"You kicked one in the face and hurled another across the room. I don't think they'll be eager to share secrets with us."

"*You* cracked one on the head too." Duncan still looked aggrieved about his van but managed an approving smile for me. The acknowledgment probably shouldn't have warmed me, but it did. And I was more kindly inclined toward Duncan, as he'd put it, after he'd driven me down here and helped out. Too bad he'd ended up with his tires flattened.

"They won't share secrets with *either* of us," I said.

Eyes narrowed, Duncan looked down the pier in the direction of the bar. "Let's try asking one of them anyway."

"With your hand around his throat?"

"Unless you want to bribe them with chocolate bars."

"They didn't look like connoisseurs of fine foods."

"So I shouldn't bring the brisket, then?"

I shook my head. "They weren't werewolves, right?" Even though I'd sensed people with power in the bar, mostly witch and warlock power, the bartender had been the only one with a lupine vibe. Those men might have been similar to the blond guy and taking a potion. Maybe they *all* took that potion.

"No."

"They were abnormally strong though. Like our mugger."

"I noticed when one shoved a pool table into my balls."

"Oh, is that what he pinned? I noticed it took you a moment to recover and push the pool table back." I eyed Duncan as we walked, again thinking about the strength that had required. I would have to consult the internet to know how many hundreds of pounds a pool table weighed, but I knew they weren't light.

"Yes, it took me a moment to bite back an unmanly squeal of pain and gird myself sufficiently."

"I'm sorry you had to go through that." The comment came out more flippantly than I meant, and in a softer tone, I repeated, "I really am sorry."

"It's not your fault, but thank you. My mangled balls *especially* thank you."

"I hope your equipment wasn't permanently damaged." I smiled for his sake, thinking he might appreciate the joke. After all, he'd brought up his *fishing pole* earlier.

"Don't worry. My equipment and I heal quickly."

"That's a relief."

He raised his eyebrows.

"For you, I mean. I don't have any plans involving your equipment."

"That's disappointing. It likes to be used."

We reached the back door of the bar, found it locked and without a handle on that side, and had to go around to the front again. The music still played, but fewer of the tables were occupied, and the back area with the pool tables and axe-throwing alley had cleared out completely. All of the brutes were gone.

Francisco eyed us warily as we approached and waved at the

broken pool sticks littering the floor. "It would have cost me less if you *had* come to collect taxes."

"Sorry," I said and reached for my purse, feeling compelled to offer to pay. But which of my budgeting envelopes would I extract the money from? It was hard to classify that experience as *entertainment*.

Duncan noticed me opening my purse and stopped me with a hand on my wrist. He held up a finger, withdrew a billfold, and laid a couple of hundreds on the bar top. I glimpsed more bills with large denominations inside and decided that he might make more than I'd thought selling his rusty finds.

"Who were those guys, Francisco?" Duncan asked casually. "We weren't expecting to get jumped when we were examining the community board."

The bartender shrugged. "They come here a lot, from *up north*, I hear them say sometimes. But they're surly dicks, so I don't talk to them. I only serve them the drink they like." He waved to a glass at the end of the bar that hadn't been picked up. The pink liquid inside bubbled and smoked.

"That looks like Pepto Bismol simmering on a Bunsen burner." I couldn't imagine wanting to drink it.

"That's one of the ingredients." Francisco lifted a bottle of the pink medicine off a shelf under the bar. "Then a number of powders I get from my druid supplier, and of course the tequila is what makes the medicine go down."

"That sounds loathsome." After hearing the rest of the ingredients, I could imagine drinking the concoction even less.

"Rue mentioned one of the side effects of that potion was stomach upset, didn't she?" Duncan asked me quietly.

"It fixes that right up," Francisco said. "And, if you have too much cactus juice—" he waved toward a row of tequila bottles on the shelf behind the bar, several labels not in English, "—I've got some hangover drinks for the morning. Stuff to help you concentrate on your spells too." He nodded toward the Dungeons and Dragons table, though half the cloaked drinkers had disappeared during the fight. "There's a reason this place is popular with the paranormal."

"With Pepto Bismol mixed with tequila, how could it not be?" I muttered.

Missing or ignoring the sarcasm, Francisco nodded firmly.

Duncan and I moved away from the bar.

"I need to find somewhere to buy new tires," he said, "in case you want to call someone for a ride home. I don't think *up north* is enough to go on, as far as locating those men, or whoever hired them, so we'll have to do more research."

"Well, Tacoma is south, so we at least know they're not selling their stolen magical artifacts to the person hiring cauldron unloaders."

"Likely not, but if my van keeps getting ravaged while I'm in the area, *I* might have to take that gig."

If he could move a pool table with a hulk shoving against it, lifting crates of cauldrons wouldn't be a problem. I almost asked again about his unusual strength, but he'd already dodged that question, and he would probably continue to do so.

"It might be healthier for you and your tires if you didn't stay in town," I said as we walked back out into the night. "If you told Chad to F off and aren't looking for the case anymore, what's keeping you here?"

"A gentleman doesn't use vulgarities or curse words when resigning from a job."

"You should have. It's the only language he understands. That and a punch to the nose."

"Physical maiming is hard to deliver over the phone. I *did* tell him that he has a woefully inadequate tallywacker if he couldn't come to you and bargain for access to his artifact himself."

"Tallywacker?"

Duncan lifted his eyebrows. "You haven't heard that term? Perhaps you're more familiar with trouser snake. Meat puppet. Or pork sword."

"*Pork sword*," I mouthed, then shook my head. "Next time you talk to him, at least tell him *I* told him to F off. And to stuff his tallywacker up his ass."

"Women are blunt in this country."

"Yeah, we like our vulgarities. Especially we middled-aged, jilted women who've learned to fend for ourselves."

Duncan gave me a sympathetic look. I waved my words away. I hadn't intended to fish for sympathy.

When we returned to his van, Duncan pulled out his phone to try to find a tire place open at night. I doubted he would be able to get the problem fixed until the morning. He must have drawn the same conclusion because he opened a ride-sharing app to summon someone to pick us up.

"What's keeping you here?" I asked again, noting how often he side-stepped answering questions.

What if his supposed conversation with Chad had never happened, and he remained on the clock for my ex? I didn't *want* that to be true, but Duncan had already deceived me once.

"Aside from needing to thoroughly magic detect and magnet fish in the copious waters here, I feel I owe you. If I hadn't accepted your ex-husband's gig, the wolf case would remain under your floor, with no one the wiser about its existence. People wouldn't be routinely attacking you."

I thought about pointing out that my intern was the one who'd been attacked over the case. The rest of the trouble had been because of my cousin.

"You don't owe me anything," I said. "You don't need to stick around on my behalf."

"Wouldn't you miss me if I were gone? Who would take you to bars where you could learn about the secret favorite drinks of potion-imbibers? If *your* potion ever upsets your stomach, you'll now know where to go."

"My stomach would have to be tying itself around my throat before I'd drink something pink and bubbling."

"Maybe that happens to those who consume the Tiger Blood potion."

"With its list of side effects, one wonders *why* they drink it," I said. "Those men were already big and strong."

"They were, but someone is always stronger."

"Maybe their tiny tallywackers lead them to feel insecure."

Duncan smiled faintly as our ride pulled up. "I knew you knew what that meant."

"I read between the lines."

Duncan opened a backseat door for me but didn't step into the car himself. He waved to the driver. "He'll take you back to your truck at the Ballard Locks."

"You're not coming?" I asked.

"Not unless you're inviting me to your home for the night." His smile widened, though he didn't look like he expected that. "My home is, of course, here." He looked toward the foggy water.

I snorted, sure he would do a little fishing before going to sleep in his van. "You're too vague and irrepressible to invite home."

"As I feared." Still holding the door open, Duncan bowed to me. "It was a pleasure spending the evening with you, Luna. As always."

"You must like getting into fights."

"I do crave adventure."

I paused, having the urge to kiss him on the cheek before leaving, but I slid into the car without taking that action. I had too many questions about him, too many reasons not to trust him. Not to *let* myself trust him.

7

THE NEXT MORNING, I WALKED OUT OF MY APARTMENT WITH THE largest coffee cup I owned, and it was filled to the brim with a potent Americano. With bags under my eyes and yawns accompanying me to the leasing office, I felt like Bolin. It had crossed my mind to make *two* huge caffeinated drinks, but since I lived a hundred yards from where I worked, it would be easy to slip back and make a second coffee later.

The parking lot came into view before I reached the leasing office, and I paused to stare. Someone with his back to me—was that Bolin?—was shooting a rifle-sized water gun into the trees near the G-wagon. A roll of paper towels, a squeegee, and a bottle of Windex rested on the sidewalk beside him.

In the nearest tree, a pair of robins squawked and left a branch when the water streamed past.

I rubbed my head as I diverted in that direction. "What are you doing, Bolin?"

He scowled over his shoulder at me. "Defending my Mercedes."

"I don't see any motorcycle gangs," I said, referring to the *last* time we'd had to defend the parking lot. The thugs who'd rode through, breaking windows, had been a lot more menacing than robins.

"The gangs are up there." Bolin waved the water gun toward the tree. "Snickering at me."

"Birds hang out in flocks, not gangs, and that's called chirping."

"That's *how* they snicker." He raised his voice to add, "After they *poop* all over your SUV."

"It's a lot shinier than the other cars in the lot." I waved toward my pick-up truck in the staff spot next to his overpriced behemoth of a vehicle. The factory paint had lost its sheen, if there had ever *been* a sheen, a long time ago.

"Thus making it appealing to *poop* on?" Bolin sprayed water into the trees again. By the time it reached the upper branches, it lacked any force, and the remaining birds didn't bother moving. "It's happening every day I work here."

"I don't think your activities are illegal, per se, but they seem odd for a druid." I waved to the water gun. "Would your father approve?"

"My father is able to park in a garage like a civilized person, so *his* car doesn't get spattered. Besides, he's not a druid, and neither am I. We just dabble. Grandfather was the druid."

"Would *he* have approved of such activities?"

Bolin sighed and lowered the water gun. "No."

"I'm surprised the birds pester you. Usually animals can sense the magic in the blood of one with paranormal genes." Even I'd been able to feel a bit of Bolin's power when I'd still been taking the potion that had dulled my senses. Now, it was easier for me to identify that he had the ability to use magic and even that it was druidic magic.

"They don't bother *me*. Just my car."

"Maybe it's their way of saying you don't have a sufficiently druidic mode of transportation." My phone buzzed in my pocket, and I pulled it out.

"Cars in general aren't druidic. Unless you mean I should get a Subaru Forester or something." His nose crinkled. "Those are very... pedestrian."

"You mean affordable to the average person?" The number had a local area code, but I didn't recognize it and debated whether to answer.

Bolin wrinkled his nose again.

"I'll take that as a yes. A druid probably shouldn't have a car at all. Maybe you can ride a reindeer to work."

"Hilarious."

"I'm just saying, you never see a reindeer with bird poop on its antlers." The phone stopped ringing, and an alert came up, saying the caller was leaving a voicemail. "Why don't you spray and squeegee my truck while you're there? I think washing the boss's car is in the job description for an intern."

Bolin looked balefully at me, but it was unclear if it was because I'd asked him to do menial work or I wasn't sympathetic enough to his plight. Maybe I should have been since I'd had to pressure wash the walkways around the complex more than once. A number of tenants hung feeders on their little patios and balconies, so birds nested in the surrounding trees by the hundreds. They did tend to leave droppings everywhere.

As I headed for the office, I tapped the recording to play the voice mail.

"Aunt Luna?" a woman with a young voice asked. "Are you there?"

It sounded like my niece, Jasmine. She was the one who'd scared away my original alchemist to ensure I couldn't get potions and would have to face the world—and its dangers—with the power of the werewolf fully intact.

"Call me back, please," Jasmine continued. "Someone came on

your mom's property last night and attacked her and wounded several pack members. I'm not sure if Emilio is going to make it."

I gaped at the phone. Who'd attacked my seventy-year-old mother? And Emilio, the salami-loving werewolf who thought I was *okay*, despite what my cousins had said about me? He was a goofy innocent-seeming guy, and I'd liked him right away. And Mom... Well, who would attack an old woman? She still had power, but she was dying. She wasn't a threat.

When I called, Jasmine answered right away.

"Luna," she blurted with relief.

"Sorry, I didn't recognize your number. Is Mom okay? Where are you?"

"Yeah, she said the bullet only grazed her."

"*Bullet?*"

Someone walked past with a dog, and I waved, then hurried to shut myself in the office so the conversation would be private.

"Yeah. Normally, it would be a super minor wound for one of us," Jasmine said, as if getting shot wasn't that alarming, "but it was a *silver* bullet. That's all they were shooting. And the one lodged in Emilio's side is more problematic, and he's already weakened from it. The pack's wise wolf is extracting it and giving him potions to stave off a magical infection, but those guys knew we were werewolves and came prepared."

My stomach sank. "What guys?"

"A gang of thugs. They were strong, abnormally so. At first, we thought they were werewolves, but they didn't smell right for that. There was another kind of magic about them."

My stomach sank further, descending all the way into my shoes. "Did one of them have long blond hair? And look like a drummer from an eighties metal band?"

Jasmine hesitated. "One did look like that, yes. I wasn't there, but Emilio caught some of it on camera with his phone. The blond bro didn't have a gun, but I guess it doesn't matter. There were at least eight of them, and they were strong enough to get the best of Aunt Umbra and Lorenzo. Only because of numbers though. And silver *bullets*. Because werewolves are strong too." Indignation filled Jasmine's voice, but then it grew smaller and quieter when she added, "Aunt Umbra and Lorenzo were lucky that Emilio was there. He'd come by to fix the internet. Having another fighter helped, and Emilio called the rest of the family. When some more of us arrived and turned wolf, the guys took off."

"I'm sorry. That's awful. I can come up there today if... Uhm, is Augustus there?"

The pack might not *want* me to come up there. After I'd been out of their lives for so long, they might object to me visiting again. Mom wouldn't. She'd been waiting a long time for me to return to the pack—she'd said as much. It was the rest of the family I had to worry about, especially my belligerent cousins.

"Yeah, but your mom wants to see you. And I don't think Augustus will do anything with Lorenzo there. Besides, he'd be stupid to worry about you right now anyway. The pack has a new enemy. How'd you know about the blond bro?"

"A hunch. I've encountered him before." I'd *encountered* him twelve hours ago.

Had he and his thugs gone straight up to Monroe after running from Duncan and me? Why? To get back at me? They were the ones who'd started everything by stealing the case.

I slumped against the wall, hating the idea that I had, whether it had been my fault or not, somehow caused my mother to be hurt. And Emilio. A silver bullet lodged in a werewolf could be fatal. If it had struck his heart, it would have killed him instantly.

"In Shoreline?" Jasmine sounded confused.

It *was* confusing. I wished Duncan and I had managed to subdue the blond man and question him.

"Shoreline, Seattle... The guy gets around." I remembered the bartender's words that those thugs were from *up north*. "He stole something from me—technically from my intern. An ancient druidic case with a wolf head on the lid."

"I'm talking to her now," Jasmine said, her mouth away from the phone. "Luna said she's seen those guys before."

"Are you with my mom now?" I asked.

"Yeah. We're in her cabin. She heard what you said about a wolf artifact and thinks you should come up here right away."

"With salami," came a masculine voice from the background.

"That's Emilio," Jasmine said.

"I gathered. If he can request meat, he can't be that grievously injured." I hoped.

"He's sweaty, pale, and moaning and complaining every twenty seconds, but his appetite is okay."

"A good sign."

"I'll be up there soon." I hung up, set the phone down, and bent forward to grip my knees.

In addition to all my other woes, the question of whether I had enough money left this month for gas and salamis trickled through my mind.

"I'll have to dig into the emergency fund." I cringed at the idea, but family members being shot had to qualify as an emergency. At least I *had* a sufficient emergency fund these days.

Three honks sounded in the parking lot. Was that Bolin with the birds again?

Irritated, I grabbed my phone and keys, intending to tell him to answer the leasing inquiries or do something else more useful than battling nature. But when I walked outside, I found Duncan in his Roadtrek idling in the parking lot. Had *he* been the one to honk? Bolin and his squeegee and paper towels had disappeared.

Duncan rolled down the window and waved cheerfully at me. "Do you like my new tires?"

I headed for the truck, not in the mood to banter, but I did observe, "They're even bigger than the last ones."

"Yes, I upgraded. In case you need to borrow my van again to run over wolves in the woods." Duncan waved toward the greenbelt where he'd battled my cousins.

"I'm sure it would be effective, but can you move? You're blocking me in. I need to— My pack was attacked by the same guys we fought last night."

The humor vanished from Duncan's eyes. "In retribution?"

"I... don't know yet. I need to go up there."

"We didn't even *hurt* the blond man. And none of the others were seriously injured."

I spread my arms, confused and frustrated, and waved for him to move his van.

He started to put it in gear but paused. "Is your brutish cousin going to be there?"

"Unfortunately. It sounds like the whole family is gathering."

"Do you want me to go with you? Do you want me to drive you up there?"

"No. You're a lone wolf. They'll attack you again."

"They treat *you* like a lone wolf. What if they attack *you*?"

I opened my mouth, wanting to say I could handle it, but could I? Even in my powerful lupine form, I hadn't been able to best my cousins, not when it had been four against one. I might have knocked Augustus off that train trestle, but they'd then knocked *me* off. And what if Augustus blamed me for the attack on Mom and wouldn't let me close enough to her cabin to see her?

"Let me take you up there, Luna," Duncan said softly. "They'll think twice about attacking you with me at your side."

"They won't think twice about attacking *you*."

"Let them." His eyes flared with feral energy, reminding me of how strong and dangerous he could be. "It sounds like your pack could use some of its weakest members weeded out."

"They are, unfortunately, not weak."

"Its non-contributing *asshole* members then."

I couldn't object to that description of my cousins, especially if it was true that they were *taxing* members of the paranormal community who were trying to do business in the greater Seattle area—in a part of that area that our pack didn't even claim. What did werewolves need with that kind of money anyway?

Still, I hesitated, loath to get Duncan involved. I didn't want him to put himself in danger on my behalf.

"Let me help, Luna," he urged softly, watching the indecision on my face. "Like I said, I owe you."

"You don't owe me anything. You just…" I groped in the air. He *had* betrayed me, and I didn't want to dismiss that, but I'd also let myself be drawn in by his charm when I should have been warier. I couldn't blame everything on him.

"Need to earn your trust," he said firmly.

"Are you planning to stick around long enough for that to matter?"

"I told you there are a lot of bodies of water to fish in here. I could be in Seattle a *long* time, and since fate is making it so our paths keep crossing…" He extended a hand, palm toward the sky.

"Our paths are crossing because you keep driving into my parking lot."

"Fate." His affable expression returned as he gave an insouciant smile and waved toward the passenger seat.

"This is a bad idea," I muttered, but I got into the van with him.

8

"Did you ever find out who the white wolf was who spotted us when we hunted together?" Duncan asked as he drove through Monroe, heading northeast toward the winding forest roads that led to my mother's cabin.

"That was Lorenzo. He and my mother seem to be an item these days."

"That night, when I looked into the side mirror, he was giving me a squinty, dangerous look."

"Because you were a lone wolf invading the pack's territory, but he stood up for me after my cousins tried to take me out on the family hunt. I don't think *he's* going to be a problem when we get there." During the first part of the ride, I'd filled Duncan in on what my niece had told me. "My cousin— *cousins* are more likely to be a problem. They're not happy with me, and you already beat up Augustus once, so he's really not going to be happy with you."

"Such a lack of contentedness. Maybe we should be taking them Prozac instead of salami." Duncan waved to the recently acquired gift boxes in the seat well at my feet.

The clerk at the farm store now knew my name and that I always paid in cash from the ENTERTAINMENT envelope. That was, alas, now empty. I'd delved into the envelope labeled GROCERIES and planned to put off my next shop until the new month. For now, I'd left my emergency fund alone.

"I don't have a prescription for that." With my envelopes in mind, I delved into my purse to extract the last of the gas money.

"I've heard it's a simple matter in this country to acquire prescription drugs."

"That's sadly true. Do you think if we tucked antidepressants into the salami logs, it would improve Augustus's mood?" I envisioned sneaking the pills into the meat, much like my tenants giving medicine to their dogs.

"If you use sedatives, his mood would absolutely improve."

"Because he'd pass out in the driveway?"

"Nobody is crabby in their sleep."

"Unfortunately, my surly cousins have all sneered at the man-made salamis. They prefer fresh raw meat."

Duncan watched as I slid five more dollars onto the growing stack under his bobblehead doll. "You know I'm going to keep all that until I have enough to buy you something, right?"

"What you do with it is your prerogative."

He'd tried to buy the gift boxes, but I didn't want anyone paying my way or to depend on a man ever again. I didn't admit it to people, but Chad's many betrayals over the years had scarred me. Maybe a Prozac prescription wouldn't be a bad idea. Or at least a therapist. My son Austin had suggested that. My older son Cameron had too, in his own way. A common refrain at home had been, *You're so damaged, Mom.* Maybe that memory shouldn't have filled me with nostalgia, but I'd been lonely since the boys had moved out.

"Excellent," Duncan said. "After a few months of driving you around, I'll have enough to buy you diamonds."

"Micro diamonds, maybe. My monthly gas budget isn't that much."

"Then I might have to drive you around for *years*." Duncan leaned forward, peering upward through the windshield.

Night was a long way off, so he couldn't have been looking for the moon. Some sunlight perhaps. We'd gotten to the point in the drive where towering firs, pines, and cedars grew close to the sides of the road, and their evergreen boughs kept the pavement mostly in shadow, even on clear days. That was more true when I pointed toward the turn-off that would take us off the main road and onto gravel, only a few sunbeams slipping through to brighten the ground. Before long, the gravel would transition to pot-hole adorned dirt.

"I think you can magnet fish your way through all the bodies of water around Seattle before then," I said.

"I don't know. There are a *lot* of bodies here." Duncan pointed to a pond to the side of the road, the trees leaving it in perpetual shadow. A beaver larger than most people's pets rolled off a mossy log and into the water.

"I don't think you'll find any cell phones in that one."

"Perhaps not. I..." His gaze returned to the road ahead. "I sense werewolves."

"We're about a mile from Mom's cabin."

"They're closer than that."

"Yeah," I said, though I didn't yet sense anything.

Even with the van's new giant tires, Duncan had to drive slowly as we left the gravel behind, passing a sign that said NOT MAINTAINED BY THE COUNTY, and rolled onto the bumpy dirt road. Several more minutes passed before my instincts plucked at me, warning me of magic. Of *beings* with magic. My family.

I pointed to a driveway barely visible ahead, thanks to ferns and trees flanking it, and an address sign mounted on a tree.

"After you turn, it's another hundred yards or so to the cabin. There's parking..." This time, I trailed off. I'd spotted movement.

Duncan slowed to a stop as four big wolves padded out of the driveway and stopped in the road, fanning out to block access. Their cool eyes regarded us, especially Duncan. They focused on him through the windshield. I recognized the dark-gray wolf that was Augustus and three of my cousins. Two of the three had been on the railroad trestle and helped knock me into the river where those hunters had waited. Hunters, I had no doubt, that Augustus had arranged to be in that spot when we came through. When *I* came through.

"That I'm guessing I won't be invited to use," Duncan said to finish my sentence.

"I haven't noticed that a lack of an invitation keeps you from parking places." I smiled at him and reached for the handle, wanting to get out and talk to Augustus before they presumed to attack Duncan. It was hard to talk to a werewolf in lupine form, since our thoughts became that of a wild animal and human concerns grew difficult to grasp, but I knew he would understand me.

"It's not my fault your parking lot is so alluring." Duncan turned off the van and reached for his own handle.

"Stay." I lifted a hand. "I'll try to keep things from escalating."

He eyed me skeptically. "Do you have the power to do that with them?"

"We'll see."

I dialed my phone as I slid out of the van, Jasmine's number. But there wasn't enough cell reception for calls. I'd forgotten that.

Palms damp, I tried to text her as I stepped in front of the hood and kept my eyes on the wolves. I hadn't brought any weapons, unless I intended to club my cousins with salamis, and there weren't any handy pool sticks to grab here. I didn't want to fight my relatives, anyway. Not again.

"I'm here to see Mom," I told the wolves, "and I have useful information about the men who attacked her."

I had *some* information anyway. How useful it would be, I didn't know.

Augustus's cool eyes, more amber than brown in this incarnation, looked briefly and dismissively toward me. Then they focused on Duncan again. The eyes of all four wolves focused on him. For now, he remained in the van, but he would come out to defend me. I knew that about him by now.

But this, I realized as I watched my cousins, was about Duncan. Not me. A lone wolf had dared come into the pack's territory. If I'd remained and become the female alpha, as my mother had once believed I was destined to be, I could have brought anyone with me to visit that I wished, but I was a stranger these days, nearly a lone wolf myself.

A growl emanated from Augustus's throat. His gaze shifted back to me, and he charged.

My heart tried to leap from my chest. Two-hundred pounds of lupine savagery, he ran straight toward me.

I dove to the side, rolling into the ferns. My phone flew from my grip. Afraid Augustus would give chase, I leaped to my feet, fingers curling into fists.

Claws clacked on something hard. The hood of Duncan's van.

The driver-side door flew open, and Duncan sprang out, paws hitting the packed dirt of the road. Yes, paws. He'd changed into a wolf.

He snarled up at Augustus, who whirled and leaped off the hood. Jaws opening, he angled straight toward Duncan.

"He's with me," I yelled. "Stop!"

The salt-and-pepper wolf that was Duncan leaped to the side, easily avoiding Augustus. As soon as my cousin landed, Duncan sprang in, his jaws a blur as they snapped for the throat. Augustus turned, meeting those snapping jaws with his own, and they gnashed at each other like fencers, teeth flashing in the dappled sun that made it through the trees.

Again, I yelled for them to stop. Again, it did nothing.

The other three wolves loped forward, clearly intending to help. I jumped onto the road again, trying to throw the power of the wolf into my voice as I ordered them to stay out of it.

A couple of them glanced at me, but they didn't slow down.

"I brought him here to help! He's my guest."

The wolves crouched, jaws opening, almost smiling as they prepared to pile on, to take Duncan down.

Fury sizzled through my veins, along with the righteous indignation of being ignored. I was my mother's daughter, damn it, and the blood of generations of alphas coursed through my body.

My skin pricked with heat as the call of the wolf swept into me. Before I had a chance to think about removing my clothes to save them during the change, I found myself dropping to all fours. Power surged through my veins, and a great lupine snarl erupted from my throat.

A yelp came from my side of the road. Duncan? No, Augustus. Duncan had knocked him into the ferns, but the others arrived and surrounded him, putting the odds at four on one. As strong as he was, Duncan couldn't win against so many. But together... together we would prevail.

I sprang into the battle, biting one wolf in the flank. Another whirled toward me, but taking his focus from Duncan was a mistake. Lashing out with the power of a cobra, Duncan bit into that wolf's shoulder. He *could* have gone for the throat, but our eyes met briefly with understanding. He knew this was my pack, my family, and wouldn't try to kill them.

They didn't deserve that solicitude, not when they were trying to kill *Duncan*.

The dark-gray wolf that was Augustus snarled and sprang

toward me with loathing in his eyes. Muscles bunching, I leaped past my ally as he tore into two other wolves, and met Augustus's gnashing teeth. His bites stung as fangs gored my snout, but I whipped my head past his attack to clamp onto his throat.

A howl sounded back on the driveway, startling me. It might have been the only thing that kept me from sinking my teeth deeper and finding the artery through which my cousin's life flowed.

My grip loosened, and Augustus backed away with a snarl of frustration and pain. I let him go. Two other wolves were already slinking into the woods, leaving trails of blood. In front of the van, Duncan stood over the fourth wolf, who was down and whimpering, and met my gaze.

Another howl sounded, so close that it made my pointed ears flicker. Duncan and I turned toward the driveway. Numerous humans, including the white-haired lean woman who was my mother, stood there. A blue-eyed white wolf, he who'd howled, sat at her side, watching us. Lorenzo. His gaze was cool when it swept over Duncan, the lone wolf intruding on pack territory.

Another whimper sounded. Duncan stepped off the wolf he'd downed.

More blood darkened the dirt road under my cousin, but he was hale enough to push himself to his feet and slink off after the others, his tail between his legs. He didn't look toward the driveway as he padded away. Our observers watched us, not the wolves disappearing into the ferns.

I stepped forward to stand in front of Duncan, my tail out straight, my muscles taut. I had to make it clear that he was my ally, that I'd invited him to enter this territory, and, as a strong female wolf, I was prepared to fight for him to be allowed to be here.

Duncan came up to my shoulder, standing side-by-side with

me. In a supportive manner, not a challenge. He would fight if I had to fight, but he was letting me take the lead in this situation.

The white wolf yawned, and his tongue lolled out in a display of indifference. That was fine. As long as he didn't lead the rest of the pack into attacking us. There were too many.

"I am pleased to see you again as a wolf, my daughter," Mom said, her voice weak, her power wan. She'd managed to walk out here, but her eyes were sunken with fatigue and pain. "But why have you brought an outsider to my home?" Her eyes closed to slits as her gaze shifted to Duncan. "Especially one who radiates dangerous power and the scent of..." Her head cocked. "Not only the Old World but an old time."

An old time? What did *that* mean?

Duncan looked at me, then lowered his torso while his hindquarters remained up. A play bow. A nonthreatening gesture of innocence.

I bumped my shoulder against his and might have snorted if that was something wolves did. Duncan could turn on his goofy side in lupine form the same as human form. In another moment, he would probably be flirting with my mother. But that would cause Lorenzo's attitude to shift from indifference to something more dangerous.

The wolf magic sensed my need to change so that I could more properly speak with my family, and it faded. Soon, my body morphed, my fur disappeared, and I rose up to two legs.

The air felt chill against my bare skin, and I remembered that there hadn't been time to remove my clothes. When I'd seen Duncan threatened, the change had come upon me with startling speed and intensity. Since clothes disappeared into the ether if they weren't removed, I now stood before my family stark naked. Fortunately, I'd dropped my phone when I'd dived away from Augustus, so it was in the dirt instead of gone forever.

Next to me, Duncan also changed back into human form. He

was as naked as I, save for a few smudges of dirt across his muscled torso, but he bowed to my mother without shame.

"Greetings, Luna's family. It is an honor to meet you—*most* of you." Duncan looked in the direction my cousins had gone, but they'd disappeared, only the scent of their spilled blood lingering. Duncan held up a finger, then went to the van and retrieved his shoes and trousers. He must have started removing his clothes when the wolves had stepped into the road, knowing we'd end up in a fight.

"Luna?" Mom prompted, not responding to Duncan.

"I came—*we* came—because of the attack."

While Duncan put on his trousers and shoes, I explained how we'd encountered those men at the bar and that the blond had mugged my intern. With such a large portion of the family looking on, I didn't mention the wolf case. For all I knew, Augustus had more allies among the half-siblings, nieces, nephews, uncles, and more cousins that stood with Lorenzo and Mom in the driveway. I finished with, "There's more that I'd like to tell you later."

"Yes. You will tell me everything in the cabin." Her gaze flicked toward Duncan, as if to include him as part of that *everything*.

I didn't know how much of him I could explain. It wasn't as if he'd been forthright in answering my questions. Such as why other paranormal beings kept sensing that he was something different from a typical werewolf.

As the family turned to head up the driveway toward the cabin, Mom walking beside the white wolf and resting a hand on his back for support, Duncan stepped closer to me.

"Are you all right? Do you want to borrow a shirt?" He lifted a hand to touch the back of my head, fingers stroking through my hair as he gazed at me.

The intimacy surprised me, though it shouldn't have—before and after a change, one's passions rode close to the surface. I caught myself leaning into his touch, appreciating it more than I should have. Especially when his fingers slipped through my hair to massage my scalp. By the moon, that felt amazing.

The memory of waking up naked with his hand on my bare skin came to mind, the aftermath of our hunt the week before. What would it have been like if we'd done more than hunt that night? What would it be like if we slipped into his van and...

No. There would be no slipping. We were standing in the middle of the road in front of my mom's place. This wasn't the time to let him make me feel amazing or anything else. If I was wise, I wouldn't *let* there be a time. Not until I knew that he wasn't still using me to find that case.

"*You* don't even have a shirt." I swatted his chest, intending the gesture to be playful and nothing more, but my hand ended up resting on his abdomen. The warmth of his taut skin under my palm and the ripples of his chiseled abdomen invited exploration.

"I can get one. I wasn't quite done undressing when your odious cousin sprang upon the hood of my van, leaving claw gouges in the paint. He's lucky I was able to keep from slaying him for such impudence."

His tone was teasing, but there was a modicum of truth to the words. I knew very well how hard it was to restrain one's wild instincts when in wolf form. Based on my past experiences, I might not have been able to.

"I thought you got pissed and changed because he sprang at *me*," I said. "His claws were threatening to gouge holes in *my* paint too."

"That would have been equally unacceptable."

"Only equally, huh. I guess it's good to know where I rank in relation to your van."

"I've known the van a *long* time. We're still new." Duncan smirked and lowered his hand, fingers brushing along my bare back and my hip before they dropped away completely.

The fleeting touch sent a zing of hot pleasure through me, and

I stepped away, turning my back so he wouldn't see the gooseflesh tightening my body. I didn't want him to know I was attracted to him, that he could so easily have an effect on me. Not until I knew where he stood.

"I will take that shirt, thanks."

His amused, "Indeed," was too knowing for my tastes.

9

WHEN WE REACHED THE CABIN, WE FOUND LORENZO IN HUMAN FORM —an olive-skinned man in his sixties with thick white hair— waiting on the porch with the rest of the family. Mom had gone inside. Thankfully, my cousins hadn't returned. I didn't want to worry about them anymore today.

Cars I didn't recognize filled the small parking area, so Duncan had to tuck his Roadtrek under a pine tree beside the driveway. His new enormous tires had no trouble rolling over protruding roots.

Duncan was fully dressed now. It helped that he had a closet— well, a cabinet—in his van that he could draw upon. He'd lent me a checkered flannel shirt and sweatpants that I'd cinched so they wouldn't fall down. My underwear had disappeared along with everything else, and without bra support, I felt like I was wandering around in oversized pajamas. Duncan hadn't had anything suitable for me in the undergarment capacity. Maybe that was good. I might have judged him if he'd whipped out a collection of women's lingerie that former lovers had left behind.

A few of my relatives had noticeable bruises, and one had a

black eye, presumably from the fight the night before. The silver bullets might have made the only grievous wounds, but it looked like numerous pack members had ended up involved. Even Jasmine—who might have gotten my text and been the one to bring Lorenzo, Mom, and the others up the driveway to intervene —had a puffy, split lip.

"Thanks for coming," Jasmine whispered to me when we got out of the van. "Augustus was supposed to know better than to attack you. Lorenzo told him to leave you alone."

I nodded. I'd been there when Lorenzo had issued that warning to him.

"He was attacking Duncan," I said, though I wasn't positive that initial charge hadn't been meant to take me out.

"Hi, Duncan." Jasmine waved shyly at him, then leaned in close to whisper to me, "He's hot."

"He certainly thinks so."

Duncan snorted. I had no doubt his hearing was keen enough that he'd caught both comments.

Jasmine blushed and waved for us to head into the cabin. We climbed the steps together, Duncan walking so close to me that I could almost feel the heat of his body.

Considering the number of sour looks we both got, I didn't mind having a bodyguard. It was possible the family wouldn't have been as grumpy if only I had arrived, and that they were mostly feeling prickly because of the attack the night before, but I didn't know that. It wasn't as if my going on one hunt with them had changed people's feelings about me. Augustus had a reason to dislike me more than the others did, but I suspected many felt similarly to him, that I'd betrayed the pack by leaving—and taking that potion for so many years.

"You wait outside." Lorenzo lifted a hand toward Duncan as he nodded for me to enter the cabin. "This is a family matter."

Duncan lifted his hands unthreateningly. "No problem. Mind

if I sniff around to see if I can catch a trace of the guys who attacked?"

"*We* already sniffed," one of my relatives said, thumping himself on the chest. "They ran off into the woods that way before jumping into trucks that were waiting on the road."

Ignoring him, Duncan looked at Lorenzo. "Mind if I sniff around?"

He might have picked out the white wolf as the pack alpha. I didn't know if Lorenzo was considered that or not, especially given that he was on the older side, but he clearly had status with the family.

Lorenzo opened his mouth, looking like he might also say something dismissive, but he paused to consider Duncan, looking him up and down. He didn't comment on Duncan seeming *Old World* or whatever others detected in him, but he did nod and wave a hand toward the woods.

"If you wish."

When Duncan turned to head down from the porch, the young man who'd spoken moved to stand in front of him, chest puffed out. I'd been about to step into the cabin but paused. Was there *already* going to be more trouble?

"Take it easy, Rocco," Jasmine said. "He kicked Augustus's ass, and Augustus can flatten you with his hind legs tied by his tail."

"He can't take on the whole pack," Rocco said. "And he doesn't belong here. What are you *doing* here, outsider?"

"I'm Ms. Valens' chauffeur," Duncan drawled, looking and sounding unconcerned by the youngster blocking his way.

"She doesn't belong here either," someone muttered under their breath.

On the crowded porch, I couldn't tell who, but my cheeks heated with the knowledge that my thoughts were correct. Augustus wasn't the only one who resented me.

"*I* asked Luna to come," Jasmine said. "She has a right to see her mom anyway."

The mutterer didn't reply.

"Step aside, good chap," Duncan said.

"It's Rocco, and I'm not a chap." The young man puffed his chest out even more and didn't move. "You'd better be polite to us, bro. You're all alone here, and you didn't bring an offering."

I lifted the gift box of salamis that *I* had brought, though I'd intended those more as presents to the wounded rather than offerings to appease the pack. Rocco didn't look at me. Nobody did. They were watching the standoff.

A lupine growl emanated from Duncan's chest.

People stirred on the porch, glancing uneasily at each other. I didn't think they wanted to jump into a fight, but nobody made a move to stop it. Even Lorenzo only watched, that indifference in his eyes again. In his life, he'd doubtless seen dozens if not hundreds of young werewolves challenging their elders. It was, after all, the way of the wolf.

I was tempted to ask Lorenzo to intervene—poor Duncan had already had to endure *one* fight because he'd come with me—but I knew he wouldn't.

"Move," Duncan said softly, dangerously.

Rocco looked off into the woods, as if he was considering it, but then he threw a punch. It was so hard and fast that it would have flattened most men—most normal human men. But he didn't feint first or do a good job disguising it, and Duncan reacted with the speed of a lightning strike. He caught the fist, halting it in midair, then slid his hand down to clasp Rocco's wrist. Duncan spun Rocco as he hefted him off the porch, then jammed him face-first against the log siding of the cabin.

Snarling, Rocco threw an elbow back, trying to catch Duncan in the chest. But Duncan evaded it, then used his bodyweight to pin Rocco against the wall.

I watched the rest of the pack, ready to jump in if others joined the confrontation, but nobody else stepped forward. If anything, they snorted or rolled their eyes. Hopefully, they felt, as I did, that Duncan had already proven he wasn't to be trifled with. Oh, if he threatened the pack or tried to kill Rocco, the others would spring in. This *was* the pack's territory, after all, but they weren't as foolish as this young pup.

"You're an idiot, Rocco," Jasmine whispered as he struggled ineffectively to escape. "If you want to pick someone to be a role model, don't let it be Augustus."

Rocco spat in her direction.

Duncan ground his face into the logs. "My ambitious young chap, aren't you done being disrespectful yet?"

"Screw you."

"A desire for that is behind your infantile display? Alas, you didn't end up in the right position to enact such a gesture."

Again, Rocco tried to free himself. His face was beet red, and his muscles strained against his shirt, but he couldn't escape. Finally, he slumped.

"Are we done?" Duncan asked.

Rocco didn't concede that, but he remained slumped, his body language full of defeat.

Duncan released him and stepped back. Not looking at him, Rocco straightened his shirt and slunk down the steps. He did glare over his shoulder at *me* before walking around the corner. I sighed, fearing I would yet regret bringing Duncan along. The pack was probably extra irritated after having intruders in here, shooting silver bullets at everyone.

Reminded of the injured, I raised a hand toward Duncan and stepped inside. As weary as Mom had looked in the driveway, I expected to find her in bed or collapsed in the easy chair in the two-room cabin's living area. But chanting and the scents of essential oils wafted from the bedroom. Through the open door, Emilio

was visible in bed, his shirt off and bandages wrapped around his
torso. A woman with a strong aura of healing power attended him.
A tray with medical implements rested on the bedside table, a
bloody lump that had been extracted lying in the middle. The
silver bullet that had struck Emilio?

"Come sit with me, my daughter," Mom said from one of the
hard wooden chairs at the small dining table.

The rest of the pack remained outside, and Lorenzo shut the
door.

"Okay." But I first held up a finger, removed a salami from the
gift box, and eased into the bedroom. Careful not to disturb the
healer, whose eyes were closed as she chanted with her hand on
Emilio's chest, I laid the salami next to the tray.

Emilio's eyes were also closed, but his nostrils twitched several
times. The salami was wrapped in plastic, but that didn't mean no
odor escaped. Without opening his eyes, Emilio flopped an arm
onto the table. He patted about, found the salami, and grasped it,
then brought it over to lay upon his chest, both hands over it, a
contented smile stretching across his young face.

Since his eyes hadn't opened, he might have done all that in
his sleep, but I murmured, "You're welcome," on the way out.

"You seek to regain the allegiance of the pack through meat
bribes?" Mom asked as I joined her at the table.

We had a view through a window into the woods behind the
cabin, and I glimpsed Duncan out there, sniffing and gazing at the
pine-needle-strewn ground.

"Regain? I don't think I ever had the allegiance of the pack." I
hadn't even been twenty yet when I'd left. Who felt allegiance
toward teenagers? "I'll be happy to give gifts to keep them from
attacking me though." And Duncan, I thought but didn't say,
doubting she approved of me bringing him up here any more than
the others did.

"It may influence those who are young and have no reason to

feel bitter toward your long absence and... choices, but they would not have attacked you regardless."

"Maybe that's why I like them."

"Emilio and Jasmine are agreeable souls. That makes last night's attack even more egregious." Mom grimaced. "Those men were after me. The younger pack members weren't wrong to come to the defense of their elders, but I regret that they were wounded."

"Yeah. Why did the men come and attack? Do you know? I'm afraid it might have been retribution, but I'm surprised... I mean, I wouldn't have guessed they knew where you live or anything about you. I didn't even think they cared about me, just the case, and they already *got* that."

"Case?"

Now that we had relative privacy, I told her everything.

Her expression changed little, though her lips flattened in disapproval whenever I mentioned Chad. I didn't know if she was offended because he'd betrayed me or because I'd married a normal human in the first place. The last time I'd been here, she'd asked about my *fertility*, as if I might still return to the pack and birth werewolf young. At forty-five, with two grown sons, I didn't feel any desire to try that, if it was even possible, but she'd suggested that the werewolf magic extended one's years of vitality —and fertility.

"Interesting," Mom said when I finished, not bringing up fertility in the story. "You say this wolf case was crafted with druidic magic?"

"Yeah. I'm not sure if it would be useful to werewolves in any way, but Chad is into our kind, so it might have more of a link than we've yet learned about." He was a werewolf fanatic, Duncan had said, and that fit what I remembered about him. "I guess I could call and try to get some information from him, but I don't want to speak with him." I winced, knowing that made me sound weak and nonconfrontational. I expected Mom to call me out on that.

"No," was what she said. "Through his actions and choices, he has declared himself your enemy. He will not answer truthfully, even if you confront him in the most logical manner. With your hand around his throat."

I snorted, though I was pissed enough at Chad that I might be able to go that far. Only the fact that we had children together, and that the boys loved him, made me care whether he lived or died.

"*Forcing* a truthful answer from him might be possible. But you say he is not in the country?"

"I don't think so. Duncan said they crossed paths in Costa Rica."

Mom looked out the window. Duncan was still ambling around out there, but he'd retrieved his magic detector. Its antennae quivered as he turned it left and right, heading through the trees.

"Duncan," Mom said the name slowly. "That is what he calls himself?"

"Yes. It's the name he gave me anyway."

Her gaze shifted to me. "He has interacted with your former mate? That does not bode well."

"I know. I told him to get lost, but then when the case was stolen... I thought Duncan might be able to help find it. I don't trust him fully, though he did apologize and say he regretted taking the gig. Apparently, Chad hired him to find the case and retrieve it. He's a professional... thing finder." I winced, but I didn't have a better term for it. "Treasure hunter, I guess you'd call him."

"I am fortunate he was not among the thugs who came last night. Even without a gun loaded with silver bullets, he would have been difficult to drive off."

"He is a good fighter, but he wouldn't..." I caught myself from saying something like *attack you* or *betray me*. Hadn't Duncan already betrayed me? And didn't I keep reminding myself that I couldn't trust him, that I needed to make sure I was with him when we found the case so I could grab it first?

Mom lifted her eyebrows. "You are attracted to him."

"What? No."

Her eyebrows climbed higher, and she glanced at my shirt. No, at *his* shirt. Even though she had to know I'd borrowed it because I'd lost mine in the change, she could probably smell him on it and maybe even tell that we'd been close of late.

"I mean, he's handsome, but I'm not having sex with him. He already crossed me once, and I'm not a dummy." My cheeks flushed with embarrassment. Was it a lie? I'd let him rub my head not twenty minutes ago. And I'd liked it. "I'm using him to help find the case. That's it." I glanced toward the window, not wanting Duncan to hear that, even if the words wouldn't surprise him, but he'd disappeared from view.

"And what is he using you for?" Mom glanced toward my chest again.

I folded my arms and glared at her insinuation. "He *says* he regrets working for Chad and owes me. I'm fully aware that may be a lie and that he's using *me* to find the case."

Except... would Duncan need me for that? With his experience, he might be able to locate it, now that I'd perhaps foolishly told him it had been stolen, on his own.

"Hm," Mom said. "Because he is attracted to you, he walks close and will defend you."

"Oh, yeah. Middle-aged women are real catches."

"That is not what you are. You are a powerful female from the strongest pack remaining in this part of the world, and, as a wolf, you are still in your prime."

"Please don't ask about my fertility again."

"I suspect your fertility is fine. And now that you've stopped consuming that odious potion, your power is more palpable. Even if you hadn't brought that one, your cousins would have been foolish to confront you."

Since they'd succeeded in knocking me off that train trestle, I didn't have her confidence in my ability to stave off their attacks. Not when they ganged up on me, and Augustus was proving that was the only way he operated.

"That one is far more dangerous than your relatives." Mom waved in the direction we'd seen Duncan walking. "You would be wise to end your flirtation with him. Find the case on your own, and bring it here. I must consult my tomes and examine it, but I believe it belongs to werewolves, and since it was brought here, in our territory..." She spread her palm.

"It's rightfully ours?" I asked skeptically, though I had no idea to whom it belonged. "Druids made it."

"Yes, as they long ago made our family artifact." Mom rested her hand on her chest. Was she talking about the medallion she'd shown me? That she intended for me to inherit? "They worked in conjunction with the werewolves of the time. Our two magics have always been complementary, both born of nature. Wolves are not strong crafters of artifacts, so we've made pacts with druids in the past, lending our power to theirs for the making. In exchange, we've guarded their kind, those who didn't fear us and were willing to ally with us."

"Oh. Huh. Maybe that's why I like Bolin." I liked that he'd used his magic to help de-mold one of the apartment units anyway.

"A druid?"

"Sort of. He's my intern and just out of college, but he said his grandfather was an actual druid, back before he passed, and Bolin has learned a few things. He can use magic."

"He may be a good resource then." Mom leaned across the table and gripped my wrist. "I need your help, Luna."

I blinked in surprise. Mom was so proud, the once- and

perhaps still-alpha female of the pack. It was startling to have her ask for help from anyone, especially me.

"What can I do?"

"The attacks are linked by the artifacts."

"The case and... your medallion?" I waved toward the bedroom. The last time I'd visited she'd retrieved its box from a drawer in there.

She grimaced. "They stole it."

"Those thugs got in here and took it? Doesn't it zap bad guys?"

"If they felt pain, they did not show it. Or they prepared themselves ahead of time. I have no doubt it's what they came for. They weren't certain where it was and ransacked my cabin as they shot at us." She pointed toward a bullet lodged in one of the logs next to the refrigerator. "They tore everything up as I lay bleeding on the floor. I threw a butcher knife and lodged it in one man's shoulder, but it wasn't enough." Her voice lowered. "Also, the change... eluded me. I struggle now to summon the magic sometimes. And the men... They were surprisingly strong." There was almost a quaver in her voice when she admitted, "I was not powerful enough to stop them. For the first time in my life, I wasn't enough."

"I'm sorry, Mom." I rested my hand on hers, wanting to comfort her, but I was also scared.

When I'd been a girl, she'd been a mountain. Strong, unflappable, fearless. A brave female werewolf from an era where you couldn't show vulnerability or the pack would sense your weakness and drive you out. Or so she'd always told me. Even last week, when she'd admitted to her cancer diagnosis and that she was dying, she'd still seemed strong and powerful to me, the magic in her blood almost overcoming her body's failings, her age.

Now, for the first time, she was showing her vulnerability, her distress at the world and how it was treating her. I didn't know what to do, but I regretted having been away for so long. My cousins weren't wrong—I *had* turned my back on my family and heritage. Not because of them but because of my own failings, of the knowledge that I was a danger to others, that I'd killed by accident—and that it could happen again. At the time, and during all those years in between, my choice had made sense to me, but now... Now I doubted it. And myself.

In that moment, I knew I had to help my mother. I couldn't cure her disease, but if I could at least get the medallion back for her, she would rest more easily. She would know it would remain with the family, passing into my hands, whether I was worthy or not. I had to at least be more worthy to carry it than whoever the thieves wished to sell it to.

"Did they speak at all?" I asked. "Anything that could hint to what they wanted your medallion for? Both artifacts?"

Mom's face hardened, the glimpse of vulnerability disappearing. "All they said was that it was open season on wolves. Then they started shooting indiscriminately."

"I wish we'd caught the blond guy. I want to question him. Badly."

"Jasmine has asked her father to use his computer skills to research paranormal dealers in the area, as well as members of the community, to learn if anyone else has had magical artifacts stolen of late. He has always been a quirky wolf who prefers spending time using technological devices instead of being out in nature, but in this case, it may be useful."

From what Jasmine had said, her father was a game developer. I imagined him asking people about real-world magic while flinging fireballs in online realms.

"We'll do our best to find the guys and get back what they stole," I said.

"We," Mom mouthed and looked out the window again.

Duncan hadn't come back into view, but she knew who I meant.

"You should not spend more time with him," Mom said. "Do

not trust him. Lone wolves, in general, are suspicious. If he challenged an alpha, lost, and was cast out, he might make such a challenge in another pack again, perhaps less honorably, to ensure he won."

"I'm not sure that's what happened with him. He said he's never had a pack."

"He *said*. Did *you* not say that he lied to you? That he worked against you for the sake of your former mate?"

"Yeah. Like I said, I don't trust him, Mom, but he knows about finding things. That's the only reason I reached out to him."

"If you work with him, you might help him in finding your artifact, only to have him disappear with them *both*."

"I won't let that happen, Mom. I'm strong, remember?" I said it half-jokingly, or at least self-deprecatingly, since I'd felt like a punching bag for life of late.

She was raising a good point. I should put together a plan, a way to make sure I could get the best of Duncan if he *did* turn on me. I didn't want to believe he would, but...

"You are strong, but he is dangerous."

"I know. I've seen him fight."

"I have not sensed a werewolf that exuded such power before. Even your father was not that strong, and he was an alpha through and through, one who few dared challenge."

"I'll be wary of Duncan," I assured her, then stood up, feeling the press of time in the weariness on Mom's face.

If I wanted to return the medallion before she grew too ill to appreciate it... Well, I might not have that long.

Before leaving, I withdrew a salami log from the box and laid it on the table for her. Salty preserved meat probably wasn't the ideal food for someone dying, but I also rested a bar of dark chocolate on it. Surely, *that* would help. It could only improve her mood.

Indeed, her eyes seemed to brighten a touch as she watched.

"I'll get your medallion back for you, Mom. I promise."

10

TWILIGHT WAS CREEPING INTO THE WOODS, AND MOST OF THE FAMILY had dispersed by the time I stepped out of the cabin. A few remained on the porch, arms folded across their chests as they gazed into the woods toward the road. Was that the direction Duncan had gone? I suspected they were keeping an eye on him—or at least making sure he didn't return and represent a further threat. I didn't see any of my cousins.

I trotted into the woods, thought I caught a hint of Duncan's scent, and headed onto paths that wove between the trees. A faint beeping soon reached my ears. His magic detector.

Following the noise, I spotted his outline near an ancient fir a dozen yards from the road. His fingers rested on the mossy bark, as if he were communing with the tree, while the metal detector in his other hand beeped cheerfully.

As I approached, I tried to see and sense him as my mother and the various other people who'd called him dangerous had. When he'd first appeared in the greenbelt by my apartment complex, whistling and wielding his metal detector, my senses had been dulled by the lingering effects of my last potion. Even then,

I'd gotten a hint of the feral power about him. I'd known right away he was a werewolf. But was he *more* than that? And, if so, what more?

Since I hadn't taken a dose of the potion at the last full moon, my magic—and my senses—had returned to me. I *could* notice his power, like the sun radiating energy. I'd gotten used to it, and his affable smile always seemed to say he was the opposite of dangerous, but when I attempted to assess him through fresh eyes, I could see what others saw. He seemed pure werewolf to me—not like those guys taking the strength-enhancing potion—but, as Mom had said, he was an especially strong werewolf.

"Hey, Luna." Unaware of my scrutiny, Duncan waved for me to come over.

"I take it your device isn't beeping due to the proximity of werewolves."

"Nope. I've programmed it not to register those right now. *They're* all over the place here."

"I did warn you about that."

"You did." Duncan lowered his voice to add, "One of your cousins is watching from the other side of the road, about fifty yards that way." He twitched a finger but didn't look in that direction, instead continuing to consider the tree. "He's in hiding, but I know he's there, so you might want to be careful what you say."

"I doubt he's working for the other side," I replied, but I did speak softly. It sounded like Mom hadn't admitted to many others yet that she'd lost the medallion. I intended to get it back before the rest of the family found out. "He probably wants to see if an opportunity comes up to kick your ass."

"I have no doubt about *that*." Duncan turned off the magic detector to stop the beeps and opened a tool kit he'd also brought. He pulled out pliers, then poked them into a hole in the moss and bark.

A *bullet* hole, I realized. He'd already used a knife or other sharp tool to cut some of the bark away, and he used the pliers to extract the projectile.

"It's silver but not *only* silver." Duncan held it up, the bullet smashed flat from striking the tree. "Whatever metallurgist made it imbued it with additional magic. Your pack is lucky nobody died." He looked at me. "Is that right? Is the kid you mentioned going to make it?"

"Emilio, and I heard it was bad, but he smiled and grabbed a salami in his sleep, so that seemed promising for his health."

"It takes a great injury to dull a werewolf's appetite."

"Yes. The men took off in trucks, from what I heard."

In the fading light, deep tire tracks in the dirt road were visible. They'd probably torn out of here at top speed.

"Is there any way you know of that I don't that would allow us to track them back to their lair?" I added.

"A wolf could follow the scent of the trucks for a while, but... probably not once they got to main roads." Duncan's brow furrowed slightly as he turned the bullet over, eyeing it from all angles. "I did catch that hint of lavender again a couple of times. Our blond thug was here with the other attackers."

"That wasn't an ingredient in that Tiger Blood potion, was it?" I asked, though I doubted someone would smell like one of many ingredients in a liquid they'd consumed hours or days before, not unless it contained something potent, like garlic.

"Rue didn't give us the full list, but I can ask her later. I'll probably go back to see if she can offer any insight into this." Duncan held up the bullet.

I touched it and felt the faintest tingle of magic. It wasn't exceedingly powerful, less than what I'd sensed from the wolf case or my mom's medallion, and I suspected it had a small enchantment designed to make the bullets more deadly for our kind.

"I need to find those guys—or whoever hired them," I said grimly.

"I know. I'll help."

I gazed at Duncan in the deepening shadows, my mom's warning about him coming to mind. I wanted his offer to help to be sincere—for *him* to be sincere. But maybe I was foolish to think he was anything other than a treasure hunter looking for treasure. Treasure that my ex had hired him to get.

Maybe I needed to visit an alchemist myself and try to acquire something that could stop him if he turned on me. My gut twisted at the thought of attacking him after he'd joined me in so many battles. We hunted and fought well together. I didn't *want* Duncan to be an enemy.

What if I could find the men and the artifacts on my own? Then Duncan's allegiance wouldn't matter. If Jasmine's dad got a lead, maybe I could figure something out. Or find a store that sold lavender-scented deodorant and was frequented by men amped up on potions.

"Are you admiring my profile and thinking of how appealing I am?" Duncan asked into the long silence.

"Oh, absolutely. It's hard for me to think about anything else."

"Unfortunately for my ego, I detect sarcasm in your tone."

"You're a perceptive werewolf."

Duncan pocketed the smashed silver bullet and lowered the pliers. "Do you need to do anything else up here? Do you want a ride back?"

"I think I'm done for now. I'm not that much more welcome here than you are. But Mom is okay, for the moment. As okay as she can be. And I... I've got work to do back home."

That wasn't untrue, as I doubtless had a long list of tenant requests after being gone most of the day, but the *work* I had in mind was figuring out a way to find the artifacts.

"Of course." Duncan gazed across the road in the direction where he'd presumably glimpsed—or sensed—whichever cousin was lurking. "Are they done harassing you? Do you know?"

"Lorenzo told them to leave me alone, but I don't know if they'll listen. He's strong, but he's older, and my cousins think they're the young shits."

"I noticed."

"I wasn't positive which one of us Augustus was after when he charged at the van."

"Both maybe. Right before I changed, I saw him snap toward you. You were fast enough to avoid it, but he wasn't holding back."

"Maybe he thought they could kill me and then say it was an accident, that they were after you."

"Even though *I've* done nothing." Duncan splayed his hand across his chest. "And I'm a delight."

I snorted. "You're a lone wolf, and they don't like you."

"Such a crime to travel solo."

"They can also sense..." I stepped closer, catching his gaze in the dying light. "Those with magic all seem to sense that you're extra dangerous." I decided to dive in and ask directly. "Why is that? Will you tell me?" Would he answer?

Duncan hesitated. "I prefer to keep my past to myself."

"Your past? Or your heritage? It's not like something that happened in your youth would give you more power, right?"

He shrugged and returned my gaze without looking away, but I could tell he didn't want to go into more detail.

I lifted a hand and stepped back, not wanting to push him. I didn't appreciate when people pried into my past, after all.

"Would you trust me more if I told you?" he asked softly.

"I guess if it was the truth and I could tell it was the truth."

He snorted softly. "I don't have a lie detector that I can hand you to hold on me."

"What? All that equipment in your van and no lie detector? That's disappointing."

"The treasures I find don't usually get mendacious with me."

"No? Those rusty forks haven't looked trustworthy."

He laughed softly, then stepped closer and wrapped his arms around me. His grip was loose, and I could have stepped out of it if I wished, but I caught myself leaning into him and wanting him to reveal... whatever he would.

"I like it when you verbally fence with me," Duncan said. "Usually, people with power are arrogant and stuck on themselves. You're fun."

"Thanks, but I'm a property manager who only gets by on what I'm paid because of the free rent. I'm the opposite of someone with power."

"You know what I mean. The power of the wolf." Duncan rested his face against the side of my head, his lips brushing the tip of my ear. Pleasure zipped along my nerves. "It has nothing to do with one's station in the human world," he continued, "though you could certainly use it to claim money and status and power there, if you wished. Most werewolves scorn everything human and prefer to be left alone, but history is full of those who used their lycanthropy to create minions and take land and wealth for themselves. You would never consider doing such. You want to win ethically and morally."

"You know me that well, do you?"

"I've seen your envelopes."

"And following a budget defines me?"

"Following the rules when you have the option not to does."

It surprised me that he valued that. He'd come to Seattle to steal something from my apartment, after all. He didn't seem that much of a rule follower himself.

I shifted my head to look him in the eyes. Only my wolf blood sharpening my vision allowed me to see his face in the deepening dark, the strong line of his jaw, the scar above his eyebrow, the way he gazed back at me with intensity, his arms tightening around me. His power seemed to envelop me as well, promising he would protect me and that I would enjoy being with him.

I opened my mouth to say that I might indeed trust him more if he told me about his past. But he must have assumed my parted lips meant I wanted to be kissed, for his mouth lowered, capturing mine.

I hesitated, conflicted on whether I wanted this. Oh, my body responded to him, nerves lighting up with longing, and I had to resist the urge to grip his shoulders and return the kiss—*hard*. But he was still a question mark, his intentions unknown. His past and his heritage were a mystery.

Despite all my reservations, the feel of his hard body and his power mingling with mine was appealing. Appealing and arousing. Before I'd made up my mind about the wisdom of the choice, I kissed him back, reveling in his touch and his interest. He found me more than *fun*. We were close enough that I could tell that.

A howl came from the driveway.

That wasn't one of my cousins. It sounded like Lorenzo, the white wolf saying this was pack territory and that this activity wasn't welcome here, not with a stranger.

Duncan growled, not breaking our kiss, and he clasped my butt, keeping me close to him, *molded* to him. Though my body sang with pleasure, I leaned back.

He released me slowly, with reluctance. A hint of that growl lingered in his voice when he shot a dark look toward the driveway and said, "I hadn't imagined the family being so involved if I chose to date a mature woman almost as old as I am."

"We're not dating. We're tracking bad guys."

"Ah." His gaze returned to me. "I was confused by your eager lip touching."

"And your hand on my ass?"

"No, that wasn't confusing in the least." He smiled roguishly and squeezed me before stepping back.

Damn if I didn't like that squeeze and want to shift closer again. But another howl came from the driveway, and I refrained.

"I'll take you home." Duncan picked up his magic detector and tool kit, and led me down one of the paths heading toward his van. "Unless you'd like to drive back to that pond, where only the beavers would be witness, and test the firmness of my mattress?"

"I would not." That might have been a lie, but since he didn't have that lie detector, I felt safe in asserting it. "Beavers are notorious gossips. And you... are still being evasive with me."

"I know." He sounded sad about it, but that feeling, if genuine, didn't prompt him to share any more about himself. He merely opened the passenger door for me.

"Thanks."

As Duncan turned the van around and drove toward the road, no wolves were visible. My senses told me that some were watching us, though, making sure we left.

For a fleeting moment, it crossed my mind that if I found Mom's medallion and returned it, the family might think more kindly toward me. They might *accept* me once more. But if she hadn't told anyone, and I could return it before the others found out, she would be the only one to know I'd retrieved it. That was okay. That would be enough. Let the feelings of the family toward me be as they would.

"I don't trust that trouble isn't going to come after you again," Duncan said, his thoughts on other topics. "I want to stay in your parking lot tonight in case you need help."

"Or in case I get randy and call you to my bedroom?"

"Is that a possibility?"

"No."

"You're sure? I haven't noticed any gossipy beavers in that area."

"I'm sure."

"All right, but you won't object if I stay close?"

"You'll find out if you wake up with a tow truck attaching chains to your van."

He snorted. "As long as the tires don't get slashed again."

"I wish those guys *would* show up and attack so we could capture them and force them to tell us what the deal is, but... I don't have anything left for them to steal. I doubt I'll see them again."

"I was thinking more of your cousins. I don't think they're done with you."

If Augustus knew the medallion he wanted his wife to inherit had been stolen, he might have been done with me, but I wouldn't speak of what my mom had told me in confidence, not with my relatives and definitely not with Duncan.

"You can stay," I told him. "In the parking lot."

"Of course, my lady." He made a hat-tipping gesture at me as he turned the van onto the pavement of the road heading back to town. "I'll pine for you from afar."

By the light of the dashboard, his gaze was more intent than teasing, and a longing crept into me, a wondering of what might have happened in the woods if my family hadn't shown up.

Nothing, I told myself firmly. I wasn't going to sleep with a man I couldn't trust. Not again.

11

I SHOVELED SNOW FROM THE WALKWAYS LEADING TO THE PARKING LOT with more vigor than the activity required. It was not, I assured myself, sexual frustration. I was way too old to have hormones that had hissy fits over denied passions.

"Tell that to last night's dreams," I muttered with a big shove.

Sweat dampened my clothes under my jacket. Two inches had fallen during the night, a rare occurrence in Seattle, especially before the official start of winter. The forecast promised temperatures would melt it by midday, but I always hurried to shovel the snow when it came, not wanting any of the tenants to slip and be hurt. I'd risen before dawn to sand the parking lot.

At least the work had given me time to think, to think and scheme. An idea was percolating in my mind. I was tempted to run it past Duncan. I looked over at his van parked in the corner of the lot, snow covering the roof and obscuring the windows. But his ongoing evasiveness made me reluctant to confide in him. As I'd been thinking the day before, it would be a good idea to find the artifacts without him at my side.

Bolin's G-Wagon rolled into the lot, its lack of snow and frost promising it had spent the night in a cozy garage. There *was* a splotch of bird poop on the windshield, something left behind from work the day before presumably. I wasn't sure whether to be amused or puzzled that the feathered locals had it out for that vehicle.

I had about finished with the walkways, so I headed over to greet him. He might have ideas about my percolating scheme and whether or not it could work. At the least, he could tell me the origins of the words I might choose if I placed an ad on that community board—that was part of what I had in mind.

When Bolin climbed out of his SUV, he didn't look in my direction. Instead, he rummaged in the back and pulled out several gray and brown objects, each about a foot high. I couldn't tell what they were until he planted one on the hood.

"Are those... plastic owls?" I asked.

"To scare away the birds, yes." Bolin put another on the hood, then four on the roof. "They're like scarecrows. The birds will see them, think they're fearsome beaked predators, and stay away."

I leaned against my snow shovel and eyed the faux raptors with skepticism but didn't suggest his scheme wouldn't work. After all, I had a scheme of my own in mind, and I hoped for support.

"Need any help placing them? It's a bit stormy today. The wind may blow them off."

"Nope. I filled them with rocks." Bolin tilted the last one to show me a plastic plug in the bottom. "If they work, I might ask if I can store them here in one of the maintenance sheds, so I don't have to carry them in the car. Once they've been out in the elements, they'll get wet." He curled a lip, probably imagining dour dampness touching his expensive leather seats.

I nobly refrained from suggesting the owls would probably

also get pooped on. So far, the birds chattering in the nearby trees weren't subdued by the arrival of the supposed predators.

"That's no problem," I said.

"Excellent." His owls placed, Bolin drew out two to-go coffee cups. After taking a breath and visibly bracing himself, he faced me and the apartment complex.

It bemused me that he needed such bracing for an office job that started at eight, but I held my snark back so I could ask his advice. "I need a favor."

His gaze fell to the handle of the snow shovel I was leaning against. "Don't you *pay* someone to do that? This place has a ton of walkways, plus the parking lot."

"I do have a service that swings through to plow around the cars if we get more than four inches."

"And the walkways?"

"They're not wide enough for a plow." I waved the shovel.

His lip curled again, and he took a deep swig from one of the cups.

"I've got them handled though. What I was wondering..." I glanced at Duncan's van to make sure he hadn't ambled out, then lowered my voice to finish. "If I was able to cobble together something that *looked* like an ancient magical artifact, do you have any druid potions that we could sprinkle on it to make it glow?"

"Sprinkle," he mouthed.

"Yeah. Douse, pour over, drench. Whatever."

"Did you know the word drench comes from the Old English *drencan*, which means to give drink to or make drunk? Also from the Proto-Germanic *drankijan*."

"I assumed it did, yeah."

Bolin squinted at me. "Sprinkling a potion on something won't make it glow, but if you give me the object, I might be able to cast an illusion on it that could do the job. You're looking to fool someone?" He looked toward the van. "That won't work on him, if that's what you're thinking."

"I'm not planning to involve him in any way. My doohickey only needs to have a wolf head and fool whoever's hiring thugs to steal wolf artifacts from innocent people." I extended a hand toward him.

"You could probably use a crayon to draw a wolf on a flattened beer can and fool the troglodyte who attacked me."

"I doubt he's *that* dumb. And he's alchemically enhanced, so he might be able to sense whether an object, a faux artifact, if you will, has any magic about it."

"I wouldn't bet on it." Bolin grimaced and touched his forehead.

"My idea is to use my fake artifact to bait a trap for him and his cronies—there are a bunch more of those overpowered guys who lurk, at least now and then, at El Gato Mágico downtown."

"I'll cross that place off my to-visit list."

"Other than the bar fight in the back, it wasn't that bad. There were some geeky wizard types playing Dungeons and Dragons." I nodded toward him.

"Are you implying those are the *types* I might fit in with?"

"I can envision you at their table."

"My ancestors were druids, not wizards." Bolin sniffed disdainfully before taking another drink.

"They looked like they would be interested in word origins. One had a wand. If you made friends, maybe he would use it to zap the rogue birds turning your luxury car into a port-a-potty."

"Funny. Have you started construction on this faux artifact?"

"Not yet. Is there any material that would be better to use than others? For glow? I've got carpentry tools and some experience there, but artifacts aren't usually made out of wood. My metallurgy skills are much more limited, and ivory-carving isn't something I've tried." I didn't even know if one could legally buy ivory anymore. "I'm not a practiced craftswoman, so I'm a little concerned about my ability to create something that includes a realistic wolf head. I might have to hire someone who can carve or sculpt." I winced, having few envelopes left with money in them for the month. Nothing had been budgeted for hiring artists.

Bolin listened to my meandering musings with a bland expression on his face. After another sip, he asked, "Do you want me to go home and 3D-print something for you?"

"Uhm, would that be... realistic?"

I'd heard of the technology, of course, but it wasn't anything the apartment complex needed, so I hadn't looked into it.

"More realistic than you chiseling a wolf head out of wood scraps, I'm sure." Bolin rolled his eyes.

Once more, I nobly held back my snark, though I did envision myself skipping around his SUV later and sprinkling birdseed on it. "If you could make something realistic, I would appreciate it."

"Sure. I can go get it started now. I've got a row of dragons and spaceships lined up in my room that I made and painted."

I smirked at him. "I *knew* you would fit in at the D&D table."

"Funny," he said again.

"Yup. I'm thinking of starting a side-hustle at a comedy club."

Shaking his head, Bolin removed the carefully placed owls and drove off.

Maybe I should have asked him how long it would take to 3D-print a wolf head. I worried that Mom's illness limited the amount of time we had. Further, if whoever had requested the wolf artifacts wasn't a local, the ones that had been gathered might be shipped off to who knew where.

An image of Chad on a dock in Costa Rica, having a package delivered into his hands, floated through my mind. I didn't know if he was behind this—I doubted he would be able to hire alchemically enhanced thugs from halfway around the world—but it was possible he was. If Duncan had told him off, as he'd implied, then

Chad might have searched for someone else to get the case for him. I didn't know, however, how he would have known about Mom's artifact. When we'd been together, I'd told him very little about the pack—all he'd known was that I'd lost the first love of my life and the pain was why I'd left my family. There was no reason I could think of that he would have guessed the pack had valuables, other than that they were werewolves. I hadn't known about the medallion myself until Mom had shown it to me the week before.

I looked toward the Roadtrek, tempted to ask if Duncan would call Chad and try to get information from him. To my surprise, Duncan was sitting in the front seat, visible through the frosted windows. Was he talking on the phone?

He noticed me across the parking lot and lifted a finger when our eyes met. Yes, he *was* talking to someone.

I headed to a patch of snow that needed removing and worked on it, but I glanced often at the van, curious who he was speaking with that had prompted him to tell me to wait. It wasn't as if we had a breakfast date and had agreed to meet, but the gesture seemed to imply...

He moved into the back of the van and out of sight.

My curiosity prompted me to walk over there. I hadn't left his window cracked this time, but I stood in the same spot as when I'd eavesdropped before and tried to hear him.

As more days had passed, the remnants of the previous dose of my potion had completely worn off, and my werewolf-gifted senses had grown stronger. They were keen enough that I could hear Duncan speaking, even without an open window.

"No, I didn't reconsider," he was saying. "I just thought you should know that someone else got your case."

My mouth dropped open. Was he speaking with Chad again? Even though I'd just been thinking about asking him to contact my ex-husband, it was hard not to seethe. The thought of them chatting—chatting and *colluding*—made me crazy.

"Unless *you're* the one responsible for that theft," Duncan added. In a leading tone? "When I wasn't able to get it, did you put the word out, offering money up here to anyone who found were-wolf artifacts?"

I willed myself to calm down. It sounded like Duncan might have called on my behalf to try to learn if Chad was behind things.

"I'm in Brazil now. How am I going to put word out in Seattle?" came Chad's voice, surprisingly clearly.

Had Duncan put him on speakerphone? Maybe he knew I was lurking and wanted me to hear this.

"I hear they have the internet all over the world these days," Duncan said dryly.

After a pause, Chad said, "There *is* that Discord server where dealers for the paranormal hang out."

He sounded thoughtful, like he hadn't considered it before but was doing so now. Or was he simply playing dumb? Maybe he'd figured out that Duncan was more on my side than his. I *hoped* Duncan was more on my side.

"There are several," Duncan said. "Which one are you thinking of?"

"The Elder Kinwalkers. I've gotten information there before."

"Oh, yeah. I've heard of that one. You might even find leads there."

"Not if someone already stole my case," Chad grumbled. "Are you sure about that? You're not still up there, sleeping with her, are you?" The jealousy in his tone was more irritating than flattering. He couldn't possibly care about who I had sex with, could he? Not when *he'd* left *me* numerous times over the years. He'd been sleeping with girls all over the world long before I filed for a divorce, threw his belongings into the parking lot, and changed the locks.

"I'm still up here. The treasure hunting is good. Who I sleep with isn't any of your business."

"Stay away from her," Chad said.

"You've got an interesting way of apologizing."

Apologizing? Had *Chad* been the one to call?

"I thought you might still be able to get the case," Chad said. "Now that I know someone *else* has it... Shit. Can you find it and get it back? I'm still willing to pay. I think that's going to be worth even more than I thought. To the right people. If you can find it, I'll cut you in big time."

Duncan hesitated.

"*No*," I mouthed but didn't say loudly enough for him to hear.

"Who are the right people? Do you have any idea who else might have wanted it? Maybe they've already got it. I described that thug to you. Does he sound familiar? I can do some research, but it would help if I knew who else is in the running. You know, willing to pay for the acquisition of werewolf artifacts."

The van side door slid slowly open. Startled, I backed up a step. Duncan wasn't surprised to see me, and the phone was indeed on the speaker setting. He'd known I was there. And thought I might want to hear?

He watched my face warily, probably not sure how I would react.

I clenched my jaw but didn't do anything to interfere with the end of the call.

"I have no idea who that guy is," Chad said. "He sounds like someone's heavy. And, no, I'm not the only one looking for werewolf artifacts right now."

"Oh? Do you plan to resell it? No offense, chap, but if I find it, I could sell it to the highest bidder myself."

"You don't know who the highest bidder is."

"I can find out."

"You're not stealing *my* artifact and selling it to *my* contact, you bastard. I hired you to fetch it, not screw me and my wife."

"She's your ex-wife."

"She's still *mine*."

"That's not what *she* says."

I nodded firmly, my face hot, my hands clenched around the snow shovel. I wished Chad were physically present so I could club him in the head.

"Stay away from her," Chad warned, "and if I find out you sold that case, I'll come up and kill you myself."

"I'm trembling with fear." Duncan hit the button to hang up and lowered the phone. Face still wary, he met my eyes. "He called me. Not for the first time since the conversation you overheard, but I didn't answer before. I thought if I did so this time, I might be able to get some useful information."

Trying to sublimate my anger—it was directed far more at Chad than Duncan—I struggled to answer. I needed a minute to stand there with snowflakes landing on my head as I fumed.

"I knew you were there," Duncan added. "Your aura of were-wolfness is stronger now that your potion has fully worn off."

"My aura of werewolfness is stronger when I'm *pissed*," I finally got out.

"Ah. I looked something up for you. Do you want to see it?" Duncan tapped his phone and held up a map.

"I want..."

What did I want? Duncan hadn't done anything wrong, other than answer the phone when my nemesis had called, and he'd had a reason.

"Me to get naked so you can ravage my firm, taut body?"

I gave him the exasperated look the question deserved, but his silliness *did* cause some of the tension in my shoulders to release. "No."

"That's disappointing."

"Also, firm and taut mean the same thing."

"If that were true, two different words wouldn't exist."

"Do you want me to get Bolin? He's my word expert."

"To discuss my firm tautness? No."

Just as well. He'd taken off in his SUV. To 3D print my wolf artifact, I hoped.

I waved at the phone. "What have you got?"

"I've marked all the lavender farms within fifty miles of Seattle." He held up a map with numerous dots on the northeastern part of the Olympic Peninsula and a few more scattered in northern Snohomish County.

"Are you planning to buy me a bouquet of flowers?" I asked before remembering the lavender scent he'd caught whenever we'd been close to the blond guy. Since I hadn't picked it up myself, it was easy to forget.

"No, I'm saving for a micro diamond, remember?" Duncan waved toward the bills pinned on his dash. "Lavender is fleeting. Diamonds are forever. The ultimate memento to remember someone by."

"You think I want to remember you forever?"

"I'd be aghast if any woman wanted to forget me."

I shook my head and rubbed my face, smiling slightly despite myself. He was goofy, but maybe I needed some goofy in my life.

"You think the lavender scent you caught was from our guy traipsing through actual flowers?" I was skeptical, especially since it was late November. Lavender season had long since passed. "Isn't it more likely he uses lavender-scented deodorant or something?"

"Did he seem like the kind of man to buy floral deodorant?" It was Duncan's turn to sound skeptical. "I don't believe there's *any* kind of man who would rub flower smells under his armpits."

"Oh, they exist, but I agree he didn't seem like one."

"If it's unlikely he's rubbing his armpits with floral scents, he may be spending time somewhere that they linger in the air." Duncan waved his phone, the map still on the display.

"He could have a lavender car freshener he picked up at a gas station."

"I suppose, though I maintain that's not a manly scent that a professional mugger would be likely to purchase."

"No? Mugging people is a tough job, and lavender is supposed to be de-stressing."

Duncan shrugged. "I'll send you the map and list of places in case anything strikes you as worth checking out. Some of these farms are in your pack's territory."

"Okay. But what was that online server Chad mentioned? You teased that out of him, right? It wasn't something you knew about?"

"I did try to get it out of him, but the name is familiar. The Elder Kinwalkers. I'll look it up, but I think it's an underground marketplace where people trade items relevant to alchemists, witches, druids, shamans, etc. A paranormal eBay of sorts."

I made a note of the name. It sounded like a good place to list a faux werewolf artifact for sale.

"Luna?" came a call from one of the walkways, one of the tenants taking her miniature pinscher around the grounds.

"Poop bags?" I guessed.

"Yes, the dispenser by the path is empty again." She waved toward the greenbelt.

"I'll fill it." Lowering my voice, I muttered, "Either people besides my tenants are using those, or the werewolves cruising through the area are taking them."

Duncan snorted. "Your cousins didn't seem the solicitous types to bag their droppings after a hunt."

"Probably not. They're on the rude and presumptuous side." I lifted a hand in a wave, intending to get back to work, but I paused to make myself say, "Thanks for researching this on my behalf."

"You're welcome. Do you forgive me for talking to He Who Shall Not Be Named?"

This time, I snorted. "He's not Voldemort. I'd feel better about you if you *didn't* chat him up regularly—"

"I don't. I just thought I might be able to get useful information from him."

"I know. I get it. It's fine." I waved again and headed away.

Judging by the expression Duncan wore as he watched me leave, he wasn't sure if it truly *was* fine. I wasn't either.

12

I DIDN'T KNOW HOW LONG IT TOOK TO 3D PRINT SOMETHING, AND I had plenty of work to keep me busy, but I kept glancing out windows as I waited impatiently for Bolin's return. When my phone rang, I had my head and shoulders under the sink in B-14, the water turned off so I could replace a leaking faucet.

"Hey, Jasmine," I answered, not bothering to crawl out of the cabinet. The fifty-something tenant worked from home doing computer stuff, so he was nearby, tapping away at his keyboard. It was probably better if my voice was a little muffled.

"Hey, Luna. Thanks for coming out yesterday. My dad is still looking stuff up, but I wanted to apologize for getting you and, uhm, your boyfriend jumped by the family. Your cousins think they run things, even though we all pay way more attention to Lorenzo and your mom."

"It's okay, and he's not my boyfriend. He's..."

"Really hot. I *love* that accent."

"He's too old for you," I said dryly.

"I'm twenty-four. Lots of people my age date older guys. Especially older guys with sexy accents. And when he was naked, he looked really... not old."

"Yeah, he's fit."

"Absolutely." Jasmine giggled, sounding more like thirteen than twenty-four.

I pulled the new faucet out of the box on the floor.

"He's into you though. That's really cool. Like I told you before, we've only kept tabs on you from a distance, but I know your husband has been gone a while. You should totes hook up with Duncan."

"I'll keep that suggestion in mind."

"Don't pay attention to what the family thinks. You know the males get surly and territorial about anyone from another pack intruding on their territory. But that's so dumb. The *females* know we need werewolves from other bloodlines to breed healthy young."

"I'm not *breeding* with him." I glared at the phone, then clamped my mouth shut as footsteps sounded.

"Sorry, just getting a pop," the tenant said, opening the fridge.

From under the sink, I couldn't see his face, but the way he hurried away made me think he'd caught the breeding comment. I sighed. It had been easier to keep my secret identity as a werewolf from getting out before my family had started talking to me again.

"If you did, you would have amazing young, I bet. But, anyway, that's not why I called."

"Thank the moon."

Jasmine laughed. "Like I said, I wanted to apologize. I knew your mom wanted to see you, but I should have realized things weren't over between you and Augustus, and that he wouldn't listen to Lorenzo. He respects Lorenzo, but he's almost challenged him for the pack a few times. You can tell. I think it's mostly because he doesn't want to rile up your mom that he hasn't. Not out of any wisdom or prudence on his part."

"He seems to lack those traits."

"Oh, for sure."

I suspected the only reason Augustus didn't want to *rile up* my mom was that he still hoped I would die—or be killed—and he could claim that medallion for his wife. I should have asked Mom more about what it did. Something told me Augustus knew more about its powers than I did. There was little doubt that it had value, perhaps value to more than werewolves, since outsiders had risked a fight with the pack to steal it.

At least I assumed those men were working for outsiders. For the first time, as I stared up at the bottom of a sink, it occurred to me that another pack might be behind things.

I hoped Bolin showed up with my faux artifact today. I ached to bait my trap.

"I didn't want you to think I set you up," Jasmine said in an apologetic tone.

"I don't. I appreciate you calling me."

"Emilio woke up and appreciates that you brought him a salami. If you ever need a favor, I think he'll do anything you wish."

"And Mom didn't think my bribe would work."

"Oh, hang on. Dad is calling. Maybe he's got some information."

Jasmine switched lines for a conversation that took a while. While I waited, I finished installing the new faucet, turned the water back on, and crawled out from under the sink.

Key tapping noises from the bedroom the tenant used as an office floated to me, promising he hadn't lurked to listen to the rest of the weird call. Good. I should have taken it outside. As I put away my tools and considered doing just that, Jasmine returned to the line.

"Are you still there, Luna?"

"Yes."

"Have you heard of a Discord server called The Elder Kinwalkers?"

"Oddly enough, that's come up recently, yes."

"Dad dug into the logs and found someone named Celtic Salves and Tonics saying they were in the market for moon-touched artifacts. That's code for *werewolf* artifacts. I'm sure of it. Dad thinks so too. He reached out to the poster but hasn't heard anything back yet. He's going to keep poking around though."

"Okay, good. Keep me updated, will you?"

"Sure. Say hi to Duncan for me." She giggled again. Maybe she was still imagining him naked.

The tenant leaned out of his office.

"I'll talk to you later, okay, Jasmine?"

"Yup. Bye."

"Sorry about that," I told the tenant as I tucked the phone into my pocket, "but everything should be working now."

"No problem," he said as I turned on the new faucet to demonstrate the water flow. "Want a Mountain Dew?"

He lifted his own can of soda and gestured to the fridge.

"No, thanks."

"Coffee?"

"I'm good." I grabbed my tool kit, afraid he was thinking of asking me out. Considering how long I'd been a shrub to most males of the species, the last week had brought more interest in that area than I'd had in a long time. Of course, Chad's possessive claim on me hardly counted.

"Okay. Here." He stuffed a hand into his pocket and pulled out two crinkled twenty-dollar bills.

"Repairs are included in the rent."

"It's a tip."

I lifted a hand to stave off the offering.

His forehead creased. "I usually give people tips if they come do work for me. And I buy Girl Scout cookies and Campfire chocolates. You know, for karma."

And because he had a sweet tooth, if that Mountain Dew was any indication.

He held the twenties out. I waffled, but there didn't seem to be any strings attached. I vaguely remembered from his lease application that he was divorced and paying child support and alimony, so he'd had to sell his house and move into the apartment. He was probably lonely. I knew the feeling.

"Okay." I accepted the generous tip, vowing to replenish my GAS envelope. Maybe the ENTERTAINMENT envelope, too, since buying gift boxes of salami had emptied it. "Thank you."

"Come by any time," he said as he walked me to the door. "For coffee or pop or Pop-Tarts."

"Pop-Tarts?"

He *definitely* had a sweet tooth.

"I'm not much of a chef, but I have a Darth Vader toaster." He pointed to the black-helmeted appliance on the kitchen counter, then shrugged sheepishly. "It was a gift from my kid. We watched all the movies together when he was growing up."

"That's sweet." Since I had an espresso machine with a penis drawn on the side, I couldn't scoff at other people's appliances, but I did not commit myself to coming by for Pop-Tarts.

Bolin knocked and stuck his head through the door when I was about to step out. "Ah ha, there you are, Luna."

"Here I am." I'd left a sticky note in the office with my location, so it couldn't have been that hard to find me.

"I have something for you." Bolin lifted a hand toward the tenant, as if to apologize for stealing me away, but his gaze snagged on the kitchen counter. "Is that a *Darth Vader* toaster? I almost bought the Deathstar when I got my own apartment."

The tenant nodded. "It's awesome, isn't it? Do you want a Pop-Tart?"

"Yes." Bolin bounced by me, pressing something into my hand on the way by.

"What is this?" I whispered after him.

He'd already made it to the kitchen where the tenant had opened a cupboard to pull out a Costco-size box of Pop-Tarts. Boxes of sugary cereal lined the shelf next to it. Duncan, with his smoker for making brisket, was starting to look like more of a catch. Maybe Jasmine was right.

"The item we discussed," Bolin said.

I turned it over, not sure what to think of it. It was a little brown wood-like stump with a wolf head sticking out of the top. A hook on top implied it was an amulet or pendant to be hung on a chain, but its bulk and heft ensured it would clunk on one's chest with every step.

"It's made from PLA and wood dust and cork, one of the material mixes we have at home," Bolin added in a distracted tone as he examined Darth Vader. He grinned widely when the tenant waved for him to do the honors and push the lever down.

"What's PLA?" I asked.

"Polylactic acid, a biodegradable thermoplastic polyester plastic material."

That was a mouthful.

"It looks like a kid's toy."

"Press the Celtic rune on the bottom." Bolin waved for me to do it outside, giving a significant nod toward the tenant.

I stepped out onto the covered walkway and found the rune in the bottom of the stump. Since Bolin had made this, it probably genuinely meant something.

"The only authentic thing here," I muttered, then rubbed the bottom. The rune wasn't a button, only an indention in the stump. At my touch, it glowed green. "Well, I guess that's something."

Would it fool anyone and prompt whoever had acquired the other artifacts to send their thugs out to get it?

"We'll find out."

13

Twilight found me in the leasing office with my finger poised over the computer's enter key. I'd uploaded pictures of my fake artifact, showing the wolf head and the glowing rune, and used my limited photo-manipulation skills in an attempt to make the 3D-printed toy look more realistic. *Usually*, those skills went toward making the units for rent appear as appealing as possible.

"I feel like I'm using my talents for evil instead of good," I muttered, twitching when someone peered in the window.

Duncan waved and held up a glass storage container with something in it. Meat?

Remembering his brisket made my mouth water. Maybe he had leftovers.

I waved for him to come in and was about to hit enter and tab to another screen so he wouldn't see evidence of my scheme, but I paused. After hearing him speak with Chad again, did I truly think he was still working for my ex? I didn't, but... did I want to trust him with this? I'd hoped to find and recover the artifact on my own, in case Duncan was still angling for it. It was hard to believe he was hanging around and putting this much effort into helping me all because he felt guilty over his involvement with Chad and felt he *owed* me.

It was possible that romantic interest, and a lack of a career that meant he had other places to be, might have him lingering, but I wasn't arrogant enough to think I was so amazingly hot that I could motivate men to risk their lives—and deal with my belligerent family—on my behalf.

When Duncan opened the door, I hit enter on the ad I'd created. It said I would sell the supposed artifact for a hundred dollars and shared a story of how I'd inherited it from a grandparent. Once the post went live, I tabbed to another window before Duncan could see the screen.

"What's that?" He walked in with the container and nodded toward the desk.

I snorted with the realization that even though I'd hidden the window on the monitor, the faux artifact rested next to the keyboard.

"An invaluable druidic werewolf artifact imbued with powerful magic," I said, though the bottom of the stump only glowed for a few seconds after being touched, so it looked like a plastic toy at the moment. A polylactic-whatever toy.

Duncan picked it up. "Did it come out of a cereal box?"

My nostrils caught whiffs of meat. Not only brisket but... "Are there smoked sausages in there?"

"Andouille and chorizo. Take your pick." Duncan put down the toy and peeled back the plastic lid.

My mouth started watering in earnest. "Those are way better than Pop-Tarts."

"I'm going to say yes, though I don't know what a Pop-Tart is."

"They don't have frosted toaster pastries in Europe?"

"They may. My werewolf genes don't prompt me to seek out such things."

"They crave brisket and sausages instead."

"Certainly, my lady. Don't yours?"

"Yeah."

When he offered the container, the hot meats wafting their delicious scents into the air, I plucked out an entire sausage, hardly caring that I didn't have plates or silverware in the office. There *were* napkins leftover from a tenant bringing a birthday cake by that summer. I grabbed some of those for each of us and waved Duncan to a seat. He perched on the edge of the other office chair while eyeing the toy.

I took a bite of the andouille, and juices ran down my chin. Delicious.

"I have a plan," I admitted, my taste buds moving me to honesty. It was possible I was far too easily swayed by delicious meat. A werewolf failing. There was a reason salami bribes worked to win over young relatives.

"Is it better than the plan I had to run my smoker all afternoon to entice you with its scintillating smells to visit me? Because that didn't work."

"I don't know if anything will come of my plan either. It's possibly more of a scheme."

"I was visited by three homeless people and a bunch of your tenants."

"Did you share with them?"

"I felt obligated. There used to be a lot more sausages. What's your plan? I assume that factors in?" Duncan waved to the toy. "I *can* actually sense that there's very slight druid magic about it."

I rubbed the rune on the bottom and showed him its glow.

"What does that do?"

"I think that's it. Glowing. I thought that would look enticing— *magical*—in the photographs." I hesitated but then tabbed back to the screen to show him the post. "I suppose the same could be done with photo-manipulation software, but if someone reaches out and wants to see it in person..."

I trailed off, feeling foolish. Seeing it in person wouldn't convince anyone that it was real. Up close, it looked like the toy it was. The wolf head was similar in profile to the one on the case, with rows of sharp teeth on display, but I didn't know if that was what had drawn the thief to the case in the first place. Mom's medallion had a howling wolf on it. No teeth.

"It doesn't hurt to try," Duncan offered after looking at the photos and post I'd uploaded on the server that Chad had mentioned, as well as in other spots I'd heard of before or found through research.

"You sound like you're being politely supportive but don't think this has a shot of working."

"I am politely supportive. That's why I brought you sausages."

"I'm not sure what else I can try if this doesn't work."

"Touring lavender farms in northern Snohomish County?" Duncan raised his eyebrows.

"They don't offer tours in November. *Or* have flowering lavender." I shook my head, still skeptical that the thug traipsed through flower fields daily and that was where the scent had come from.

The phone in the leasing office rang, an avocado-green rotary model that was older than I was. The owners of the complex kept saying they would replace it with something modern when it stopped working, but it had proven resilient.

"You didn't put your name and number in the posting, did you?" Duncan asked as I reached for the phone.

I hesitated. "Not my *name*, but I did need a phone number someone could call. And the phone needed to be close by so I'd hear it ring." I answered, worried I'd done the wrong thing, since whoever had researched me enough to know where my family lived probably knew the number for the complex too. Maybe I'd made a mistake. "Sylvan Serenity Housing."

Duncan waited with his eyebrows raised.

"We do have some availability, yes," It was a perfectly mundane call that had nothing to do with magical artifacts. "A couple of two-bedrooms and one three. Yes, dogs from most breeds are allowed."

"And wolves," Duncan whispered with a smirk.

I held my finger to my lips, gave the rest of the requested information, and made an appointment for the person to come see the units.

"We do require at least a 650 credit score," I said. That was on the website and in all the ads, but people tended to think it didn't apply to them.

The prospective tenant didn't cancel the appointment, so I put her in the calendar for the following day.

"Ah, the credit score," Duncan said, "a rather unique American invention that rewards a person for going deeper and deeper in debt."

"While making the payments in a timely manner each month." *That* was what my employers cared about.

"You'd think a more ideal tenant would be one who pays in cash for items and doesn't have any debt."

"We're okay with those people too." Given my own bruised history with debt, I *enjoyed* leasing to those who'd also clawed their way out. "You just can't be in debt and behind on payments. Are *you* debt-free, Duncan Calderwood?"

"Of course."

"You should have mentioned that when you first asked me out. After being married to a deadbeat who took out loans I didn't know about and stole the kids' college money, I'm particularly attracted to men who can make ends meet without credit cards."

"I guessed that from the envelopes." Duncan grinned. "But I didn't think you would be wooed by the finances of someone who lives in his van. You were somewhat snide about the idea of me making a living as a treasure hunter."

"I was snide about the rusty forks and forty-year-old bike locks. Had you pulled golden chalices out of Lake Washington, I might have believed your career had more financial stability."

"Gold isn't magnetic."

"Ah, so the chalices are down there, and you just don't have the right tools?"

"I have *all* the right tools. Trust me." His eyelid shivered in what I took as a wink, though it was subtle, and I wasn't *positive* that was a sexual innuendo. It probably was.

I was debating on an appropriately snarky response when the phone rang.

"Sylvan Serenity Housing." Again, I kept myself from including my name, as I usually would. Just in case.

"Is this the owner of the wolf artifact?" a man with a raspy voice asked.

The hair on the back of my neck rose.

"This is Janette, yes," I said, using the name I'd put in the ad.

"I'm an interested buyer, but I need to see it in person."

"Of course."

With his keen ears, Duncan probably heard both sides of the conversation. He crossed his arms over his chest and leaned his hip against the desk.

"Are the batteries included?" the caller asked.

I blinked. What?

"Uh, I don't think there are batteries. Oh, are you asking because of the glow? I'm not quite sure what that is but probably some phosphorescent paint." I imagined Bolin being aggrieved at the suggestion that his druid enchantment was something so pedestrian.

"I see." Did the speaker sound more interested? "I see," he repeated. Yes, he sounded eager, almost triumphant. "Where may I view it?"

Duncan shook his head. Warning me not to invite the guy

here? No, I couldn't even if I'd wanted to fight on my home turf. If this was the man who employed the blond thug, the blond thug who'd already been here, he would know it was a set-up.

"The convenience store on Bothell Way by the teriyaki restaurant," I said.

That was close to where Duncan and I had gone for our first date, a date of fine dining and battling my cousin's wolf and mongrel-dog minions. If we had to fight again, we were both familiar with the area. I assumed that he would come with me.

"I get off work at eight," I added into the silence.

"Let me see what I can arrange."

"If you like what you see, it's a hundred dollars."

"That item isn't worth more than fifty."

"It's worth a hundred alone for the glow," I countered, figuring I should haggle. It would be suspicious if I was willing to give away such a fine find.

"The phosphorescent paint," the man said dryly.

"It's *nice* paint. And I'm willing to drive over there to show it to you."

"I could come to you," the man said. His raspy voice already made him sound creepy, but that added to it.

"The store is good. And my boyfriend will be with me, just FYI. He's a karate blackbelt and a body builder."

Duncan raised his eyebrows.

The caller chuckled, not sounding concerned.

"Eight o'clock tonight." He hung up.

"Do you think that worked?" I worried it had been too easy. That guy had to have been monitoring those sites if he'd pounced so quickly.

"I'm not certain." Duncan looked at the time on his phone. "I am concerned that I only have three hours to learn the skills of a karate blackbelt."

"What makes you think *you're* filling the role of my boyfriend?"

"Of course I am. You've been aching for me since I told you I don't have any debt."

"So almost ten minutes."

"Yup." He smiled, but it faded as he considered the toy. "That did seem easy and... unlikely."

"Do you think we should bring more backup?" If the thugs were lying in wait and had rifles loaded with silver bullets, having another werewolf along might not be enough. Worse, I could get Duncan shot.

"Do you *have* more backup?"

"Uhm, I could call Bolin. Or the ladies in my book club. One of them has knitting needles like fencing rapiers."

"You could call your family." Maybe that was who he'd had in mind in the first place.

"Oh." I grimaced at the thought of asking my sick mom for help. And the males of the pack... Other than Lorenzo and the injured Emilio, there weren't many prospects who might assist me. "If someone with silver bullets shows up, I don't want to get more werewolves into trouble. Besides, I'm not sure who among them I could trust to help."

"I guess it's the two of us then." Duncan picked up the toy with a bemused smile and examined it.

"And the knitting lady if I call her."

"I think we can handle it. What shall we do to kill time until eight?"

"I have another leaky faucet to replace." I waved to a box sitting on the desk. "The tenant works the evening shift so I was waiting for him to head out before going over."

His eyes crinkled. "Can I help?"

"I'm still waiting for you to rake the leaves out there," I said, though I'd done that myself when the forecast for winter weather had come. It was much easier to rake leaves when they weren't covered with snow.

"Ah, yes, I remember you assigning me that duty."

He hadn't done it, though, since that had been right before I'd overheard him speaking to Chad on the phone the first time—the time I'd believed it a great betrayal. After that, I'd driven him off.

"As I recall," he added, "you were enticed by the idea of me doing it shirtless."

"As *I* recall, it was Grammy Tootie I promised would be enticed by that."

I grabbed the faucet and headed for the door. There was time to complete the task, and I felt obligated to finish everything on my workday to-do list before taking off to attempt to hunt artifact thieves. That was, after all, the kind of thing one did after hours.

Duncan followed me out of the office, but I paused before taking more than two steps. Three matte-black Teslas were rolling into the parking lot, the license plate lights dark so they weren't legible. I sensed magic about the vehicles—or maybe in those riding inside—and my instincts reared up, warning of danger.

"It's those men again," Duncan said, though he couldn't have seen through the tinted windows. He pulled me into bushes to the side of the walkway. "The man on the phone might have seen through your ruse and been calling to verify that you were here."

"Then that saves us the trip of having to drive to Bothell," I said with determination.

If the blond thug was one of the people in those cars... This time, I would catch him and question him.

The Teslas stopped, and two windows rolled down enough for the muzzles of rifles to stick out.

"Silver bullets," Duncan warned, his grip tightening on my shoulder. "Get down."

How he could be certain, I didn't know, but I didn't want to be shot with *any* type of bullet, so I let him push me lower and behind a garbage can that would offer more cover than the bushes. Two more muzzles appeared, bringing the total number of rifles to four.

One of the car doors opened, but the interior was dark, and we couldn't identify who was inside. Not by sight, at least. Duncan, crouched close beside me, inhaled sharply. Maybe he could *smell* the occupants.

"Get inside, girl," someone called through the open door. "Come with us, or we'll shoot up this place and kill your tenants."

Duncan stirred. "They didn't come for an artifact. They came for you."

14

With four rifles peeking out car windows and aimed in my direction, I wasn't inclined to obey the command to *get inside, girl*. Since night had fallen, and Duncan and I were crouched behind a garbage can, the gunmen probably couldn't see us, but that didn't mean they couldn't do plenty of damage.

I clenched my jaw. I couldn't let these people endanger my tenants. It was nothing but luck that nobody returning home from work was in the parking lot at that moment, but that wouldn't last.

"I'm going to try to get them to chase me away from the complex." I pointed out a route across the lawn that would take me behind bushes and toward the parking lot from the side. "I don't want them to open fire on this property."

I tapped my pockets where I usually kept my phone and car keys, but the keys were in my apartment, and I had left my phone on the desk in the office. Damn it. I would have to lure these guys away on foot.

"I can distract them while you get away," Duncan offered.

"By what? Hurling sausages at their windshields?"

"That would be a blasphemous use of good meat."

"We're not joking around, girl," the same man called from the Tesla with the open door. The other vehicles were circling the parking lot. "We *know* you're here."

I eyed the lights of the leasing office, suspecting that Duncan was right, that the phone call to the land line had been a way of verifying my location. Whoever the man in charge was must have guessed right away what I was trying to do when I posted that ad. And he was trying to do something else, nothing good for my health.

"Just stay here," I told Duncan, then slipped out from behind the garbage can.

Staying low, I jogged toward the sidewalk running past the property, intending to use the mailboxes, trees, and bushes to stay hidden until I was in the street. And then... Then I would have to hope the men truly did want to snag me, not shoot me, because I would be an easy target running down the pavement.

Before I made it, a tenant in a minivan rolled into the parking lot. I winced, recognizing the vehicle. It belonged to a mom with two kids.

Hopefully, they weren't with her, but I couldn't count on that. Instead of running into the street, I hurried toward the parking lot. I would have to give myself up to ensure there wasn't violence. Maybe Duncan could help me escape later.

Anger at the situation and frustration that I'd inadvertently brought it down upon the complex surged through my body. Magic mingled with the emotions, the call of the wolf. It urged me to take my lupine form to battle the threats.

I tried to sublimate the call, certain a wolf wouldn't be effective against cars and guns—especially guns loaded with silver bullets. Besides, I needed my wits about me to protect the tenants and figure this out.

One of the Teslas halted abruptly. Two of its doors opened, and men surged out. They weren't facing me or the minivan but the walkway in front of the leasing office. A salt-and-pepper wolf stood there, brown eyes toward the intruders, jaws parted to reveal fangs.

Damn it, what was Duncan doing? He would be as vulnerable to silver bullets as I.

He lifted his snout toward the night sky and howled.

"That's her ally!" one man yelled as he got out of his car, a rifle in hand.

It was the blond guy, and he reeked of magical power. Had he quaffed a fresh dose of the Tiger Blood potion?

I reached the parking lot from the side but didn't rush out, instead using the big metal cluster mailboxes for cover. How *much* cover they would provide, I didn't know. They were meant for keeping out parcel thieves, not stopping bullets.

"If it's me you want," I called, leaning out, "I'm right here."

With their rifles in their hands, the intruders spun toward me. They were all huge and *all* oozed magical power. Their fingers rested on the triggers, but they didn't pull them.

"That's her." One man raised his voice. "Get in, girl, and send your wolf boy away."

As if I had that power over Duncan.

I took a step away from the mailboxes, but the minivan lady had parked.

"Mom," a young voice cried. "Those men have guns!"

"Stay inside!" their mom barked.

Another car swung into the parking lot, another tenant coming home. Damn it. This was about to turn into—

The blond guy swung his rifle toward the minivan and fired at it.

"No!" I shouted.

I started toward them, but a different man raised his rifle to fire at *me*. Instincts more than any stunning brilliance warned me an instant before he pulled the trigger. I dove to the pavement. The bullet that shot from his rifle left a silver trail in the air before slamming into a mailbox.

"Watch out for the other wolf!" a man yelled.

Two more rifles fired at Duncan.

The fury and frustration that had been simmering inside me shifted to a boil, overflowing with magical urgency that coursed through my veins. Heat seared my skin from within, and a fearsome tingle of power burned through me. Before I could leap to my feet, the change began, clothing disappearing into the ether as my body morphed. By the time I stood again, it was on all fours as a wolf.

Fear of the men and those magical bullets should have made me hesitate to charge them, but rage over them attacking Duncan and my tenants took me over. *More* than took me over. I was barely aware of anything but the need to destroy those who dared trespass on my territory.

Rifles fired again, aiming both at me and toward Duncan on the walkway. No, my ally had reached them. Dodging bullets as he ran, the salt-and-pepper wolf sprang toward the gunmen.

I also dodged as I ran, but a bullet grazed my shoulder before it struck a lamppost. Though searingly intense, the pain didn't stop me. I leaped at the blond man, knocking his rifle aside as I rammed into him.

He staggered, managing to shift his strong legs to brace himself and stay upright, but it didn't matter. Guided by the magical instincts of the wolf, I snapped my jaws for his throat.

He got a hand up to block me and clipped my chest with a powerful blow, but I caught his arm and sank my fangs into it. The man screamed, strong muscles jerking as he tried to break the grip and fling me away. But I was strong too. I held on, sinking my fangs in deeper.

His allies turned toward us, but they couldn't shoot me without risking hitting him. When I landed, I made sure to stay close, using his body for cover. He ripped his arm up and out of my grip, leaving the taste of blood in my mouth. Before he could back away, I sank my jaws into his thigh. He yelled and flailed wildly. Most of the attacks went awry, but a strong punch slammed into my spine. I hung on, gnashing my teeth and sinking them in deeper.

More shots fired nearby, but men also screamed. My wolf ally was attacking the intruders.

My foe punched me in the back again. I released my grip on his thigh and sprang at his chest. This time, I succeeded in knocking him to the pavement. He flung his arms over his neck and face, shouting for help, but I was merciless in dealing with the threat. Rational thoughts disappeared, and the savage animal in me took over.

I tore out his throat, then spun to face another enemy. Barely registering that it was another of the big enhanced men, I charged.

Tires squealed loudly as one of the vehicles sped away, and I paused, startled. A powerful kick knocked me flying. It hadn't come from my target but from one of the other men. Shoulder twinging, I hit the pavement and rolled. Faster than lightning, I leaped up to spring again.

Someone fired, and a bullet clipped the pavement inches from where I'd been.

"He wants her alive," someone barked.

"She's *killing* us! They *both* are."

Snarls came from a fight Duncan was engaged in. I rushed toward the man who'd kicked me, driven by savage wildness, the need to defend my territory—the need to kill.

My target tried to club me with his rifle, but I ducked low, and the blow missed. I barreled into him, jaws snapping as I bit into his belly. He cried as he fell back. Someone else fired, but the bullet flew wide, one of their allies yelling as it struck him.

Chaos covered the parking lot, and my thoughts scattered, only instincts driving me. I eviscerated my foe.

Tires squealed again. The vehicle hadn't been leaving. The driver had come around and was heading straight toward me, the car oddly silent, no smell of gasoline in the air.

At the last instant, I recognized the danger and jumped away. The driver had meant to hit me, to knock me flying. Instead, he ran over one of his own downed allies. The obstacle made the vehicle careen into a lamppost, the crash assaulting my sensitive ears.

Near me, Duncan knocked aside a man who'd been aiming a rifle at me. I met his eyes, silently acknowledging that I appreciated the help.

One of the cars tried to zip out of the parking lot with two men, those wise enough to flee, but the vehicle angled toward me before leaving. Another driver attempting to take me out.

I tensed, but the salt-and-pepper wolf sprang in from the side. He landed on the hood of the car, startling the driver. The man swerved, drove over a curb, and smashed into a sturdy cedar. Duncan leaped off before impact, before the front of the vehicle crumpled.

The driver-side door flew open, a man with a rifle scrambling out. The wolf sprang upon him, knocking the weapon to the pavement with a clatter.

On the passenger side, the window rolled down. My instincts processed the threat before the rifle fully thrust out, and I dodged before the shot fired. A silver bullet streaked away, disappearing into the night.

The rifle shifted to follow me, but I rushed in before the human could shoot again. My jaws clamped onto the cold steel of the barrel. The man didn't release the weapon, and his grip was strong, but my magic and fury made mine stronger. I tore the rifle from his hands, flinging it away, then leaped halfway through the window. He screamed and tried to crawl to the other side of the car to escape me, but I was too fast. I caught him by the neck and crunched down, halting the scream—and his life.

Sensing movement behind me, I dropped out of the window. None too soon. Another bullet streaked past, this one glancing off the roof of the car.

The gunman stood behind me, utter terror widening his eyes. Swearing, he fired again. Though I saw the finger squeeze in time to duck, the bullet parted the fur on the top of my head. Fear as well as my ongoing fury propelled me forward, and I reached him before he could shoot again.

I leaped, magic and power taking me into him so quickly that even his enhanced blood wasn't enough. He couldn't get his rifle up fast enough to block me, and I tore out his throat. As a wolf, I felt no remorse, no concern about possible ramifications, only the satisfaction that I was ending the threat to my territory.

Fortunately, Duncan didn't come close while I was in that state. In the haze of leaping and charging and snapping jaws, instincts having overtaken me, I might not have known friend from foe. I kept fighting, snarling and attacking anyone close until the battle fury faded and all lay still around me.

15

In the aftermath of the battle, with all my enemies down or escaped, the apartment complex grew quiet, the distant roar of the freeway noticeable as it wafted through the trees. The smell of burning rubber from the men's tires lingered in the air. All but one of the cars was gone, the one that had crashed into the cedar, faint protesting beeps coming from the console. For whatever reason, those cut through the animalistic haze in my mind, and awareness slowly returned.

I remained in my wolf form, muscles warm from the fight, my shoulder burning from the bullet that had grazed me. At least it hadn't lodged in. I had little doubt that it, like the bullets that had been used on my pack, had been made from silver. Enchanted silver with the power to kill a werewolf. A shudder went through me, and I shook my head and body, as if to fling water from my fur coat. I wanted to fling off the taint of those men.

Movement behind me made me spin in that direction, tensing in case a new threat had arrived.

But it was my ally, the salt-and-pepper wolf. Duncan. He, too, remained in wolf form, watching me with his brown eyes.

He'd battled against the same enemies as I but hadn't come too close. Maybe he'd understood that the animal had overtaken me and that, in the midst of the fight, I might not have known friend from foe. I was relieved he'd recognized the danger and had stayed away. In this form, I could easily sense his power and knew he wouldn't have been easy to kill, but a memory percolated through my mind. Long ago, the love of my life, the werewolf Raoul, had also been stronger than I, but he'd been in love and hadn't wanted to hurt me. Because of his hesitation to strike aggressively, I'd ended up killing him.

The sour taste of torn clothes and human blood tainted my tongue. I lapped up the remains of melting snow to wash it away. Voices sounded near the human structures. People who lived in the dwellings. They were whispering. Watching.

As more of the wolf magic faded, I realized I would soon change back. Duncan caught my gaze, then pointed his snout toward the woods. He trotted a few steps in that direction and paused to look back at me, his eyes telling me to follow.

Yes, I couldn't remember why the watching humans mattered —what did a wolf care about such things?—but something told me they did. Besides, it was never wise to change in front of potential enemies. During a transition, one was vulnerable.

I padded into the woods after Duncan, my ears flickering at the roar of traffic. The urge to travel far from this hive of humanity crept into me, the longing to find a serene place to hunt, but the wolf magic ebbed further. With trees all around, my muscles, bones, and skin shifted, returning to their human form. Soon, I sat on my butt in damp pine needles, and the awareness of my life as a woman returned to me. As well as awareness of the pain in my shoulder. I grimaced and wrapped a hand around it.

"Luna," Duncan said before stepping close to crouch beside me. He'd also shifted back and was as naked as I, the night's darkness the only cloak for our nudity.

"I'm here," I said, meaning mentally rather than physically. Of course he could see that my body was there. But he'd been fighting with me and had witnessed me losing it, seen my conscious thoughts vaporize as the beast took over. I eyed him warily for judgment.

"They hit you," was what he said. "Are you okay?"

"I've been better." I released my wound, my palm damp with blood, but barely glanced at it. I was talking more about how I felt in the aftermath of killing those guys—of completely *losing* it with them. Oh, I wouldn't mourn their deaths, not when they'd mugged Bolin and *shot* my mom and Emilio, but I'd wanted to question them. All this had been for naught. We were no closer to finding out who'd sent them and where the artifacts were.

"Let me help you back to your apartment. We'll dig out your first-aid kit."

"Are those dead bodies?" someone screeched from the parking lot. The mom with the kids had made it into their apartment, but other people were arriving home.

"I need to call the police and report... something." Numbness crept into me. Numbness and exhaustion. I didn't want to deal with the police or anyone else tonight and wished I could crawl into the bushes and be left alone.

"We'll do that while we're patching up your wound." Duncan squeezed my uninjured shoulder. "We might want to take a circuitous route to your apartment though. Your tenants would wonder about our nudity, especially the ones who watched us head this direction as wolves."

"*Most* people don't believe in werewolves." Even Bolin didn't, or hadn't. I thought he might be putting two and two together now that we'd spent time together. "They're not going to connect our nudity to the wolves who killed those guys."

Unless they'd seen us change, but we'd done that in the

bushes, so I hoped there hadn't been witnesses. The security cameras might have caught it, but I could delete the footage.

"They'll probably think we were having sex in the woods," I added. Though the damp pine needles under my butt didn't lend themselves to ardent passion. It wasn't the time of year for trysts in the forest.

"And that you came away from the experience bloody?" Duncan pointed at my bloody shoulder. "I would prefer people *not* think sex with me leads to that outcome."

"Afraid it'll lower the odds of other women in the complex propositioning you?"

"It very well might. If you're not going to give in to my advances, I'll have to find another female to satisfy my urges."

"I told you Grammy Tootie is available."

Duncan rose, offering me a hand. "I'm glad you can still make jokes."

"It's a defense mechanism. I can always be snarky." It didn't mean I wasn't distressed by the night's events.

I accepted his hand and almost hugged him when he helped me up. I longed to collapse in strong arms and let someone else deal with the aftermath.

But I didn't. Once on my feet, I released his hand and straightened my back. I was the property manager. When bodies and crashed cars littered the parking lot, handling them was my duty.

With Duncan walking beside me, I headed through the woods until we could step out onto the lawn in the back of the complex, out of view from the parking lot and where there were fewer lights. I hurried toward my apartment. My phone was still in the leasing office, but I could grab it later. Once I was clothed.

We slipped into my apartment, and Duncan pointed me toward the couch. "You were kind enough to tend my wounds there when I was bleeding, so I'll do the same for you."

"Thanks, but mind if I put my robe on first? It's a little nippy."

He glanced at my chest before lifting his gaze higher. "Yes, that's a good idea. I might otherwise be distracted."

"There's blood and dirt all over me." I scraped my fingers through my hair and dislodged dead leaves and fir needles. "And less than desirable other things."

"You, of all people, shouldn't be surprised by what *doesn't* faze a werewolf." Since Duncan had seen me retrieve my first-aid kit before, he knew where it was and fetched it, as well as dampening a towel with water to wash my wound.

Before heading to the couch, I made myself grab the phone in the kitchen. Attached to the wall by the fridge, it was almost as old as the rotary phone in the office. I dialed 9-1-1 and felt the weight of my lies as I fabricated a story for the dispatcher. I said feral coyotes or dogs instead of wolves had attacked strangers who'd been on the property for some unknown reason.

Meanwhile, Duncan spread paper towels on the couch, winking at me when he caught my eye. I snorted softly. He'd done that for himself when I'd told him not to bleed on my furniture. I had a feeling he was doing it now to amuse me, or at least lighten my somber mood.

The dispatcher said the police were already on the way because they'd received numerous calls about coyotes or wolves. I didn't try to disabuse her of the notion that wolves had been involved. It didn't matter that much. As long as nobody figured out there had been *were*wolves—and that I was one of them.

A knock on the door made me jump. Was that the police already? I hurried into my bedroom to grab my robe.

Less concerned about propriety, Duncan answered the door naked.

"Oh, uhm, hi." That was Bolin, not the police. "Is Luna here? There's been... an incident."

"Has there?" Duncan asked innocently, then called over his

shoulder. "Luna, are you here, or are you so exhausted in the aftermath of our lovemaking that you can't talk to anyone?"

"Funny." I winced at the pain in my shoulder as I shrugged into the robe, then stepped out of my bedroom. "Bolin, I didn't know you were still here."

"Showing an apartment. It's on the calendar."

"Yeah, thanks for handling that. Things have been chaotic lately."

He looked toward the parking lot, though it wasn't visible from my door. "Tell me about it. The police just got here. I think it's the same officers as last time."

"I don't suppose you'd like to talk to them?"

"I don't know what happened. Are you okay?" Bolin squinted at my robe. "Is that *blood*?"

"I'm not positive what exactly happened either." That wasn't a complete lie. Everything that had occurred while I'd been afflicted by the battle lust of the werewolf was a haze. "But if you already have a rapport with those officers..."

"Last time, they called me a spoiled punk."

"Maybe rapport isn't the right word."

"It's not, but I can talk to them."

"You can tell them I'll be out in a minute."

"Ten minutes," Duncan corrected and pointed to the first-aid kit.

Bolin looked like he might say something snarky, perhaps about all the nudity in my apartment, but he glanced at the blood on my robe again and didn't. "Okay."

He left, shutting the door behind him.

I was relieved Bolin was here and could talk to the police, at least to start with. They would inevitably question me. Having to lie made everything awful, but it wasn't as if they would believe the truth if I shared it. Despite the long-term presence of the

Snohomish Savagers, most of the local authorities simply believed what the naturalists told them, that wolves lived in the area. *Most* of the time, we didn't change in the city. This had been... an accident.

"If they'd met me where I'd asked, this wouldn't have turned into such a debacle." I slumped down on the couch and, at a finger twirl from Duncan, eased my left arm out of the robe. "I mean... it probably still would have since *I* was involved, and I totally lost it, but it wouldn't have happened in front of my home—and the home of three hundred residents."

"*Losing* it was understandable." Duncan perched on the edge of the couch next to me, still stark naked.

If I hadn't burned Chad's clothes—literally—I could have offered him something, but they wouldn't have fit well anyway. Duncan was taller and more muscular than my ex, and my boys had still been on the lanky, if not gangly, side when they'd lived at home. I couldn't imagine the handful of things they'd left behind fitting him either.

Duncan watched my face as he dabbed the towel over my wound. It stung, but I'd hit the ground and rolled after being shot, so dirt mingled with the blood. Even with the regenerative power of the werewolf, cleaning wounds was a good idea.

When I didn't respond, Duncan said, "They were shooting at us, and they're the same brutes that hurt your family."

"I know."

It was a half-hearted agreement. It didn't bother me that I'd changed—Duncan had changed too. It bothered me that I'd lost my sanity—my rational mind—and turned into a killing machine. *Again.* My history with that was the reason I'd fled from my family all those years ago and started taking the potion. I'd longed to be a normal human woman, for nothing like that ever to happen again. For twenty-six years, it hadn't. But now... things had changed. *I'd* changed.

"It wasn't even my family they maimed, and I shifted," Duncan offered.

"You said you don't have a family."

"I don't, but if I *did,* their maiming would upset me. It would make me furious."

I stared at the coffee table. "It was more than fury."

"I know," he said softly. "I saw."

That made me grimace. I appreciated that he'd been there to fight with me, but having a witness to my insanity... I could have done without that.

"I hate how dangerous it is to others when it happens," I whispered.

"I understand now why you took that potion."

I grimaced again. Just how insane did I look when I lost it like that?

"When I was growing up, I rarely saw anyone else in my pack go that crazy," I said. "Completely lose their minds—and control."

"I've gotten that way a couple of times in my life."

I looked at him, surprised by the admission. From what I'd seen, it was hard to rile him up in human *or* wolf form. Maybe he was only saying that to make me feel better.

Duncan shrugged, reading the doubt on my face. "It's what the werewolf blood does to you, what comes with it. Great power, great stamina, great regenerative ability—" he nodded to my wound, "—but the stronger your magic, the more it can consume you."

"And turn you into a freak."

"Usually, that's what people call *me.*" Duncan smiled and switched from the towel to gauze from the first-aid kit, pressing it against my wound to stop the bleeding that his cleaning had stirred up again.

"Well, you are... odd."

He was more than that. I thought of all the warnings people

had voiced about him. And, when I'd been in my wolf form, I'd noticed his atypical power for myself. Strange that I remembered that when much of the battle was a blur.

"Yes, I am." Duncan glanced down, then away. "You might want to, er, cover your... womanly curves."

Not looking, he waved vaguely toward my chest. The robe had slipped low.

"It's hard to leave my shoulder bare without other things being bare," I pointed out.

"Perhaps a blanket." He looked resolutely at the first-aid kit as he pulled out antibiotic ointment and bandages. "Or..." His gaze shifted to the roll of paper towels on the coffee table.

"I'm not using Brawny to cover up my boobs," I said tartly. "You're a lot more naked than I am."

"Yes, that's problematic as well. I'm trying not to let myself be inappropriately, er, to have a..." He glanced down.

"Tallywacker problem?" I suggested.

"Quite."

"Yeah, it would be weird to get aroused by giving a woman first aid."

"The *first aid* is not the reason for my tallywacker's interest."

"That's good to know. Wounds aren't supposed to be stimulating." I took mercy on him and shifted the robe to cover my breast.

"No," he murmured, his gaze following my hand. He swallowed then made himself focus on applying the ointment. "I don't think you're in the mood to have me stimulated right next to you, so I'm trying to control myself."

"You're a polite medic."

"I do try. Brace yourself."

The ointment stung, but his touch also felt good. It was a professional application, not a gentle caress, but it turned out he wasn't the only one feeling stimulated this evening. A part of me was tempted to lower the robe again and lean over to kiss him. But

I had things to do, and remembering the garish scene outside quelled thoughts meandering toward the idea of sex.

"When has anyone called you a freak?" I asked. "Aside from your atypical career choice, you're more on the handsome and charming side."

That was an understatement. When I'd first seen him, I'd had no trouble imagining him modeling for a men's magazine. The little scar above his eyebrow and the gray dusting his hair did nothing to detract from his handsomeness, and there was nothing wrong with the rest of his body either. I caught myself glancing down, though I'd already seen him naked a few times and didn't need to reaffirm his fitness. Ah, and he *was* aroused, wasn't he? This time, I was the one who looked away, embarrassed by my desire to let my gaze linger.

"It's the wolf blood and the magic in it that makes me different from the norm." Duncan had to have noticed my gaze, but he didn't comment on it. His expression looked a touch smug and pleased, but he only continued his ministrations, bandaging my wound after finishing with the ointment.

"*All* werewolves are different from the norm," I pointed out, though a part of me wanted to ask for clarification.

Would he give it? I'd asked a couple of times now what his deal was.

"Most werewolves are born into a pack and learn the ways of our kind."

"And you didn't? Did you lose your mom when you were young?"

A long moment of silence passed as Duncan bandaged my shoulder, and I didn't think he would answer. He hadn't before, and nothing had changed. Or had it? He looked contemplatively at me, as if he was considering...

"What?" I asked softly.

He took a long breath—a bracing breath?—then exhaled it

slowly. "Fifty years ago, before such things were common, before science had advanced as far as magic... I was created in a laboratory."

I stared at him with my mouth dangling open. I didn't know what dark past I'd expected him to have, but that wasn't it.

"Why?" I managed to ask.

"The scientist who was responsible sought power and prestige. He wanted to bring back the werewolves of old, those that could turn not only into wolves, but into the bipedfuris, the great two-legged creatures of the legends, beasts who could bite humans and spread lycanthropy. As you're probably aware, we don't know many with that power anymore. It died out, or so the stories say, as magic faded from the world, destroyed as more and more of the wilderness was cut down, technology replacing what was."

"I've heard the stories, yes." I tilted my head as I considered him. "So... you were an experiment? Like with DNA splicing or the magical equivalent?" Fifty years ago, we hadn't been sequencing DNA and doing the kinds of cloning experiments that were possible now. If his story was true, it had to have been achieved with magic.

"Sort of, but splicing wasn't involved. Lord Abrams—that was the scientist's name—acquired some centuries-old DNA—I think that's exactly what it was—from a werewolf who died long ago, high on a mountain in the Alps. He was buried for centuries under a glacier, his remains largely preserved by the ice. Abrams decided he would clone that werewolf so that he had a living, breathing specimen from that time." Duncan touched his chest. "In part to study, in part to use. Abrams raised that werewolf, having tutors brought in to teach him to fight and to educate him so that he could be useful. Abrams' goal was to send him out to spread lycanthropy with his bite, to create an army of werewolves that they could control together."

"Can you do that?" I whispered.

"I can." Duncan watched me warily.

Expecting a negative reaction? Horror? Fear?

I considered my feelings, but the story didn't change much for me. Since I was *already* a werewolf, it wasn't as if his bite could do anything to me. Except sting. But biting wasn't what I worried about with Duncan.

"For a time, I served him. He was, as strange as it seems, like a father to me. But when I grew closer to adulthood, I longed for freedom and to be my own man. As I read more and more books, I realized he was evil and that I, if I continued to serve him, would be the same. He probably should have forbidden reading, for great knowledge lies in the pages of tomes, but he never did. That was his mistake."

"You escaped?"

"Eventually. It took a few tries." Duncan glanced at his wrists.

The scars I'd noticed before also drew my eye. I'd wondered what had made them, and handcuffs had crossed my mind. But, from their width, they must have been more like shackles. Imagining Duncan strung up in a mad scientist's dungeon made me wince with sympathy.

"It wasn't easy to get away, as Abrams knew intimately what I was and my capabilities. He had prepared his abode and laboratory well. But eventually, I got my opportunity. And I left to be my own man—my own *wolf*—and see a world I'd only read about in books. I was also intensely curious and wanted to meet more of my kind. But that never went well. The werewolves of this time don't know *what's* different about me, but they all sense that I am not like them. They either hate or fear me—often both."

That wariness remained in his eyes. Was this why he hadn't told me? He thought I would judge him?

Hell, it wasn't as if *I* could judge anyone. Not an hour ago, I'd completely lost my faculties, and it hadn't been the first time.

"I've been driven out of many countries by werewolves and

others with paranormal senses, those who realize what I am." Duncan smiled without humor. "You see, *I've* been called a freak, and worse things, many times, so, as I said, I understand completely why you'd want to take that potion. It crossed my mind to wonder if it would work on me, but I can't imagine giving up the wolf. I love that part of myself, running through the moonlit woods and hunting, the smell of nature, the excitement of the chase, of the takedown." He closed his eyes and took a deep breath, as if he were imagining escaping to the wilderness at that very moment.

I rested a hand on his arm. "What happened to the scientist? Did you slip away, or did he come after you?"

I almost asked if the guy was *still* after Duncan, but he had to be dead by now. All this had happened decades ago.

"The night I escaped, it was after an argument, and I was angry. I lashed out, and... in the process, I burned down his laboratory—half his castle was destroyed. He was inside at the time and died, his body charred to a crisp." Duncan grimaced.

"He had a *castle*?" I asked, focusing on the less grisly aspect of the story.

Duncan probably didn't want to dwell on how his escape had resulted in the death of his creator. But his creator had been his *captor*. I couldn't feel sorry for the passing of someone like that.

"Well, this was back in Europe. Castles are easier to come by over there." Duncan managed a more genuine smile, though that concern lingered in his eyes, like he worried I would realize at any moment that he was a freak. "As to the rest, I didn't mean to kill him at the time, but I don't regret ending his ambitions. The things he wanted me to do... Some of the things I *did* do..." Duncan shook his head and stared at the coffee table, though I doubted he saw anything on it.

"Have you told your story to many people?" I asked, though I thought I already knew the answer. After all, before now, he'd been evasive with me.

"No." He returned his gaze to mine. "After tonight, I thought you might understand. One werewolf freak to another." He smiled wryly to make it clear he was using the word because others had applied it to him. To us. He didn't see me that way.

My belly fluttered with an emotion I couldn't quite name. Nervousness? Anticipation? Attraction? Maybe all of those things.

He lifted a hand to trace my jaw, and a tingle of desire swept through me, making me want to scoot closer to him on the couch. Making me want *him*.

"Your blood, your lineage, the power that is so great that it threatens your control," he murmured. "You must also be closer to those ancient werewolves than most are."

"I could ask my mother, but I don't think glaciers and DNA were involved in my birth." I scooted closer, the robe drooping and my lips parting. We'd kissed before, and in that moment, I wanted nothing more than to kiss him again. And more.

He leaned forward, his hungry eyes promising he wanted the same.

As our lips met, his fingers trailed from my jaw and down the side of my neck, their teasing touch rousing my entire body. They slipped under my robe, caressing my bare breast, as if he'd longed to do exactly that since he walked in.

I gripped his shoulders and leaned so close I was almost in his lap. His masculine scent mingled with that of the wilds, and his power enveloped me, arousing me.

A firm knock sounded at the door, and reality rushed back in —and the reminder that I needed to deal with it.

With great reluctance, I drew back, our lips parting. "I need to answer that, to go out there and make sure we don't both end up arrested."

"I know," Duncan said, his gaze holding mine. His dark eyes

were intense, and I knew without a doubt that he wanted to ignore the door, sweep me into his arms, and carry me to the bedroom.

I licked my lips, wishing we could do that. Instead, I said, "You probably need to let go of my boob."

"I don't want to." A hint of humor replaced some of his intensity.

"I don't want you to either."

"Good." He gave me a final stroke before kissing me and scooting back. He swallowed and rose from the couch. "I think you'll live, patient."

"Thanks," I said quietly, my gaze on him as I pulled my robe over my shoulders and cinched it closed.

"Luna?" came Bolin's call through the door. "The police want to talk to you."

16

Duncan opened the door before I reached it, revealing Bolin standing outside with two police officers, a man and a woman. Their guns weren't drawn, but my stomach knotted as concern about everything coming out tangled within me.

What if they demanded to see tonight's footage from the security cameras? Before I had a chance to delete it? What if my story was so pathetic that they saw right through it?

I hated the situation and that it would force me to lie. I tried to be an honorable person, damn it.

Instead of waiting for them to start the questions, Duncan ambled out the door. "I need to check on my van. I heard there was a ruckus in the parking lot."

The male officer reached for him, took note of his nudity, and reconsidered. The female eyed his nudity, including his lower regions, and then looked frankly at me.

"I guess we know what the property manager was up to at the time," she told her partner.

I grimaced. Someone must have pointed out that I lived here and wondered why I hadn't made an appearance yet.

"I'm sorry," I said. "I can change and come out if that's what you need."

Duncan continued past them.

"Wait, sir." The female officer stepped after him, then gripped his arm when he didn't stop. "The tenants said you've been hanging out in your van in the parking lot. We need to question you."

"Hanging out?" Duncan turned to face her.

To my senses, he exuded power, and I thought of the story he'd just told me. I assumed a mundane human couldn't feel his magic, but the officer let go, uncertainty in her eyes. She took a step back and glanced at her partner.

"I've been courting my lady." Duncan tilted his head toward me.

"My lady," the woman mouthed, much as I had when he'd first used the term.

"He's from Europe," I said, as if that might be a suitable explanation for his eccentricities.

No, he was from a scientist's laboratory, if that tale was true.

Bolin was standing back, pointedly not looking at Duncan as he waited. When our gazes met, he dug something out of his pocket to hand to me. My phone from the office. He'd probably tried to call me before leading the police to my apartment. My nudity-filled apartment.

"I need to check on a couple of things," Duncan told the police while giving me a significant look that I couldn't interpret. What did he want to check on? A minute earlier, he hadn't seemed to have anything pressing on his mind—anything except *me*. "If you have questions for me later, I won't leave the premises."

The female officer looked toward her partner again.

"*I'm* not grabbing him," the man said.

"We'll talk to him later." The furrow to the female officer's brow suggested she wasn't sure why she hadn't handcuffed

Duncan and demanded answers immediately. Maybe she *had* sensed his power, at least on a subliminal level, and her subconscious mind had decided it would be better not to start something with him.

Unfortunately, they hadn't decided the same about me. Wearing no-nonsense expressions, they turned to face me. The male officer lifted a tablet open to a report.

"I didn't see what happened out there," Bolin told me, "but I informed them that one of the dead is the man who mugged me a few days ago and that there's a police report on the incident on file." The way he held my gaze made it seem like he was sending a silent message along with those words. Saying he *had* seen some of what happened? But that he was trying not to get me in trouble?

"And you think you're the reason they came back?" the female officer asked Bolin.

"I suppose it's possible."

I shook my head, not wanting Bolin to lie, even if it was to help me.

"Do you have any idea why they'd want you?" she asked, not looking at me.

"No. I mean, unless they wanted to kidnap me and ransom me or something. My parents own this place and numerous other large multifamily properties. They've done well for themselves."

"Huh." The male officer tapped notes into his tablet.

I hesitated, torn between wanting to protect Bolin and realizing his explanation might seem plausible to the police, at least as a reason why over-muscled thugs had shown up. Nothing I could say would explain the wolf attack, not without confessing to everything.

"We'll look into that." The male officer lowered his tablet, and the pair's focus turned back to me. "Were you here with... Shit, we didn't get his name. That guy. Were you with him the whole time? According to witnesses, there was shooting and some kind of huge dog fight. No, a dog *attack*. There are dead men all over the parking lot out there, their throats torn out."

"*Dogs* weren't responsible for that," the woman said grimly.

"Wild animals, then." The man held a hand out helplessly.

"I was with Duncan the whole time," I said.

That, at least, wasn't a lie. Never mind that we'd been responsible for the torn throats...

"He's distracting," I said, though I doubted they would buy sex as a believable reason that we hadn't heard the commotion.

"I'll bet." The woman glanced in the direction he'd gone. "We still need to talk to him. If he's staying in the parking lot, he might have seen some stuff."

"He's been with me for hours," I said.

True again.

She eyed me. "Hours, huh?"

I nodded firmly.

"You want to get his number on the way out?" the male officer asked her.

She shot him a dirty look, though her cheeks also turned pink. "I just want answers to our questions. For the record."

"Of course."

The officers asked me if I'd spotted anyone unusual on the premises that day, if there'd been suspicious activity recently, or if any of the tenants had been acting oddly lately.

"You've worked here twenty years?" the man asked to finish off the questions.

"More than. Nothing like this has happened before." I spread my arms in what I hoped was the picture of innocence.

If nothing else, it was another true statement. I'd managed more of them than I'd expected, mostly because the police hadn't asked any questions that implicated *me*. Even if it had been somewhat mortifying to have Duncan naked in my apartment when they'd arrived, it was probably saving my ass. Sex *did* apparently seem like a reasonable alibi. Not that police who knew nothing about werewolves and the paranormal world would have a reason to think a forty-five-year-old woman would have something to do with throats being ripped out...

"All right. We're going to speak with some more of the tenants and see if anyone saw more than *big dogs attacking* and men driving in and shooting at them." The female officer shook her head, as if she couldn't believe any of this.

"Okay," I said.

"You come with us." The man pointed at Bolin. "I want to hear more about your family and why someone might be after you."

Bolin grimaced—he probably didn't care to lie either—but he didn't object. He did, however, give me a long look over his shoulder as he trailed them back out to the parking lot.

I rubbed my face. Later, I was going to have to sit down with him for a private chat. After all that had happened, I owed him an explanation. And, after all that had happened, he might believe it.

Though the police hadn't requested it, I washed myself, changed into a new set of clothes, and headed to the parking lot. Ambulances had arrived, as well as more police cars, and their flashing lights threw the entire front of the complex into reds and yellows. Paramedics were putting the bodies onto gurneys and wheeling them to the ambulances, though I knew without a doubt that they would go to the morgue, not the emergency room.

Would there be autopsies? Would someone figure out that strange alchemical substances had coursed through their veins? I had no idea.

I spotted Duncan darting out of the shadows behind a tree and toward the black Tesla that had crashed into a cedar tree. He'd found a moment to put on clothes, including a black leather jacket, the pockets bulging with who knew what. There was just enough light to make out a credit card or maybe a hotel key card in his hand.

Confused, I walked across the lawn toward him. He looked like he was trying to avoid notice, so I also stuck to the shadows. A police car idled not far from that Tesla, but the driver and passenger had gotten out and joined their colleagues. The pair of officers who'd questioned me were on the far side of the parking lot; they'd been mobbed by tenants who were all trying to speak at once and share what they'd seen.

Trusting they were suitably distracted, I trotted over to join Duncan. He'd reached the Tesla, its matte-black paint swallowing the flashing lights instead of reflecting them, and was trying to peer through the driver-side window. Despite the tint, a glow was visible inside, the light from the big rectangular display on the dash.

"The doors on those lock automatically, I think," I said when I reached him. The windows that had earlier been down enough to allow rifles to fire through them had rolled up of their own accord.

I was surprised the display was on when there wasn't anyone inside. Or *was* there? I also tried to see through the window.

"They do." Duncan held up the card, waving it around the window. "I sneaked over to the driver before they picked up the body. He had this in his pocket. I thought he might." Duncan moved the card to the frame between the front and back door, and the locks released with a soft *clunk*. "Ah, that's the spot. I've only ever test-driven one, and it was the funky truck."

"I don't think you could fit all your equipment in that."

"Nope. I've got to stick to my van." Duncan opened the door, and eased into the driver's seat. "Watch out for me, will you?" He nodded toward where the police were trying to calm down the exuberant witnesses.

"Yeah, but you might not want to get your fingerprints on anything."

He'd been about to touch the glowing display and paused, his index finger dangling in the air. But he shook his head and tapped it. "My fingerprints aren't in a database anywhere."

"Off the grid, are you?"

"You know why." He smiled when he met my eyes, as if pleased we now shared his secret.

For some reason, that touched me. I was glad he didn't regret telling me his story.

He tapped a navigation bar on the display while I watched the police to make sure they didn't run over, outraged that we were messing with the crime scene. Since the crime scene sprawled all over the parking lot and front lawn, it was a lot for them to monitor, and nobody had noticed us in the car.

"If they were smart, they wouldn't have ever inputted their home base," Duncan murmured as he scrolled, "but they probably didn't expect their car to crash and be invaded, so maybe..."

I glanced over and caught Sylvan Serenity Housing at the top of the recent destinations. Other recents included a hardware store, a gun range, a charging station, and... I leaned in and squinted even as Duncan muttered a soft and triumphant, "Hah."

"TBL Luxury Perfumes and Potions?" I read.

The other stops made sense—they'd wanted guns and rope to use on *me*, presumably—but why that one? Given that TBL Luxury Perfumes and Potions was in the GPS as the name of a public store, I didn't assume it had anything to do with the paranormal, not *real* potions. Unless that was done on the side.

"That didn't come up when I was looking for farms, but I'll bet they have lavender products." Duncan tapped the destination, and a route popped up on the map. It was up north, near Arlington. "I should have known to expand my search beyond farms, especially considering, as you pointed out, we're past the season that any flowers would be blooming."

"Well, those guys didn't look like the perfume types, so not guessing that was understandable."

"I don't think they were *wearing* any, as the whiffs I kept catching weren't that strong, but if they worked there and passed in and out of the building, that could account for the scent."

"Why would thugs specializing in stealing and kidnapping work at a perfume and potion store?"

Duncan had tapped in the name on his phone and said, "It looks like the factory where they make the stuff, not only a store."

"Oh, well, if they work at a perfume *factory*, that makes much more sense."

Duncan gazed blandly at me. "Your snark is more appealing when you're naked."

"Really."

He grinned. "Yup."

"Is *everything* about me more appealing when I'm naked?"

"Oh yes. I trust the same is true of me."

I folded my arms over my chest.

"You *didn't* enjoy my nudity?" he asked.

"It was all right."

"I hope to get another opportunity to more thoroughly share its appeal with you." Duncan leaned over and patted the passenger seat. "Shall we visit this potion shop?"

I stared at him. "In the stolen crashed car of our enemies? After you told the police you'd stay in the area for questioning?"

Duncan leaned forward, looking out the windshield toward the crumpled front of the car still mashed against the cedar. He didn't glance at the police officers, but they were still distracted, with more and more tenants coming out to surround them.

"The damage doesn't look that bad," he said. "I think that's just the trunk up there. There aren't any errors on the display, so I doubt the car will explode if we drive it."

"Oh, would it *warn* us first before blowing up?"

"I should think so. This is modern technology, after all."

"I'd be more comfortable in your van." I didn't object to riding in electric cars, just electric cars that belonged to other people and had recently been crashed into trees.

"So would I, but that bobby is standing close to it."

"That what? Is that like a tallywacker?"

Duncan snorted. "No. Don't you watch any British TV?"

"I'm too busy with work."

"I believe you. This place seems to come with a lot of issues." Duncan patted the passenger seat again.

"Most of those issues started after you showed up," I muttered. "We can take my truck."

"Do you have money for gas?" He arched his eyebrows.

I hesitated. I did not, but this was an emergency. I could—

"Look, if the potion place happens to be a front for the master-mind behind the artifact theft, it might be a good idea to drive up in a car they'll be expecting."

I wanted to keep arguing, mostly because I didn't trust the huge mass of batteries that powered the car not to blow up on the freeway, but he had a good point.

"Fine. But if this breaks down, you're paying for the Uber."

"Fair."

After slipping into the car with him, I spotted Bolin. He was looking in our direction, but he didn't do anything to indicate to the police what we were doing.

"I'm starting to like that kid," I admitted, though that had been true since he'd used his burgeoning druidic powers to annihilate the mold in one of the apartments.

"He doesn't miss much," Duncan said. "I think he's figured out what we are."

"As long as he doesn't tell his parents."

Duncan looked over at me.

"My employers. He's their kid. That's why he's interning here."

"Ah."

Since the police weren't talking to Bolin at the moment, I grabbed my phone and called him.

"Yes?" he answered in a dry drawl.

"We've got a lead on who sent these guys."

"A lead? Like the navigation back log in the car?"

"Yeah, Duncan found a likely spot that it's been today."

"That's pretty good for a Boomer to think of looking at that," Bolin offered.

I shot him a scathing look through the windshield as Duncan backed the Tesla away from the tree. "We're Gen X, not Boomers. I'm *almost* a Millennial, FYI."

"He's got a lot of gray in his hair."

"It's silver, and Gen Xers aren't that young anymore." I shook my head. Why was I arguing about this? "Thanks for handling the police. I really appreciate it."

"No problem. I think... I owe you one."

"You don't owe me anything. I don't even pay you."

"My parents don't either, other than my allowance."

"The allowance that's six figures a year?"

He hadn't told me that, but I had my suspicions. Either that or his parents had bought him that car and paid for the insurance on it. And hadn't he said he had his own apartment?

"It's a generous allowance," Bolin agreed. "But I meant the thugly blond guy who beat the snot out of me. Some kind of wild animal ripped out his throat. I'm not a vengeful person, but I'm going to admit I'm not as horrified to see him dead as some other people might be. The bastard hurled me against a post and smashed my face. I'm lucky I'm the cerebral type and don't need to make my way in the world as a model."

"Yeah, your spelling-bee skills are sure to pave the path to a lucrative future."

"Those aren't my *only* skills."

"Oh, sorry. I forgot you play the violin too."

"You're kind of snarky tonight."

"You called me a freaking Boomer."

"Touché. But anyway, I'll take care of this. Like I said, I appreciate that you... or *something*... made sure that guy won't go after me again."

The thug had only gone *after* Bolin because he'd been carrying the wolf case, but I didn't point that out. Whatever his reason, I was glad to have him helping out. I wouldn't have expected someone that young to have the maturity to stand out here and field all the questions and whatever requests the police were making.

"Thanks, Bolin."

"No problem." He hung up.

We'd driven away from the apartment complex, so I couldn't tell if the police had returned to question him. I hoped he would be all right. As I slid my phone into my pocket, my shoulder twinged from the movement, and I grunted softly. The pain wasn't that bad, but I grunted again when I realized I didn't have my purse or even my ID with me.

Maybe that was for the best. Then, if we were captured and searched, my belongings couldn't give me away. Except that probably wouldn't matter. Whoever had sent the thugs to capture me... already knew who I was.

"You doing okay?" Duncan asked after my grunts.

"I'm fine. A bit sore, but these seats are surprisingly comfortable. And warm." I wiggled my rump. "Did you turn the butt heaters on?"

"I haven't poked around to figure out how to do that. The previous guys must have."

"I'm bemused that those brutes were riding around with soothing heat warming their asses while they were plotting our demise."

"All humans crave creature comforts. And it was only *my*

demise they were angling for. They wanted you alive for something." Duncan gave me a significant look as he drove the car onto the on-ramp for the freeway.

"Yeah, I caught that too. It's probably unwise of me to head up to their headquarters in the very car they sent to snatch me."

"That might have been an impulsive idea."

"*You* came up with it."

"I know. I'm the impulsive one. I was worried about the police rounding me up if I lingered, but, now I wish I'd grabbed a few more things from my van." Duncan touched one of his bulging pockets but didn't show me what he had in there. Not enough to storm an enemy fortress, I guessed.

"You might have been wise to get out of there," I said. "They're probably going to cordon off your suspicious van with caution tape and flashing lights."

"Suspicious? It's a perfectly normal camping van, refurbished and improved since its original build in the nineties."

"A perfectly normal camping van with tires big enough to roll over park benches."

"And surly werewolves."

"They did come in handy in that instance." Technically, I hadn't rolled *over* anyone. But knocking whichever of my cousins that had been flying was possibly another reason they didn't like me. "Maybe the police won't check it. I don't know what happens when a bunch of people are slain by wild animals in a suburban apartment complex. The authorities might not have a standard operating procedure for that."

"The van's interior is a little quirky, I'll admit. If they search that, their interest in wanting to question me may intensify."

"Do you have condemning equipment inside? Stuff more suspicious than magnets and SCUBA gear?"

Duncan hesitated, and I didn't know if he was taking a mental inventory of the contents or he didn't want to answer the question.

After a long moment, he admitted, "There are some underwater demolitions."

"Demolitions? As in *bombs*?"

"Incendiary devices with explosive kinetic potential." He sounded like Bolin giving one of his word origins.

"So, bombs."

"Yes."

I should have asked him *why* he had bombs, especially since he left his van in my parking lot so often—I hoped they were professional-grade and not some unstable homemade version. Instead, influenced by my current predicament, I peered hopefully at his pockets. "Did you bring any along?"

Duncan looked over at me. Wondering if I seriously wanted some?

I didn't *usually* long for weapons, but these were trying times.

He slid a hand into one bulging pocket, withdrew a metal sphere with a clip in the top, and offered it to me. By habit, I started to reach for it, like someone accepting a square of chocolate, but I froze.

"Is that..."

"An M67 fragmentation hand grenade, yes. I brought two with me. Just in case."

I hadn't truly expected him to have bombs—or grenades—in his pockets, but... who knew what we would face? They might come in handy.

"Uh, that's all right. I've only seen them used on TV. I'd better stick to what's in my pockets."

"You brought weapons?"

I pulled out a half-consumed bar of dark chocolate. I'd needed a little fortification before leaving my apartment. It was fancy enough to be in a cardboard container in addition to the foil wrapper inside, so it wasn't in danger of melting.

"That should make the bad guys quail." Duncan returned the grenade to his pocket.

"If we fall down a well, we can survive on the extra calories." I put the chocolate away, knuckles brushing the locket we'd found together. I'd been keeping that close since its magic had been helpful. "Are there grenades in your other pocket too?"

"That one has a small magnet on twine and a lock-picking kit."

"By your standards, a small magnet is probably the size of my head."

He slanted an amused look in my direction. "Your *head* wouldn't fit in my pocket."

"The size of a lemon?"

If he could fit two grenades in his pocket, he ought to be able to fit lemon-sized magnets in there.

"Amalfi Coast or Meyer?" Duncan asked.

"I... don't know how big an Amalfi Coast lemon is." I'd never even heard of the variety.

"Perhaps, one day, we can take a trip to Italy, and I can show you some in person."

I started to shake my head, but... couldn't I travel somewhere exotic now? With the boys gone, I didn't have to worry about their school or sports schedules, and I'd dug myself out of debt, so I could hypothetically take a vacation. I even had an intern, at least for the moment, who could take over my work for a few days.

"You seem like someone who could use a vacation," Duncan offered, glancing at the map. Outside, the scenery along the freeway had transitioned from the lights of suburban houses to dark fields and trees.

"Tell me about it."

A phone rang, startling us enough that we both twitched. It wasn't my ringtone. Since Duncan looked in confusion at the car display, it probably wasn't his either. The call didn't pop up on the screen, so the phone wasn't paired to the Tesla.

As the phone rang again, I peered around and patted between the seats. Finally, I spotted the lit screen in the seat well behind Duncan, next to one of the rifles that had been used to shoot at me.

I picked it up but hesitated. "We probably shouldn't answer, right?"

Duncan shrugged and took the phone from me, hitting accept before it dropped to voicemail.

"Yeah?" he answered in a flat tone, not bringing the phone close to his mouth. Was he trying to subdue his accent?

"Is this Dox? Or Ballinger? You get her yet?"

My blood chilled. It was the voice of the raspy guy who'd called the office after I posted the ad.

"We've got her," Duncan said. "We lost Dox."

I grimaced, sure his attempt at an American accent wouldn't be enough to fool the caller. The guy would recognize the voices of his subordinates, surely.

"Is the male werewolf dead?" Maybe the speaker didn't care about his subordinates.

"Yeah," Duncan said.

"Okay. Bring her up. The scientist thinks she's the key to figuring this amulet out."

Amulet? Did he mean my mother's medallion?

"Okay." Duncan hit the hang-up button, then looked at me. "Did I sound like the guy whose phone that was?"

"How should I know?" I had no idea which of the men Dox and Ballinger had been.

"The caller is either going to be waiting for us with open arms or semiautomatic weapons loaded with silver bullets."

I leaned forward, tempted to drop my face between my legs. "Do you think two grenades, a lock-picking kit, and a magnet will be enough to allow us to be victorious?"

"I'm hoping those will get us inside when we reach our destination. It's our two sets of werewolf fangs that will allow us to be victorious."

"I'm not sure I'll be able to change again so soon. I don't have to tell you that the magic bleeds off, and it's usually a once-a-night thing. For some, it's only once a night during a full moon."

"You've got a lot more power than that. I can tell. And so do I." Duncan reached over and touched my arm. "We'll be all right. *And* we'll get the artifacts back for you and your family."

"I hope so," I whispered, watching the dark landscape outside as we headed farther north and into farmland. Farmland and, apparently, at least one perfume factory.

17

As we took an exit that would lead us toward the town of Arlington, my phone rang. My first thought was that Mr. Raspy was calling back, but this was my phone, not the one we'd returned to the back seat. Jasmine's name popped up, and I answered, hoping she or her father had learned something useful. According to the GPS map, we were only twelve minutes from our destination.

"Are you okay?" Jasmine asked before I could utter a *hello*.

"Did you hear about the attack at the apartment?" I guessed, though I didn't know how she would have, unless my cousins were still spying on me. Reminded of the wolf we'd heard howl near Ballard, I considered that a possibility.

"It's on the *news*. Sylvan Serenity, that's your place, right? Not that I really need to ask when the media is saying four guys were killed by wild animals. Did Duncan do that? I *knew* he was dangerous."

"Really," Duncan murmured.

"We... fought them together." I didn't think Duncan had lost control the way I had. I didn't ask him, and, with my hazy memory of the fight, I couldn't be certain, but I suspected he had only injured people, helping to keep the brutes off my back. All those deaths might be on my shoulders.

Since the men had been attacking me and had threatened my tenants, maybe it was all justifiable, but it sat uneasy with me. Losing control like that *always* sat uneasy.

"Oh, gotcha," Jasmine said. "Well, that must have been an epic fight. Are you okay?"

I touched my shoulder. "Yeah. It could have been a lot worse. It was the same guys who attacked Mom and Emilio. They had rifles with silver bullets."

"Damn, you're lucky then."

"I am, but I wish I'd been able to capture and question one of them to figure out who's behind all this and where they are." I eyed the navigation map. It was possible we were about to learn the answer to both those questions. It was also possible we were visiting a random shopping spot where the driver had stopped to pick up a gift for his girlfriend.

"They wouldn't tell you? Or... Oh yeah. Are they *all* dead? Or did some get away?"

"I... think some got away in the other cars, but it's kind of a blur."

I looked over at Duncan, realizing Mr. Raspy might have gotten a different report from one of the men who'd escaped. Would that complicate things? Another report wouldn't necessarily contradict what Duncan had said. The men in the other cars had left before the fight had been over. For all they knew, their comrades had prevailed and had indeed captured me in the end. We'd more likely be in trouble if Mr. Raspy knew his subordinates well enough to recognize their voices on the phone. I would cross my fingers that he had a lot of underlings and found them interchangeable.

Duncan only lifted a shoulder. Most likely, his memories of his time as a wolf were also hazy when he returned to human form.

"Okay," Jasmine said. "Well, I'm glad you're alive. I've got a lead for you, and it might help."

"Good."

"Like I told you, my dad has been combing through those servers, digging up logs and going down rabbit holes—whatever computer stuff he does in the basement with all his robots and spaceships dangling from the ceiling and shelves behind him."

I blinked at this new information about her father and envisioned Jasmine rolling her eyes. When she'd first said her dad worked at a software company as a game developer, I hadn't thought much of it, other than deciding he might be the first *geek* werewolf I'd encountered. Later, I would have to ask her where he'd come from since I didn't remember anything about him from my youth. I assumed he was from another pack.

If he'd been a lone wolf, and our pack had eventually accepted him, maybe there was hope that my relatives would stop trying to kill Duncan. I looked wistfully at him. But with the power he emanated that all magical beings could sense, he was more threatening than a geek werewolf waving robot toys around.

"He found another wolf-related artifact that was mentioned in a couple of different spots about four months ago," Jasmine said. "There was a picture of it. A goblet or a chalice, I guess you'd call it. It was gold with tiny jewels, and the jewels made a wolf head on the side."

"I guess there *are* chalices in the Seattle area," I murmured, thinking of my conversation about them with Duncan. "Or was this not a local find?" I asked Jasmine, realizing those servers might be global.

"It was in Bellingham. A guy dug it out of a storage unit full of crap that his mom left him when she passed. From what Dad could uncover, the owner had been a lover of one of the Cascade

Crusher pack's male wolves years ago. No, I guess it had to have been *decades* ago. The lady who passed was ninety-three."

"You don't think a werewolf could have fallen for an older retired lady?" I asked dryly.

"No. And ew."

I snorted since I'd reached the age where retired folks didn't seem all that old anymore. Of course, Jasmine had a long ways to go before she reached that stage of life. She probably thought *I* was well on my way to ancient.

"Anyway, she must have gotten the chalice from her male lover or was holding it for him until he came back, but then he died or something. Whatever. The point is that her son figured out where to put it up for sale, and someone with the name Erik Burlington bought it, after lots of people bid a ton for it. That's a fake name, Dad thinks, but it was dropped off at a warehouse in Arlington. The warehouse is owned by the Tumwater Tonic Corporation. They've got businesses all around Puget Sound that specialize in perfumes and stuff like that."

Our faces lit by the display, Duncan and I exchanged long looks.

"Do they own TBL Luxury Perfumes and Potions?" I asked.

"I don't have a list of their companies, but, like I said, Dad thinks their headquarters is up in Arlington. Do you want the address to check it out?"

Duncan read the address of our destination off the map.

"Did you hear that, Jasmine?" I asked. "Is that it?"

"Yeah, how'd you know?"

"Just a hunch."

Nerves tangled in my gut. We were only four minutes from our destination now.

"Thanks for the research," I told Jasmine. "I'll let you know if anything comes of it."

"Welcome. If you find the guys and kick their asses, make sure you tell your mom that my dad helped, okay? *He* didn't ask for credit, but I know he wishes he could fit in with the family more. Nobody shuns him, but most of my cousins and aunts and uncles don't talk to him much or invite us to all the hunts."

"If you mean Augustus and his thugly brothers, it's probably the lack of common interests. From what I've observed, they aren't the robot types."

"That's the truth, but, really, *no* werewolves are the robot types." Jasmine lowered her voice—maybe she was calling from her parents' home. "Dad's kind of a nerd," she whispered.

"He sounds like a good guy."

"He's offered tech support to everyone in the pack. *Some* of the family appreciate it. Some of them just throw their router across the room if it stops working and get a new one."

"Ah, Luna?" Duncan asked, a weird note in his tone.

We were two minutes away now, driving back roads that ran near Arlington. House lights were visible from the road, but the homes were on acreage, so it felt like we were still in the country.

"I need to go, Jasmine. I'll talk to you later." I hung up and asked Duncan, "What is it?"

He lifted his hands from the steering wheel and gave me another significant look.

"Did you activate the self-driving? Teslas have that, right?"

"They do have that, but I didn't touch anything." His hands remained in the air, not on the wheel.

"Can you brake and deactivate it?" I had no idea how the self-driving feature worked.

Duncan tried pumping the brake. The autopilot didn't disengage.

He toggled the levers and tapped different spots on the display, but nothing happened. Only the navigation map with our route remained, the screen showing us getting closer and closer to our destination.

The car signaled and made a turn of its own accord.

"That's ominous," I said.

"I concur."

18

No longer accepting input from Duncan, the Tesla took us to a property surrounded by fields, with a stone-paver driveway wider than many streets. Mounted among artfully placed boulders forming a pond and waterfall, a plaque read TBL Luxury Perfumes and Potions. Spotlights shone upon it, and many more lights lined the long driveway as it meandered through a tidy lawn. It ended at a fountain in front of a blocky adobe building— or maybe that qualified as a *mansion*—that brought to mind architectural styles of the Southwest rather than Washington State. Up here, quality homes were, of course, made from logs.

Signs pointed to a gift shop and offices, so maybe it wasn't a mansion but the company building, though balconies and glass doors on the second story made me think at least part of it might be living quarters.

Before reaching the turnaround, the Tesla signaled and headed onto a side driveway that led toward a large corrugated-metal building, a garage with multiple tall roll-up doors. Beside and beyond it lay fields of low shrubs that I thought might be lavender. Those fields were dark, obscuring the details. *Most* of the area the car was heading to was dark, save for a few lights by the doors. A high stone wall appeared to enclose more buildings, maybe an entire compound, between the garage and the adobe structure, but we couldn't see over it to guess what was inside.

As the Tesla approached, one of the roll-up doors opened.

"What are the odds that it's taking us right to your stolen artifacts?" Duncan asked.

"Low. Everyone knows you don't store valuable magical items in garages."

"Your wolf case was in a heat duct under the floor."

"Only because my ex is an idiot. Had I known it was in the apartment, I would have found a more appropriate hiding place."

"I watched you put it in your sock drawer under your tube of, uhm, female cream."

"Estradiol. I figured you were thinking of coming back for it, so I put it there to dissuade you."

"It almost worked. When I snuck in, I had to poke gingerly all through that drawer looking for it. Little did I know you'd moved it."

"Yup. I knew you were sus from the beginning."

"Sadly true." Duncan looked curiously at me as the car rolled silently into the dark garage. Something about that silence, the lack of engine noise, was disconcerting. "Where *were* you keeping it, anyway? Before the thugs got it."

I debated whether to tell him. That hiding spot wasn't being used anymore, and I didn't *think* he still had plans to retrieve the case and ship it to Chad, but...

"Your intern had it when the mugger came and stole it," Duncan reasoned. "Was he keeping it somewhere?"

"He and his dad were studying it."

"Because of the druidic connection?"

"Yes, and because who *wouldn't* want to study a magical wolf case?"

"I can't imagine not wanting that hobby. Were they the ones to translate the writing on the bottom? About the bite of the werewolf?"

"Yes."

"That's useful," Duncan said. "I've read and researched a lot over the years for my various treasure-hunting adventures, but I'm not a linguaphile."

"From the conversations I overheard between you and Chad, it sounded like he knew a little more about it."

"Do you want me to call him back?"

"No. We can ask whoever is trying to capture me when we meet him." I waved to the garage around us as the Tesla parked. "Presumably, he knows why he's interested in it and other werewolf artifacts."

"One would hope."

The door rolled down behind us. No lights, save for the screen inside the car, were on anywhere. If whoever worked here had expected allies to return, wouldn't they have left a light on?

"They might have figured out that the wrong people are in their car." I glanced at the phone lying in the back seat. During the call, Mr. Raspy hadn't given any indication that he'd been suspicious of Duncan's voice, but... that didn't mean he hadn't figured out our ruse.

"It's possible. We'd better get out while we can." Duncan pressed the button that opened the door, that *usually* opened the door. Nothing happened.

"We may have to break the windows." I pressed the button that should have rolled mine down and wasn't surprised when it didn't budge.

"I think these cars have manual overrides for the door." Duncan patted around the armrest. "In case the electrical goes out."

"Or the car goes into servant-of-an-evil-overlord mode and won't release you?"

"Exactly." He dug into the cubby under the armrest. A *thunk* sounded, his door releasing. "There we go. It's in there." He pointed at my door, then stepped out.

I'd no sooner found it than a man door near the roll-up door opened. Two big thugs stood silhouetted there, one with a rifle gripped at his side. The other held what might have been a handgun or knife.

My senses picked up magic, both from them and the weapons. I darted around the car to use it for cover.

One man flipped a switch, and blinding light filled the cavernous garage. Duncan also ducked behind the car, but it was too late. They'd spotted us.

"Radomir was right," one barked, raising a rifle. "That's not Ballinger."

They lunged behind stout metal support posts, as if we might have firearms too. If only.

"Now could be the time for grenades," I whispered to Duncan.

"We might want to catch one of them to question," he replied softly.

I winced. That hadn't gone well before. But since I didn't have a reason to feel protective of my territory or tenants under my watch here, maybe I could refrain from turning into a wolf. If I *wasn't* a wolf, however, I wouldn't have a way to fight armed men amped up on potions.

"Come out from behind the car, you two." The rifleman stood behind the post but leaned out enough to point his firearm in our direction.

I didn't see the knifeman but sensed that he was on the move. The garage was filled with crates, rolling drawer-cabinets, machinery, a tractor, and a big auto that looked like a mix of a tank and an

SUV. The man followed the wall, staying behind those items to try to circle behind us.

"If you lower your gun, we'll be happy to come out for a chat," Duncan said.

"That's not how it works, buddy."

"That's the girl Radomir wants," the man circling to get behind us called.

Who was Radomir? The boss? Mr. Raspy from the phone call?

"I don't think they're armed," he added.

"That's what you think," Duncan muttered, then stepped out and threw something at the gunman.

Assuming it was the grenade, I ducked lower and wrapped my arms around my head.

The rifle fired three times as Duncan leaped back behind the car. Leaving silvery trails in the air, the bullets zipped across the warehouse and clanged off whatever they hit.

The rifleman cursed as a clunk sounded. I lowered my arms enough to eye Duncan. He crouched with his back to the car and was pulling in twine. Was that attached to the lemon-sized magnet we'd discussed?

Footsteps thudded on the other side of the car. Duncan pulled faster. Whatever he'd snagged on the magnet caught on the rear tire. He lunged to grab it and bring it back behind cover. The man's rifle was stuck to his magnet.

By the time its owner sprang around the car, a dagger in his hand, Duncan rose to one knee and aimed the rifle at him.

"Drop the knife," he said.

The guy froze and raised his hands above his head, but he didn't drop the blade.

"To your right," I whispered, glimpsing the second man near the tractor.

He leaned out, gripping a handgun and aiming at us.

Duncan whipped the rifle toward him and fired. So did his

target, but Duncan ducked in time. I flattened myself to the cement floor.

The bullet pierced the rear car window that Duncan had been crouching in front of, and a spiderweb of cracks appeared. The closer man took advantage of the distraction and leaped toward Duncan.

Using the butt of the rifle, Duncan struck him in the chin. I ran toward the man who'd fired at us, not sure if Duncan's bullet had caught him. He'd disappeared behind the tractor.

I spotted the handgun on the floor, along with spatters of blood, and plucked it up. I lacked experience with firearms, but I gripped it in both hands as I stepped around the tractor.

Face scrunched in pain, the man leaned against one of the giant wheels and held his bloody hand to his chest. He cursed when he saw me and kicked toward my wrist, trying to knock the gun away. His speed startled me, but I managed to leap back and avoid his boot.

"Stop." I pointed the gun at his chest and reminded myself that these men had more speed and strength than typical.

A loud *thud-crunch* came from Duncan's fight. Someone being slammed into the car? Hard enough to dent it?

My foe didn't obey my order to stop. He inched forward in a crouch, his arms spread as if he would tackle me, and I could see the calculation in his eyes as he debated whether he could spring upon me before I could shoot him. Or maybe he was debating if I *would* shoot him.

"Where are the artifacts you stole being held?" I didn't know if he'd had anything to do with the thefts, but, by now, I believed they were on this property. Or at least that they had been at one point.

He lunged in, slapping toward my gun hand. Again, I avoided his attempt to knock the weapon away, but frustration simmered inside of me, and my skin tingled with a hint of magic. Duncan might be right. I might have the power to change again tonight.

Trying to sound as calm and cold as possible, I said, "If you won't tell me, I've no reason to keep you alive."

"You barely know which end to point at me," he said.

From Duncan's fight came the sound of a fist connecting with flesh, then another thud. Something heavy toppled and clattered to the cement.

"And yet, I took care of the guys who were originally driving that car," I said.

For the first time, a hint of uncertainty darkened his eyes.

"Where are the wolf artifacts?" I asked.

"I have no idea."

"Who's your boss? Do you have any idea about that? About who signs your paychecks?" I squinted at him. "And forces you to drink those potions that make you limp and give you the runs?"

A grunt of pain came from the fight—it didn't sound like Duncan. Another crash followed.

Maybe thinking he was out of time, the guy in front of me leaned to the side, as if he would run to the left to escape me. I shifted the gun to track him, but he lunged back in and dove for my midsection.

Cursing, I fired.

The bullet took him in the top of the shoulder, but he still rushed in close, barreling into me with one arm wrapping around my torso. He took me down, but he thrashed at the pain of the shot and cried out in my ear. I drove my knee up into his groin, cracked him in the head with the handgun, and managed to squirm away from his grip.

As I rose to my knees, ready to shoot again if needed, Duncan sprang into view behind my attacker. Fury burned in his brown eyes. He had to be on the verge of changing too.

But it was with human hands that he grabbed my foe under

the armpits and threw him into the tractor with stunning force. These men weren't the only magically enhanced people here.

Duncan leaped after him, slamming the heel of his palm into our enemy's jaw. His head jerked back, cracking the metal frame of the tractor. The man slumped, the fight going out of him, but Duncan grabbed him again and threw him past me and into stacked barrels. When he struck them, they tumbled, and he collapsed with them falling on top of him. He didn't move.

I pushed myself to my feet. "I was trying to question him."

"Did I get in the way of that?" Duncan looked me up and down for wounds, but the blood on the floor was theirs.

"Him being a turd and attacking me got in the way of it."

"I had a similar experience with the other bloke." Duncan led me back to the car and picked up his magnet, rolling up the twine to tuck it back into his pocket.

The man he'd been fighting lay bloody and not moving. I didn't ask if he was dead.

Duncan also picked up the rifle. "That was noisier than I would have preferred. Whoever runs the security at this place is going to know we're here."

A blinking red light in the shadowy corner of the ceiling caught my eye, and I pointed to what had to be a camera. "I think they already know we're here."

Duncan grunted in agreement. "They probably did before we arrived. When the car took over."

"Yeah."

He looked around the garage, pointed at a man door in the back, and led the way toward it. By now, there might be more armed people heading to the garage from the front.

"Let's see what we can find in that direction," Duncan said.

"Before the rest of the security detail catches up with us?"

"Exactly." He paused with his hand on the door and tilted his head.

Somewhere nearby, a wolf howled. A *young* wolf.

The voice didn't sound familiar, not like the wolf who'd called when I'd been walking around Seattle with Duncan. This wasn't one of my pack; I was fairly certain.

"We won't have much time before reinforcements arrive," I said when Duncan didn't stir for a long moment.

A hard-to-read expression had crossed his face—maybe he recognized or was trying to place that howl?—but he only nodded and pushed open the door.

19

Leaving through the back of the garage led us into a stone-paver courtyard behind the stout wall we'd seen from the front. A towering metal building without windows shared it on the opposite side, and to our right stood a tall wrought-iron double gate large enough for trucks to pass through. Beyond it lay the lavender fields, stretching off into darkness.

Visible behind the metal building, the upper portion of the adobe mansion caught my eye, and I pointed to it. If I were a rich thief with a perfume corporation, I would keep my stolen artifacts in the house, not a garage or other outer structure.

Duncan nodded, but it looked like we would have to go through the metal building to reach it. As we approached, I spotted vents high on the wall and caught floral whiffs, as well as other scents I couldn't name. Lavender *was* in the mix, one of the stronger odors. Maybe that was the mixing or manufacturing facility.

The howl sounded again, wafting in from the fields.

"Could another pack be behind all this?" I hadn't heard of any wolves coming into the area from Canada or across the mountains, but it wasn't as if I'd been in the loop with my own pack these past years.

"It's not like werewolves to hire outside heavies." Duncan gazed toward the gate and the fields.

"Yeah." I'd had that same thought before Mom's medallion had been stolen, deciding my cousins probably weren't behind all this. "But would a werewolf work for someone else? That's not like our kind either."

Duncan hesitated. Thinking?

He finally said, "No," in agreement and headed across the courtyard. He glanced toward the tops of the stone walls. More cameras were mounted there, and powerful lights kept the area bright. We were anything but hidden, so I was surprised we hadn't yet encountered more men.

A soft *click* floated across the courtyard from behind us. The sound of the door we'd exited locking.

Duncan gave it a long look over his shoulder, then gazed back at the courtyard walls. About twenty feet high and smooth, they lacked handholds or any way to climb them. I wondered if Duncan's magnet had enough twine attached that he could use it like a rope and grappling hook.

"I keep waiting for cannons to pop out of the top of the wall and open fire on us," he murmured.

"Cannons? I think they use big exploding artillery weapons these days." I wasn't an expert on ammunitions, but cannons sounded antiquated.

Duncan smiled faintly. "Yes. But cannons were common in the books of my youth."

"When they were calling people *my lady*?"

"Precisely." He reached the metal door to the windowless building and tugged on the handle. It was locked without a visible keyhole.

"Now that we're trapped, it *does* seem a likely time for cannons." I eyed the gate. Maybe we weren't entirely trapped—with Duncan's strength, he might be able to push the iron bars apart—but I doubted what we sought was out in those dark fields. "Will your magnet befuddle that lock and open the door?"

"Not likely. Locks are usually made without magnetic materials for that reason. If there were a keyhole, I might be able to *pick* the lock, but I don't see anything."

I wondered if that lock-pick set was how he'd gotten into my apartment when he'd planned to swipe the case himself. Probably.

"Guess you're not supposed to come in this way," I said.

"Not unless you're invited."

"Or have grenades?"

"One could work. They're noisy though."

"They already know we're here."

"Likely, yes." Duncan considered the edge of the door and the hinges. Would his magnets work on *them*?

It was the metal handle that he gripped with both hands.

I raised my eyebrows. He'd torn apart a motorcycle, so maybe...

Duncan put one foot on the wall next to the door and leaned back, shoulders flexing. The feral magic I could always sense about him, the power of the wolf, intensified as the tendons in his neck stood out. With the snapping of something metal, the door released and flew open.

I lunged to keep it from banging against the wall as Duncan sprang away. He caught his balance and raised his fists, as if he expected enemies to charge out.

All that exited the door were powerful floral scents. I could also hear something gurgling and thought of a witch stirring a cauldron over a fire.

"You're rather strong," I remarked as Duncan slipped inside, "even for a werewolf."

"You're strong too. I've seen you carrying toilets around."

"Carrying a ninety-pound toilet isn't on the same order of magnitude as ripping a stainless-steel door off its hinges." I joined him inside, putting my back to the wall.

"I think the hinges were made from cold-rolled steel so not quite as strong."

"Oh, in that case, I'm sure a toddler could have popped that door open."

Duncan held a finger to his lips. Eyes probing the shadows, he murmured, "We're not alone."

Inside, the building was dark save for LEDs glowing from machinery and computer equipment. In the shadows above, a metal catwalk followed the wall, possibly running all the way around the interior. It allowed access to vats taller than we were.

This had to be the laboratory where the perfumes and potions and who knew what else were made. If the hired help wandered through here regularly on the way to the garage, it could account for the scents Duncan had picked up so often.

He pointed toward the catwalk about halfway back along one wall. With the shadows deep there, I might not have picked anything out, but whatever it was—no, *whoever* it was—must have turned his or her head slightly. For a second, the reflection of green LEDs appeared in a pair of eyes.

I still had the gun and raised it, but I hesitated to fire at a human being who wasn't immediately threatening our lives. For all I knew, that was some minimum-wage security guard who knew nothing of his boss's nefarious doings and was simply paid to monitor the laboratory. Duncan hadn't brought along the rifle he'd liberated from our attackers, but, since he could rip doors from hinges, maybe he didn't feel the need.

The person, perhaps noticing us looking, vaulted the railing and jumped down from the catwalk. I gaped. That was fifteen feet above the concrete floor. The figure landed in a deep crouch, disappeared behind a couple of vats, and then reappeared, running down a center aisle toward a door on the far side of the building.

It was lit better than the catwalk, and when the person glanced back, I glimpsed brown hair flopping in the eyes of a boyish face. It was boyish, I realized, because *he* was a boy. Maybe eight years old.

I lowered the gun.

Not moving, Duncan stared after the kid. I thought I caught a hint of the lupine about the boy before he darted through the far door. If so, that could have explained the easy jump from a height that could have broken a leg, though it wasn't a feat *I* would have tried.

"Is he the werewolf we heard outside?" I wondered.

Duncan stirred, as if pulling himself from a daze. He must not have expected a child spy either. "I think so."

He led the way down the center aisle, advancing slowly and glancing into the alcoves and aisles along the way. More than once, he peered up at the catwalks.

The place had my gooseflesh stirred up. As we passed vats, the intensely floral smells almost enough to give me a headache, I sensed magic within more than one. Whatever was sold at the gift shop wasn't *all* this company produced. I wondered if the alchemist Rue had heard of this place.

Surprisingly, we reached the door the boy had disappeared through without trouble. I kept expecting boobytraps or for guards to leap out.

This door wasn't even locked. Duncan eased it open, revealing a wide, well-lit hallway with a couple of windows looking toward the fields. Timber posts and ceiling beams supported the plaster walls, and the floor was made from rustic Saltillo tile. The hallway had to lead into the adobe mansion.

A closed door between the windows led outside, but Duncan

passed it by with only a glance. He, too, believed that what we sought wasn't hanging out in the lavender fields.

We passed under another camera with a glowing red LED.

Nervous, I wiped my hands on my trousers. The wait for something to jump out at us was as stressful as if tanks with shell guns had rolled into the hallway and opened fire.

A door at the far end was made from wide-plank wood, and I trusted Duncan could force it open if he needed to, but when he tested it, it wasn't locked.

"Other than the two garage attendants," he murmured, listening at the door and not yet opening it, "it's like we're being invited in."

I almost snorted at the term *garage attendants*, as if those guys had been positioned there to park cars and wipe windshields.

"The thugs at the apartment complex *did* want me to come with them," I said.

"They didn't have similar feelings about me."

"True. Maybe you should be walking behind me."

"A gentleman cannot hide behind a lady."

"Against the rules of your old books, huh?"

"Precisely." Duncan opened the door and peered into a large room with a fountain in the middle and a guest-relations counter at the far side. Nobody waited at that counter, but this area looked more like the lobby of a Southwestern-style hotel than a home.

Duncan stepped out, considering the options before us. There were multiple doors that exited from the lobby and also wide steps leading to the upper level. Perky yellow and blue sunburst tiles set into the risers drew my eye.

Duncan sniffed at the air. "Explore randomly or follow the boy?"

"You can track him?"

With the odors from the perfume laboratory clinging to us, I would be hard-pressed to track a rotisserie hot dog to its spit.

"He smells of the fields, fresh earth on his paws—feet." Duncan pointed toward the stairs.

Despite his words about being unwilling to hide behind a lady, I marshaled my courage and stepped past him, intending to lead the way. Duncan glanced at me but didn't allow it. He matched my pace so that we climbed side by side.

The wide hallway at the top was carpeted, a timber railing open to the lobby below and closed wood doors lining the opposite wall. Another wood door at the end stood open, office furniture visible inside.

As we walked together toward that office, I *did* catch an earthy scent, as if the boy had been out digging holes. If he'd been in his wolf form, and the howl suggested that, he could have been digging for moles or other critters that got busy at night.

Duncan paused well before we reached the open door, stopping me with a hand to my wrist.

"There are people inside," I murmured, sensing more of the big brutes with magical potions flowing through their veins. I also thought the boy was in there, and I smelled a cigar burning.

"Yes." Duncan looked like he didn't want to continue, like we would be walking into a trap.

I withdrew the locket and rubbed it, as I had before going on the hunt with my cousins. That night, its magic had seemed to help me with the injuries I'd taken. I might need its help again.

My nerves tingled, and Duncan eyed me, probably sensing its magic. I showed him what I had. Since he'd been the reason we'd found it, he must have been pleased to see that I'd kept it. He nodded to me.

I held it out, offering it to him, in case he also wanted to draw upon the slight protection of its magic. He hesitated, glanced toward the office, and then shook his head. Something told me he knew more about this place, these people, and what was going on than he was letting on. I didn't know how that could be possible, but a throat cleared in the office. This wasn't the time for a discussion.

Setting my shoulders, I walked in ahead of Duncan.

20

When I walked into the office, the two magically enhanced men that I'd sensed stood to either side of the door. They wore security uniforms, their muscles practically bursting the seams. One tensed, reaching for me before pausing and glancing toward an ornate mahogany desk across the room.

A wispy-haired man of sixty-ish wore a business suit and sat in the chair, watching me. To his side, between the desk and a huge gun safe against the wall, stood a thin bald man a decade or two older than he and wearing medical scrubs that included rubbery blue gloves. They looked like the kind someone wore to handle corrosive chemicals but pinged my senses as slightly magical.

Duncan growled as he stepped into the office beside me, looking at the security guards. At a nod from the wispy-haired businessman, the one who'd reached toward me continued to do so, taking the handgun from my grip. Since we were outnumbered, the guards also carrying firearms, I let him.

Somewhat surprisingly, Duncan didn't object to the man taking the weapon from me. His gaze had locked onto the old guy in gloves. Was that... recognition in his eyes? It was hard to tell. Duncan's face had grown hard and masked.

Interestingly, I didn't sense magical blood from either of the older men, though the fellow with gloves had something in one of his pockets that gave off the vibe of a strong artifact. The businessmen also wore three rings on one hand, and at least one emanated power.

"Welcome," he said in a familiar raspy voice. Was this the guy the guards had called Radomir? He looked to his comrade. "Nice of the girl to deliver herself."

The girl. I almost laughed. It had been a long time since anyone had called me that.

"She is not as powerful as I expected," Radomir added, lifting the hand with the rings.

Maybe one was the equivalent of Duncan's magic detector.

"So sorry to disappoint," I muttered.

"Not standing next to him, no," the older man said, speaking for the first time. His accent reminded me of Duncan's, of the Old World. "But that is to be expected." His voice soft, he looked at Duncan and added, "Isn't it, Drakon?"

Uh, Drakon?

"It's Duncan now. I'm not a monster."

"A dragon isn't a monster. When they visited this world, they were majestic and powerful. Such a namesake should never have been spurned."

"Maybe I was spurning the one who gave it to me."

I scratched my jaw, considering Duncan out of the corner of my eye. "Is this... the scientist you told me about?" I whispered.

"Yes. Lord Abrams."

"He looks good for a guy who was charred to a crisp."

The old man—Abrams—looked curiously between us. Surprised Duncan had told me about his past?

"Why do you want her?" Duncan asked coolly. He seemed to

be addressing Abrams rather than Radomir, the person I would have guessed was in charge.

"Research," Abrams said. "Answering the questions of the universe so that we may create solutions for the world."

Well, that wasn't vague.

As Duncan glared at Abrams, I scanned the room, hoping to spot the wolf case or my mom's medallion. I could sense more magical items present—perhaps in the desk?—and there was no doubt these guys had something up their sleeves and believed they could beat us if we turned wolf and started a fight. I couldn't help but feel that if the stolen artifacts were here, we might be able to come out on top and get them. Duncan hadn't pulled out his grenades yet.

The boy was crouching in the corner, mostly hidden behind a filing cabinet, but he leaned out enough to reveal curious brown eyes. The mother in me gawked in horror, thinking of my sons when they'd been that age. In the lair of villains was the last place I would have wanted them, especially when a battle might break out. The men had to expect Duncan and me to fight, didn't they?

"Nobody here has been able to activate the amulet." Radomir glanced at the boy, then opened a drawer in his desk. "From what my men told me... men who are now dead..." Annoyance flickered in his blue eyes, as if *he* wasn't the one who'd started all this. "This amulet glowed, hinting of the power that can be commanded, when the old woman touched it."

"My mother?" I scowled at him for describing her as an old woman.

"I thought she might be," Radomir said softly, watching me, as if I'd already given something away. "Come forward, girl."

He laid Mom's medallion on his desk, still in its black velvet-covered box, and opened the lid. Unfortunately, it didn't zap him halfway across the room for his presumptuousness. He pushed the box across the desk toward me, an invitation.

"What else have you got in there?" I nodded to the desk, hoping he had the wolf case too.

Radomir leaned back in his chair and started to fold his arms over his chest, but he paused and touched his chin thoughtfully. "Will you touch anything I draw out?"

"Not if you've got venomous snakes in there."

He smiled, the gesture not reaching his eyes. "I keep those elsewhere."

Thinking of the weird vats and equipment in the laboratory, I muttered, "I'll bet."

"You think she might rouse the embedded sentiences in the other artifacts?" Abrams asked.

"She might. If her blood is as special as you think."

My blood? Other than having had powerful werewolves for parents, there wasn't anything unique about my blood.

"She is from an old line, perhaps one of the originals, the first werewolves created long ago by the very visiting dragons that we spoke of," Abrams said. "Despite the dilution of many, many generations, the magic flows strong through her veins. She is not some inferior spawn of a bite."

"I didn't come here to learn about my lineage," I said, though, another time, I would have found the information interesting. "But to take back what you stole from my mother. And my intern."

Radomir grunted but delved into the drawer again. He withdrew the wolf-lidded case. "This did not belong to that boy *or* you. Or the mortal human who acquired it in recent years. It was stolen from the castle of a vampire who held it for centuries. Of course, he was not the rightful owner either, but having had it for hundreds of years, most would consider it his."

"The druids and werewolves who made it didn't believe that, right?" I asked, curious about the true provenance of the case. The medallion I wanted to return to Mom, but, if I could get the case, I would feel obligated to find its proper owner. As I'd assumed, it didn't sound like Chad had any right to it. But a *vampire*? I'd heard stories that a few existed in the world, but I'd never encountered one.

"No," Radomir said. "Their descendants would consider it theirs, most likely."

I almost said that Bolin might *be* one of the legitimate descendants, but I didn't want to give these guys a reason to hunt him down.

Watching me as he did so, Radomir withdrew a few more items from his drawer. A chalice with a jeweled wolf on the side came to rest by the case—was that the item Jasmine's dad had looked up? After that, he added a dagger with a wolf-headed grip, an Old West revolver with a wolf carved into the ivory handle, and finally a silver platter. Engraved in the center, a wolf showed all its teeth, the image identical to that on the case. It had an inscription that might have been in the same language as the words on the case, but I was too far away to tell. Too bad. I wanted to copy it for translating. I wanted to know if any of these artifacts had the secret to the bite, and I caught myself drifting a couple of steps closer to the desk.

Duncan grunted in warning and stopped me with a hand to my arm. Shit, I hadn't meant to move. I was drawn by the magic, but the last thing I wanted was to obey these guys' wishes.

The two security guards shifted, their hands drifting to their firearms as they watched us. Radomir slid a hand along the inner edge of his desk. I thought he might draw out more artifacts, but he merely folded his arms afterward.

Lord Abrams lifted a hand of his own in a quelling gesture toward the guards as he looked at Duncan. "Do not stop her, Drakon. Her touch may be revealing. We already know yours will not be."

He looked toward the boy, which also prompted Duncan to

consider him. The kid ducked fully behind the filing cabinet to dodge the scrutiny.

"You have power, Drakon," Abrams continued, "but are not, I believe, the correct sex. For all time, it has mostly been the wolf wise women who've handled artifacts and retained power for the pack." He nodded toward me and continued softly. "Come forward and touch it, girl. Luna."

His using my name creeped me out. Not only because he'd researched me—*spied* on me—from afar but because *he* was creepy. Though Duncan was fully dressed, his clothes hiding the shackle scars on his wrists, they came to my mind.

"Touch it," Radomir said in a more stern tone. "We don't have all night."

"Expecting a hot date?" I muttered.

"I *do* have a companion waiting. We can't *all* be dedicated twenty-four-seven to our research." He gave Abrams an arch look.

Duncan still gripped my arm, not hard but firmly.

I looked over my shoulder at him. "I'll touch them. I want to see too." With my back fully to the men, and shifting to block my face from the guards by the door, I mouthed, "Be ready."

If I could grab the artifacts, and we could fight our way out of here, we could escape. In the tractor if not in that awful car with a mind of its own.

Duncan hesitated, not looking like he wanted to let me get close to those guys, but he did release me.

I walked slowly to the desk. Since I already knew the medallion would respond to me, and the case hadn't done anything except zap me when I'd handled it, I touched the chalice first.

It tingled warmly under my finger, and an image came to me of a furry werewolf that had taken the in-between form. On two legs, it stood on a rocky bank and held the chalice up to capture the spray of a waterfall. A glow came from within the cup, and the werewolf drank the water before dropping the chalice and roaring at the moon.

The two men exchanged looks. I drew my hand back, not certain if they had been able to tell that anything had happened. I didn't know the significance of what the chalice had shared.

I touched the platter, and it zapped me the same way the case had. I jerked my hand back.

"Different creator," Radomir said with a laugh.

He shook his hand, and I wondered if it had zapped him too. The case probably had. It hadn't even allowed Duncan to touch it until he'd rubbed some special goo on his hand.

"Same as the case, possibly," Abrams said.

I touched the revolver, though it didn't emanate as much magic as the other artifacts. Since it looked like something from the 1800s gunslinger era, I doubted druids had been involved in its creation. The faintest of warm hums emanated from it.

"That one was supposedly made with Navajo magic," Radomir said. "I didn't pay that much for it. I'm not sure it has anything to do with werewolves. We were arguing earlier if that's even a wolf on the grip. It looks coyote-ish."

Abrams lifted his eyes to the ceiling. "A coyote skinwalker is their term, their legend, for those with werewolf magic. There were few real werewolves roaming those inhospitably dry lands, but one or two may have passed through over the years, lending their power to the creation of an artifact." He nodded to the gun.

"The medallion, girl." Radomir pointed his chin toward it, sounding impatient. No doubt because of the hot date we were keeping him from. "That's from your own pack. I want to know what it can do." He lowered his arms and leaned forward intently in his chair. "What *you* can do with it."

"I merely wish more data for my project." Abrams withdrew a phone and started recording me.

"Great," I muttered, imagining a viral video of me being zapped across the room to land on my ass.

"I know what you want," Radomir replied to Abrams. "You can keep researching all you like. Touch it, girl."

His insistence made me want to do the opposite. I looked back at Duncan, and he nodded, a hand in his pocket. Gripping one of the grenades?

I might have been reassured, but then he glanced back through the open door. Movement on the wide stairs drew my eye too.

More of the hulking, magically enhanced men were striding up. They came in pairs, walking side by side, and there had to be twenty total. Some had guns while some were merely flexing their powerful arms. Jaws set and eyes determined, they all looked to be itching for a fight. Further, they wore camo flak vests as well as neck guards. To fend off wolf bites at their throats.

I slumped. Even with Duncan's two grenades and our combined fighting power, we were in over our heads.

21

RADOMIR HELD UP A FINGER, AND THE TWENTY ARMORED MEN stopped in the hallway a few yards back from the door.

"Touch it now, and cooperate with me," he told me, "and perhaps I'll let your lover walk away."

Abrams stirred, but he didn't object. Maybe he'd long ago written Duncan off as lost.

"I understand he's recalcitrant and unwilling to properly bend his knee to an employer," Radomir added.

"*Employer*, right." Duncan had shifted so that his back wasn't to any of the security thugs, and he could monitor them while also watching me and the men behind the desk. He met my eyes briefly. His hand was still in his pocket.

The new arrivals hadn't changed anything for him. He was still ready to fight.

I didn't know if *I* was. This was starting to look suicidal. Unless one of these artifacts could do more than share a vision with me.

"All right," I said, conceding but only to buy time to think. Reaching forward, I rested a finger on the wolf head in the center of the medallion.

It startled me by glowing much more strongly than it had in Mom's cabin. Silver light bathed the faces of the older men and gleamed off the windows in the office. Either the medallion's reaction to me was stronger because my potion had fully worn off now or... it knew I was in trouble.

I had no idea how to properly use an artifact or summon its magic, but I imagined it getting brighter and brighter, then lashing out with magic at the two men. They were the leaders here. If we took them down—

The medallion *did* intensify its glow, the silvery light growing so bright that I had to look away. Unfortunately, it didn't hurl great beams of power at my enemies. Radomir grunted and reached over the artifacts, grabbing my wrist.

I reacted on instinct, lunging over the desk to punch him in the face. His nose splattered under my fist, and he released me as he cursed and reeled back.

Footsteps thundered in the hallway—the security men charging toward the office.

Duncan slammed the door shut. I almost laughed at the idea of that stopping the army, but then an explosion ripped from the hallway, the floor and walls shuddering all around me. Duncan had also thrown a grenade out there.

Screams of pain as well as curses sounded, and my stomach churned at the thought of men's body parts being blown off. Something heavy flew across the office, clipping the back of my shoulder and almost knocking me to my knees. The door. The explosion had blown it from its hinges.

As if that weren't enough, gunfire opened up. It came both from the hall and from within the office—the two security men inside with us.

At that point, surviving was all I could think about. I dropped to my hands and knees and scrambled behind the desk for cover, hardly caring that the two older men were probably already crouched back there.

Smoke filled the air, and wood snapped. Support beams giving way?

A roar sounded near the doorway. Duncan? It sounded like his voice, but it wasn't human. And wolves didn't roar. What the hell?

I lifted my head, surprised Radomir and Abrams weren't beside me behind the desk, but they'd run toward the metal safe in the corner of the room. Yes, that would provide better protection than wooden furniture.

More gunshots and roars came from the doorway, along with the sounds of cracking wood. Maybe that had nothing to do with support beams. Maybe Duncan was ripping things to pieces.

He was farther from me than Radomir and Abrams, and the smoke made it hard to see him well, but he stood on two legs, not four, as he hurled things about. Maybe he hadn't changed. Or maybe...

The realization struck me even before the smoke cleared enough to see him clearly. He'd become the in-between, the *bipedfuris*. He'd warned me that he could, but I hadn't entirely processed that.

On two sturdy legs, he was covered in salt-and-pepper fur. It wasn't as thick a pelt as when he became a wolf, but there was no mistaking that this was Duncan.

His muscled torso had broadened, his neck had thickened, his legs and arms had grown more powerful, and he was taller, his head higher than the doorway. His face had elongated to form a fanged snout, but it wasn't as pronounced as a wolf's snout. It was deadly, though, and his strong jaws snapped with the same strength as those of a wolf. Instead of paws, he had furry hands, but great sharp claws extended from his fingers, and he used them to rake at his foes, tearing into those flak vests as if they were T-shirts. He was terrifying.

But, since he was attacking our enemies, I didn't worry too much about him. Oh, I didn't want to risk running in front of him, but I understood that he was buying me the time I needed.

I grabbed the wolf case off the desk, wincing as it zapped me, and thrust it into my jacket pocket, hoping the padding would keep its magic from repeatedly knocking me on my ass. I thought about taking some of the other artifacts, but then I would be the thief. All I wanted was— Damn, where had the medallion gone? Had it fallen off the desk when the floor shook?

On hands and knees, I padded around, wincing when a bloody man flew out a nearby window. Glass shattered, pelting me.

"He's going to kill them all," Radomir snapped. "Can't you control him?"

"Maybe," Abrams said.

I sure hoped not. The older men were still by the big safe. I wished Duncan would attack *them*, but at the moment, the security guards were the bigger threat.

I peered under the desk, still patting around, broken glass biting into my hand. Where *was* the medallion?

I tried to sense it with my werewolf instincts. It was... by the filing cabinet?

The kid. I'd forgotten about him. Whose idea had it been to let him come in here anyway?

He'd opened a window near the cabinet and looked like he was thinking of climbing out. His eyes were wide as he watched Duncan hurling people around—*killing* people.

The medallion dangled on its chain from the boy's fingers. At his age, he might have taken it because he wanted its power, or he could have taken it because it was glowy and cool.

"Hey, kid," I called softly, trying to be heard over the noise of battle but not wanting the masterminds in the other corner to notice me.

The boy looked at me with bright, curious eyes. If the battle scared him, he didn't show it.

"Definitely a werewolf," I muttered.

He held up the medallion as if to confirm.

"That's my mom's, okay? I need it back."

He shook his head, and he opened the window farther. He *was* planning to climb out.

"Wait, kid." I moved toward him, debating if I could catch him before he scrambled over the sill. I lifted a stilling hand, as if he were a wild animal I might tame. "I'll trade for it." I patted my pockets. They weren't as loaded as Duncan's had been, but I *did* have my stash. "Chocolate with sea salt and cacao nibs."

I didn't mention the part where it was *dark* chocolate. Kids usually sneered at its lack of sweetness.

And, judging by his puzzled pause, the boy might not have encountered cacao nibs before.

Duncan, still in his bipedal form, roared again. The booming noise echoed off the walls. He sounded like an enraged lion, and the boy looked at him with wide eyes and reached for the windowsill.

"It's kind of like a Nestle Crunch," I blurted, waving the bar while silently apologizing to the makers of the fine chocolate for the comparison, especially since the only similarity was the crunch.

"Oh." Face bright, the boy focused on me again. No, on the chocolate bar. He held his hand out.

I pointed firmly at the medallion. "Trade."

Something flew between us, smacking wetly on the wall before sliding down it. My gorge rose. A severed hand.

That disturbed the kid less than the roaring werewolf. He skittered forward, holding out the medallion and pointing at the chocolate. We made the trade, and he shimmied out the window faster than I could consider if I should grab him and try to protect him.

More guns fired, bullets slamming into the wall above me. Ducking low, I stuffed the medallion into my pocket. The case kept spitting magical sparks at me through the fabric of the other one.

Duncan roared again, and a man screamed. Not wanting to see more flying body parts, I didn't look. Even for a female werewolf, the carnage was enough to make me queasy.

A few seconds passed before I could safely reach the window and look out to make sure the kid hadn't fallen and broken bones. A pile of clothing lay on the pavers down there. A small wolf with a narrow build loped to the wrought-iron gate with my chocolate bar in its mouth. It—*he*—glanced toward the window, briefly meeting my eyes, then slipped out between the bars. He barely fit, but he escaped. Good. At least someone had.

I pushed the window open enough that Duncan and I could slip out through it, then turned to call to him. In that form, would he understand me?

"She's getting away," Radomir barked.

They'd slid the safe aside to reveal a hidden doorway, but they hadn't left yet. Radomir and Abrams were looking straight at me. Radomir looked like he wanted to run over and grab me, but the gunfire hadn't stopped yet. Nor had the roars.

The handful of remaining men seemed too dumb—or too altered by magic—to stop fighting Duncan. They either fired at him or tried to club him with makeshift weapons because they'd lost their guns. Judging by the broken and warped metal on the floor, Duncan had torn some of those guns to pieces. A few of the wiser men were running, but they had to navigate around a huge hole in the hallway floor, with the entire railing blown out into the lobby.

"She's of no concern to my plans," Abrams said calmly.

Radomir glanced at the desk. "She grabbed the artifacts."

Abrams's eyes narrowed, and he lifted something in his hand. The magical artifact I'd sensed earlier? I pushed the window open wider, planning to flee after the kid—the drop from the second story wasn't *that* far, and he'd survived it—but I couldn't leave without Duncan.

Abrams didn't point the device at me. He pointed it at Duncan.

"No," I blurted, lunging in his direction, certain that the item had more power than the guns that could barely slow down a werewolf in Duncan's state.

Energy hummed in the air, crackling over my skin, and a narrow orange beam shot toward Duncan's head. A laser?

Duncan halted his attack, and I was terrified the beam was a weapon that would blow his brains out. It struck precisely at the scar near his eye, seeming to *connect* to it.

His back stiffened so much that his head jerked back, but that didn't break the link. The beam shifted, tracking his movements, staying connected.

Whatever it was, it wasn't a laser. But it *did* hurt him. Duncan grabbed his forehead, his face contorting, as if a dagger had been driven into it.

Heat flushed me, and magical energy coursed through my veins. A feeling of protectiveness for Duncan called to the wolf in me, enticing it to come forth again tonight. With the change threatening, I didn't have time to remove all my clothes. All I managed was the jacket, afraid those artifacts might disappear if I changed with it on. I tossed it away to ensure it didn't change with me, but, in my haste, I flung it out the window. Hell.

Fur sprouted from my arms, and my bones and body transformed, the wolf overtaking me.

Radomir must have recognized the new danger, because he backed into a dark tunnel beyond the hidden door. Abrams glanced at me, but he kept his device pointed at Duncan. I crouched, intending to rush him and tear whatever it was from his grip.

Duncan lowered his furred head and stared at Abrams, as if transfixed. The beam still ran from the magical device to his scar.

The two remaining guards in the office, both injured and down, used the distraction to crawl out the door.

As I finished changing, my front paws dropping to the floor, Abrams spoke firmly to Duncan in another language, then pointed at me.

Now fully a wolf, I surged toward Abrams. Surprisingly spry for an older man, he jumped back into the tunnel and hit a switch on the wall. The safe slid back into place.

I snapped my jaws in frustration as I tried to lunge around it to stop it from covering the door, but it was heavy and inexorable and only bumped me to the side.

Frustrated, and thinking like an animal now instead of a woman, I bit at the plaster wall, some notion that I might be able to get through *it* coming to mind. That man had hurt Duncan. I wanted to kill him.

An ominous snarl came from behind me.

I backed up enough to turn to face Duncan, a conflagration of emotions sweeping through me. An ancient part of me recognized the bipedfuris as a superior form, a form even more powerful than that of the pure wolf. My instincts told me to lower my head before this being, to accept him as the alpha. But I recognized his magic, his aura. He was the one who'd fought and hunted by my side. He was the one I wanted to mate with.

Duncan threw his furred head back and roared, the muscles in his entire body flexing with dangerous power. Blood dripped from his wounds—from bullet holes—but the injuries did nothing to diminish him, nothing to make him less terrifying.

His eyes, the same brown hue as always but wild and animalistic—and entirely devoid of recognition—locked onto me. They weren't the eyes of an ally, a mate.

The beam had disappeared with Abrams, but the scar on his forehead throbbed with magic and glowed orange.

His eyes dark with the promise of my death, Duncan advanced toward me with his jaws parted, his sharp fangs gleaming.

22

AFTER ROARING AGAIN, THE THREATENING ROAR OF AN ENEMY, Duncan sprang onto the desk.

With devastating certainty, I knew he was after me—and that he could kill me. He lashed out with those long claws, aiming for my head.

I ducked and ran around the desk, my paws slipping on the wooden floor. It was almost the end of me because Duncan leaped off, trying to land on me. Fear made me sprint to the open window. I felt the swipe of his claws as they scarcely missed gouging into my hindquarters.

My paws skimmed over the windowsill, and I sailed out, tail tucked between my legs. I landed on the pavers, my joints handling the drop easily in this form, but I had no way to open doors or gates as a wolf.

Glass shattered above me, Duncan pounding the window with his furred fists and knocking out panes. My instincts wanted me to race for the nearest exit, but I glimpsed something on the ground. My jacket. I could only vaguely remember why it was important to the human part of me, but I risked falling glass to rush back and snatch it with my jaws. Items clattered in the pockets, and I remembered the artifacts through the haze of my wolf thoughts. The medallion that belonged to my mother. Yes, I had to escape with it.

With the jacket dragging on the pavers, I turned toward the wrought-iron gate. The fields beyond it called to me. Out there, I could run fast and escape a two-legs. The bipedfuris was more powerful than a wolf but not *faster* than a wolf.

As if to deny my thought, Duncan sprang through the destroyed window. He landed in a deep crouch in front of me, blocking the way to the gate. As he spun toward me, claws slashing, I leaped to the side and ran around him. The jacket gripped in my jaws almost tangled in my legs, and I barely resisted the urge to fling it away.

Medallion. Important. I had to return it to my mother.

With the bipedfuris pounding after me, determined to tear me to pieces, I reached the gate. The smell of fresh air and farmlands enticed me, but I couldn't squeeze between the bars. Unlike the young wolf who'd gone that way, I was full-grown, and I almost got stuck trying to ram myself through.

Instincts warned me of Duncan's approach. I dropped the jacket outside the gate, then whirled back, snapping my jaws as his claws raked at me again.

I bit his furred wrist as it blurred toward me, but his blow knocked me sideways. Pain made me yelp as I tumbled across the pavers and crashed into a stone wall.

The entrance to the smelly building was open—the door lying where it had been ripped from its hinges—and I ran toward the entrance. I didn't want to go in there, but there were few options. Maybe if I could lose my foe inside, I could circle back and escape. And the strong, odious odors should mask *my* scent.

Duncan ran after me, footfalls heavy in the bipedfuris form, and I had no trouble keeping track of his position behind me.

Sprinting inside, I raced around vats and machinery, the terrible scents invading my nostrils and clinging to my fur.

Faster than the bipedfuris, I outpaced him. Then I realized it wasn't only my speed that allowed that. He'd stopped. Instead of following me, he waited by the entrance, believing I was trapped.

Was I? The memories of the passing I'd made as a human wafted hazily through my mind, images of wooden beams and a red-tiled cave floor. Another way out.

But when I weaved between the vats and reached the far side of the building, the stout door was closed. I grasped the latch with my jaws, trying to manipulate it, but it was locked. Before, the humans here had invited me in, but now... now they wanted me trapped with the bipedfuris.

Duncan's thunderous roar echoed through the building, reverberating off the walls.

Growling, I turned toward the far entrance, facing the wide center aisle. At the end, he crouched in front of the doorway with his arms spread, his furry form silhouetted against the light of the courtyard. There was no choice. I would have to face him to escape. I might have to kill him.

He crouched lower as I approached, this time stalking with purpose straight down the aisle. There was no point in hiding. I willed my werewolf power to be great enough to match his and prowled closer.

He waited, saliva dripping from his fangs and his claws glinting as they reflected the small colored lights in the building. There was so much tension in his muscles—in his entire body—that he looked like he might be slow to react.

His face contorted. In rage? Pain? Blood saturated his coat in numerous places, but he looked like he was combatting something internally. Or maybe... Was he fighting the magic of the one who'd sent him after me?

In another form, this male had almost become my mate. Maybe he did not wish to battle me.

As if agreeing, Duncan threw his head back and roared again. Not the roar of battle lust but of frustration.

A faint howl drifted to us from somewhere outside. A young wolf.

Panting from his internal battle, Duncan cocked his head, half turning to look toward the gate. I took advantage and rushed him, jaws opening as I locked on a target that would make any male cry out in pain. He might be conflicted, but I was not. I could not be if I wanted to escape.

Not as distracted as I'd hoped, Duncan whirled back toward me, but his internal war and his interest in that howl had bought me a second. I lunged, jaws snapping.

He shifted enough that I bit his inner thigh instead of his genitals. My fangs sank deep, and it had to hurt, but he didn't cry out. His arms came down, fists striking my back.

The weight of the powerful blows made my legs give out, and I dropped to the ground, but I hung onto his thigh, teeth latched on. I tried to shake my head, to knock him off balance as I dug deeper into flesh and muscles. He spun, stumbling into the door frame but managed to rake his claws down my back.

Fiery pain made me gasp, releasing the bite. With a roar filled with his own pain, Duncan struck me again. I had nothing to hold on to and went flying, again tumbling across the hard pavers of the courtyard.

With blood soaking my fur, I leaped to my feet. I couldn't fight him. He was too strong.

Again, I sprinted to the gate. I latched onto one of the vertical bars and threw all my weight into pulling on it, willing my werewolf power to help me, to bend the iron. Its foul metallic taste filled my mouth, but I only bit and pulled harder.

Not far behind me, Duncan roared again. He pounded across the pavers, racing toward me.

The metal bent slightly. I kept pulling.

Pants came from right behind me, and I didn't have to look to know Duncan had reached me, his claws raised to tear into my flank. The iron bent a little more. Was it enough?

I released it and pushed through the gap and out the gate. I glanced back as I snatched the human garment from the ground, reminded of the valuable magical things inside.

Duncan stood right where I'd been, his clawed limbs raised, as I'd imagined. He could have gotten me, but he'd hesitated.

That didn't mean I was safe, so I backed away. The bipedfuris had the power to bend the bars, if not rip the gate entirely from its mounts.

But he pressed the heel of a clawed hand to his forehead, to the still-glowing scar there. With his legs trembling, he fought the magic coercing him. His battle with himself was buying me time. I turned and ran into the fields. Only once did I pause to look back, just before the gate would have disappeared from view.

Duncan knelt on the pavers, his head bowed. I paused, tempted to go back to check on the one I'd almost made my mate. But the human scientist walked into view, stepping fearlessly up to the bipedfuris, his magical device in hand. He touched it to Duncan's forehead, to the scar.

With a feeling of lament, I realized Duncan was theirs now, that man's new minion. No, his *old* minion, returned to serve again.

Security men appeared in the courtyard, powerful flashlights in hand as they shined them between the bars in my direction. Atop the courtyard walls, floodlights came on, brightening the fields.

I dared not stay. I turned and ran into the night.

23

THE NEXT DAY, I DROVE THROUGH MONROE ON THE WAY TO MY mother's cabin. After the chaotic night, I hadn't heard from Duncan, and I doubted I would. He belonged to that scientist now. Lord Abrams.

The thought of him serving them, and of them sending him after me, made me shiver. I'd been contemplating if there was any way I could return and help him escape, but they seemed to have programmed him to attack me. I couldn't overcome the bipedfuris. I'd barely escaped with my life.

After fleeing the night before, I'd run hours in my wolf form, despite the pain from my wounds. The magic hadn't subsided until I'd made it south of Everett, miles having passed under my paws. But there'd been miles more to go, and the jacket, with my phone and artifacts in the pockets, was the only clothing I'd escaped with. Once I'd been barefoot in my human form, my modesty barely covered, I'd called Jasmine to pick me up. Traveling miles through suburban streets as a wolf wouldn't have been daunting, but as an almost naked human with numerous wounds? No, thanks.

Once we'd reached the apartment complex, I'd thanked her for her help, let her bandage my bloody gouges, and then gone straight to my bedroom. I'd collapsed unconscious for more than ten hours.

When I'd woken, with afternoon drizzle dampening the lawn outside my window, I'd been shocked that none of the tenants had come to my door, looking for assistance. Maybe they had, and I hadn't heard them. Maybe they'd been too scared after the battle in the parking lot to wander out of their apartments at all. I grimaced at the thought and vowed that whatever happened to me in the future, I would do my best to keep it from affecting the people here.

Would that be possible? I hoped so, but Radomir and Abrams were still alive. Unfortunately. And I'd messed up their place and taken the artifacts. Only the ones they'd stolen from me and my mom, but... did that matter? They might feel vengeful anyway.

And what of Duncan? They could send him after me at any time. Unless he could escape on his own and get out of range of that device. He had once, hadn't he? Maybe he could do so again.

"Let's hope," I said softly, turning into my mom's driveway.

Right away, I hit the brakes. A white wolf stood, waiting for me, as if I were expected. Jasmine must have told them I would come by today.

I rolled down the window. "I have something for my mother."

Though I didn't know how many in the pack she'd confided the loss of the artifact to, I assumed Lorenzo was in the know, so I picked up the velvet-covered box and showed it to him. I trusted he could sense its magic, especially in his wolf form.

He padded to the side of the road. An invitation to pass?

When I drove by him, he sprang into the back of the truck. That startled me, and I barely avoided clipping a tree next to the winding driveway. In the rearview mirror, his tongue lolled out. Amused, was he?

"You're spry for an older gentlewolf," I called out the window.

He tilted his head back and howled.

That howl was familiar. He'd been the one to catch Duncan and me hunting to the east of the city, but this particular vocalization reminded me of the day we'd been talking and eating brisket at the Ballard Locks.

"Were you in Seattle recently?" I drove slowly as the cabin came into view between the trees. Only my mom's Jeep was parked out front.

Lorenzo's tongue lolled out again. I didn't think I would get an answer, but after I parked, he jumped down from the back of the truck, not as a wolf but as a man. He was lean and fit, despite the creases at his eyes and whiteness of his short hair.

"I'm not spying on you," Lorenzo told me, "but your mother is concerned that your cousins might still be plotting, so I am..." He turned a weathered palm toward the cloudy sky.

"Watching me?" I debated if that was the same thing as *spying*. I supposed not if he'd had protective rather than nefarious intent.

"Watching *out* for you. When I can. I'm also spending time with Umbra, bringing food when she's not up to hunting."

"I'm sure she appreciates that."

His white eyebrows twitched. "She assures me she's not an invalid and is capable of fending for herself until the day she dies."

I snorted. That *did* sound more like the proud woman who was my mother. "Okay, then *I* appreciate it."

"Good." Lorenzo gazed toward the empty passenger seat of my truck. "You did not bring the strange outsider."

"No, he's... indisposed."

That prompted another eyebrow twitch.

"When I saw you with him near the canal," Lorenzo said, "I did not know if you considered him a friend or foe."

"Yeah, I didn't either."

"I announced myself to let him know the pack is watching over you."

I nodded, glad it had been my mother's mate rather than my cousins. "He figured you weren't there for the brisket."

Lorenzo nodded toward the box I gripped and extended his hand toward the cabin. "Your mother will be pleased to see you. And that."

He didn't follow me inside. I found Mom in her bedroom, the curtains and a window open, despite the late autumn chill. A cheerful bird chirped out back, and fresh air flowed in, so I couldn't blame her for the choice.

She lay in bed with a book in hand but her eyes closed. Emilio must have healed enough to return to his own home.

Mom still looked wan, despite her regenerative magic. I reminded myself that, unfortunately, the attacking thieves hadn't been the only thing to plague her this year. How much longer did she have, I wondered. Maybe I would call up that alchemist and ask her if there were any magical treatments to help fight cancer. Even if there were, would Mom accept them? She'd said no to the normal human offerings.

Her head turned toward me, and her eyes opened, focusing first on my face and then on the box.

"You've retrieved the medallion. I am pleased."

"Good." I smiled and set it on her bedside table, then perched on a hard wooden chair, the only seat in the room.

"It is the only thing of value that I have to leave for you. And I was sworn to keep it and protect it. It holds power for the pack, power to keep us together and protect us."

That was vague, and I wondered if she actually knew what the magic it held could do. Unlike the wolf case, it didn't have any inscriptions that I'd noticed. No ancient words hinting of its use.

"Losing it was distressing for many reasons," Mom added.

"The guy who ordered it stolen is unfortunately still alive. I got into his compound and was able to find this and also the wolf case that my ex-husband stumbled across somewhere. There were other artifacts too. All with wolves carved or engraved in them. All magical. I was a little tempted to grab everything, but then *I* would be a thief."

"If they were of the werewolf, they've more right to be held by our kind than by a mundane human. Or... was this thief something else?"

"He had some magical items, but I believe he was fully human." I shrugged apologetically, wishing I'd learned more. As soon as Abrams had compelled Duncan to attack me, I'd lost interest in anything but surviving. "He also has a lot of minions that were amped up on potions. I'm not sure we've seen the last of them."

"I will speak with Lorenzo, and we will prepare the pack and our territory. We will not be surprised again if men with silver bullets arrive."

"Good," I said, though I regretted that I hadn't been able to put an end to the threat. At this stage in my mom's life, preparing for battle was the last thing she needed to worry about. "I'm not sure what he wants, but he and a scientist are awfully interested in werewolves, and our artifacts, for some reason."

"We are an interesting people." Mom managed a smile.

"That's true."

"I'm glad you've remembered this."

Since I'd lost it in the parking lot against those men, I was more conflicted about my decision to stop taking the potion, but the world seemed to want me to be a werewolf right now. And, since I knew it was what my mother wanted, I nodded my agreement toward her.

"Will we see the lone wolf again?" From her tone, it was hard to tell if she wanted that or hoped Duncan had left the area permanently.

"You seemed concerned about him."

"Yes, but I have been thinking about that. He was powerful. Were he to become a trusted ally, perhaps he would be tolerable."

"I'm positive my cousins don't want the pack tolerating him."

They didn't even tolerate *me*.

"What *they* want is immaterial," Mom said. "If they keep troubling you, we will kick them out of the pack."

I didn't know if she and even the sturdy Lorenzo were a match for all of them, but I didn't say so. The last thing I wanted was to be responsible for a brouhaha within the pack.

"Duncan helped me get the artifacts back," I said to change the subject. I also wanted her to know that he had assisted me, that he wasn't a bad guy. I almost told her that he could take the two-legged form, but he'd confided his story to me in private, so I felt compelled to keep his secrets.

"Did he? That is good." After a thoughtful pause, Mom added, "As I said, he *is* very powerful. I believe he is from an ancient bloodline without much dilution."

"Yeah."

"When you two came before, you should have brought him in to meet me."

"The brute squad on the porch wouldn't have let him enter. Besides, he was busy sniffing lavender."

"You will bring him for an introduction next time," Mom stated, an order rather than a request.

That would be a hard order to obey if Duncan was in the clutches of a new master. No, a very *old* master.

Not wanting to disappoint my dying mother, I said, "I'll see what I can do."

"Good." She yawned and closed her eyes.

I patted her hand and left the medallion, as well as a few squares of chocolate.

EPILOGUE

THE PRESSURE WASHER RUMBLED ON A LOW SETTING AS I PERCHED on the two-story roof of one of the buildings in Sylvan Serenity and sprayed moss off the shingles. In the Pacific Northwest, moss was as ubiquitous as mold. Early that summer, I'd applied a chemical that was supposed to retard its growth, but the stuff here thumbed its fuzzy green nose—inasmuch as moss had a nose—at the various solutions I tried every year.

"Maybe Bolin has a potion that could address this." Alas, it would take gallons and gallons of a *potion* to handle the roofs on all the buildings. I imagined him standing over a cauldron with a mixing paddle the size of an oar and decided he was unlikely to do that in his apartment. "Or a spell."

Letting the moss guide me, I climbed to the apex of the roof. It was *not*, I told myself, so I could check on the parking lot again but only because I needed to clean both sides.

Duncan's van remained in the same spot it had been before we'd driven up to Arlington. It had been three days since our battle there—since I'd had to battle *him* there. Even though I believed he belonged to Abrams now, I couldn't help but hope he would find a way to escape.

The thought of not seeing him again—or of having him arrive as a mind-controlled enemy—was distressing. I'd just started to like him. No, that wasn't true. I'd liked him more than I should have from the beginning. But I'd started to *trust* him. That meant everything, but now...

"Luna?" came a query from the walkway below. It sounded like Bolin.

I turned off the noisy pressure washer and picked my way to the edge, glad the weather had warmed and the roof wasn't slick. We'd had a couple of clear days, with more sun predicted, so I'd taken the opportunity to get this task out of the way.

Bolin stood at the corner of the building, eyeing one of the downspouts spurting out water and bits of removed moss.

"It's the weekend," I said. "You don't have to be here, do you?"

Usually, he showed up from eight to five on weekdays, as if this were a normal job. For an intern, it was. For me... Well, it kept me busy most of the time. Especially when my personal life added to the maintenance load. I'd spent the last two days cleaning up the crashed in, died in, and otherwise maligned parking lot. I'd been appalled by the price of a new cluster mailbox. The post office had told me to get stuffed when I'd gone down there and implied it was USPS property and that they should replace it. Of course, I didn't have to pay for the expenses out of my pocket, but I tried to keep the business's bills down—and make as few insurance claims as possible.

I looked toward the parking lot, twitching in surprise at the blue Mercedes SUV that had arrived since the last time I checked. Bolin's auto was ensconced in... I wasn't sure what to call it. Some kind of transparent protective bubble.

"Guess that's one way to fend off bird poop," I muttered.

Bolin followed my gaze, looking a little smug, but answered my question instead of commenting on his new solution. "Some potential tenants made appointments with me yesterday. When you were battling the post office."

"I could have handled the weekend showings."

Bolin hesitated. "The redhead was really cute."

"Ah." I debated if using one's job as a property manager was an appropriate way to meet girls, but I didn't think any business ethics books mentioned it. It wasn't as if he was a psychiatrist—or psychiatrist's intern—trying to hook up with vulnerable women coming in for therapy. "This place was in the news, I understand. We're lucky potential tenants haven't been scared away."

"They're actually coming *because* of the news story. Well, more the social-media speculation about werewolves being involved. There were some videos that made it onto the internet…"

I winced, imagining my furry black ass all over one of those sites of video clips. Since nobody had confronted me about it, I assumed—at least *hoped*—there wasn't any footage of Duncan and me changing. Someone might have witnessed it, however, if tales of werewolves had arisen.

Bolin was gazing up at me, his eyes too knowing for my tastes. I'd liked it better when he hadn't believed in werewolves.

"That's a draw?" I asked.

"Apparently so. Some people are big fans of werewolves."

I thought of my ex and grimaced.

"Some people believe that they can find one, ask to be bitten, and become werewolves themselves, and that they'd then be much more badass than they are as humans."

"Huh." I didn't like where this conversation was going.

"If werewolves existed," Bolin said slowly, watching me, "they wouldn't *really* be able to do that, right?"

"Not anymore."

Judging by his disturbed expression, that might not have been the answer he wanted. It was good that I hadn't added on that at least *one* werewolf in existence in this century might be able to do that.

A sporty red Mustang pulled into the lot, heading for one of the guest spots.

"I think that's her." Bolin straightened his shirt and scraped his fingers through his hair. "*Them*, I mean."

Two twenty-something women got out of the car, and he hustled over to give them a tour of the available units and perform whatever awkward flirting he could manage. I didn't worry about my collegiate spelling-bee champion being inappropriate in any way.

I was about to start the pressure washer again when movement near Duncan's van caught my eye. No, *in* his van.

Either someone had broken into it, or he'd returned.

Nerves battered my gut. Abandoning my task, I hurried to the ladder and descended. As I reached the ground, the side door in the van slid open, and someone with wavy salt-and-pepper hair hopped out. It *was* Duncan.

Wary, I paused. Was he here under Abrams's control?

With his back to me, Duncan rummaged under the bed in his van. Werewolves under bad-guy control didn't *rummage*, did they? He started whistling cheerfully.

My wariness faded, and a relieved goofy grin may have sprawled across my face as I headed in his direction.

Bolin was leading the women toward the nearest building—okay, the redhead *was* cute—as I passed them. His eyes widened at my expression, and he paused to look toward Duncan's van.

"Are you *sure* you two aren't dating?" he called after me.

I only lifted a hand in a vague wave of acknowledgment because Duncan had turned at the words, and my relief grew stronger. Relief and *pleasure*, though that was probably the last thing I should have felt after he'd tried to kill me.

No, he'd been magically *commanded* to kill me. Or so I assumed.

He was in his handsome human form now and smiled at my approach. The scar on his forehead no longer glowed.

"You're here," I blurted, coming to a stop in front of him.

A few faint bruises darkened his jaw, and he looked stiff when he withdrew something long and narrow and wrapped in cloth—was that *velvet*?—from his van. But, otherwise, he appeared to have healed in the last couple of days. Of course, his clothing could have hidden much. I distinctly remembered biting him in his thigh.

"I'm here." Duncan looked me up and down. "Are you okay? I worried when I was…"

"Captured? Imprisoned? Suborned?" I rolled my shoulders. The wounds I'd received were healing, but I was stiffer than normal too.

"It's kind of a blur, but I collapsed in that courtyard and was out for a while." He didn't mention Abrams standing in front of him with that device. "I woke up naked in a ditch outside of Smokey Point."

I blinked. "They dumped you? Are you certain?"

"I'm certain about the ditch. That's about it."

"But I thought." My gaze drifted to his scar again. "After the scientist, uhm, took you over…"

Duncan winced.

I held up an apologetic hand. "Nothing that happened was your fault."

"I'm not sure that's true, but I… I wasn't expecting what we got that night. That's for certain."

"Even grenades and lock picks can't prepare you for being taken over by a mad scientist."

"A mad scientist I had assumed dead these past thirty years, yes. After I woke up in the ditch, it took me a couple of days to recover enough to walk back here. I didn't have my phone or clothes or anything. I *still* don't have my phone."

"You may need to spend my gas money on one of those instead of micro diamonds."

"What's on the dash wouldn't buy the power button, but I'm fine financially." Duncan waved dismissively, his expression saying that *money* wasn't his problem.

I might have been envious, but he was a man who'd just learned he had a more profound issue to deal with. Why hadn't Radomir and Abrams kept him? To use like the rest of their minions?

Reluctantly, I admitted that just because Duncan was free didn't mean he wasn't, or couldn't become, one of their minions again. They might have released him into the wild, knowing he would return to me, on purpose.

A grim thought. I was glad I'd warned Mom that there might be more trouble.

"I'll get a new phone soon," Duncan said, "but I needed to come here first. To make sure you're okay and to apologize profusely to you. And also..." He glanced at the Roadtrek. "To thank you for not having my van towed."

"I was thinking of selling it."

He leaned back and clutched a hand to his chest.

"Only if you didn't come back," I hurried to say. "All that stuff inside looks valuable. It might be able to help me along with my goal of buying a four-plex." I considered the expensive-looking SCUBA gear and other equipment and electronics. "Maybe even *two* fourplexes."

"So you're saying you would have grieved vastly and longly over my passing."

"Longly? Is that a legitimate form of that word?" I looked to see if Bolin was nearby, but he'd accompanied the ladies into one of the units.

"Of *course*. I've read many a book, remember? It's from Old English. There's also a similar word, *longlice*. It means at length or for a long time."

"Goodness. You may need to chat up my intern."

"He doesn't interest me as much as you. And *he's* not who I came to apologize to. And offer gifts to."

"You didn't bring lavender perfume, did you?"

Before we'd had our adventure, I hadn't minded the scent, but I didn't want anything to do with it now, especially not anything from that company.

"Ah, no. Those who cast me into that ditch didn't toss any in with me."

"That's rude. What if you'd woken up smelling foul and needed a little perfume?"

"There was rainwater in the ditch that kept me washed. It was, however, chilly." His grimace and the brief haunted expression in his eyes were the only indications that he'd been miserable.

I wished I'd known where he'd been dumped so I could have retrieved him. Had he walked all the way back here while cold, naked, and injured? Thirty miles or more?

"I'm encouraged that you're not shooting at me," Duncan said quietly, watching my face.

"I don't have a gun."

"That being the only reason for your restraint? However inadvertently, I betrayed you again."

"I gathered your big furry body was used against your wishes."

"Yes."

"Do you think it'll happen again?"

He hesitated. "I don't know what Abrams is doing or why he

let me go, but I'm afraid that, now that he knows I still live, he may want to use me again. And you did take back the artifacts that they stole from you."

"Thus ensuring they'll continue to think of me as an enemy?"

"Or a tool. That is what I was to Abrams."

I lapsed into silence, not sure how to continue the conversation. Since Duncan had admitted he might be forced to attack me again, I should have asked him to walk out of my life and not return. If he were off treasure hunting in the Southern Hemisphere somewhere, he wouldn't be a threat, especially if his lord scientist remained here. Why that guy had set up camp in the Pacific Northwest with Radomir, I couldn't guess, but they clearly had plans involving werewolves.

"You mentioned gifts?" I asked instead of requesting that Duncan drive off in his van and never return.

His face brightened. "I did. After a man wrongs a woman, gifts are required. In many cultures."

"In all, I should think. It's just right."

"Quite. Hold out your hands, please." Duncan had set down the velvet-wrapped item while we'd spoken, but he plucked it up now. He rested it across my arms, then held up a finger to indicate there would be more. He drew out a gift-wrapped box of truffles, then a stack of dark-chocolate bars wrapped with a ribbon. The one on top said...

"*Lavender*-raspberry dark chocolate?"

"Yes. To make you laugh. There are other flavors that might be of more interest. One on the bottom is dusted with ground espresso."

"That sounds promising."

"The ideal way to start the morning." Duncan plucked another box out of the van, the gold ribbon and wrapping as fancy as the contents. "Dark-chocolate-covered bacon strips."

"Yum."

"And one more." He withdrew another box, this one clear, allowing a view of the item inside. A caramel apple dipped in dark chocolate and nuts and drizzled with white-chocolate sauce.

I might have started salivating a bit at that one. Apples weren't traditional wolf treats, but my human taste buds had always enjoyed a crisp, tart Granny Smith.

Duncan placed it on top of the pile. "I would eat the apple first while it's fresh."

"Where did you get all this stuff if you had to walk naked back from Smokey Point?"

"There's a factory outlet mall on the way. I'm not sure why candy would be considered something from a factory, especially when the shops appeared to make it fresh there, but several occupied the mall. For the female proprietor at one, my nudity wasn't a problem. She even took pity on me and gave me a canvas tarp to wear."

"Sexy. Do you still have it?"

"I do." He waved into the van. "And now that I've been reconnected with my funds, I'll send her money to pay for her wares. I try not to accept charity when there are others who need it more."

I eyed his bruises and thought of the scientist who could control him against his will. "You may need at least a little charity."

"Possibly." Duncan waved to the velvet-wrapped item. "That's the most important gift. I found it years ago and could never bring myself to sell it. A part of me may have one day foreseen the need for it."

Curious, I handed him the sweets and unwrapped the larger gift.

"A sword? A *magical* sword?" I could sense power within it and held it out, considering the bejeweled hilt and engraved blade. Were those Celtic runes? I would have to ask Bolin. For all I knew, it was Swahili.

"It came out of a lake in Ireland."

Probably not Swahili then.

"It isn't rusty at all," I said.

Not even begrimed. Duncan must have painstakingly cleaned it if it had been in the lake since a time when swords had been carried regularly in the world.

"It was in surprisingly good condition when I found it. Freshwater, in general, isn't as corrosive as seawater, and I think the magic in it is protective. I had a specialist look at it, and he said the alloy was also atypical." Duncan held my gaze and said with significance, "It has silver in it."

I met his eyes. "Are you giving me the means to..."

"Kill me if I'm forced to come after you again. Yes."

Even in my wolf form, I hadn't been strong enough to defeat him, not when he'd been the bipedfuris.

"I'd prefer not to do that," I said.

Duncan offered a lopsided smile that took the seriousness from his eyes. "I'd prefer you not need to do that."

"Yet you're giving me a silver sword."

"Just in case."

"Okay." I set the gifts aside and hugged him.

"Ah." He returned the embrace and rested his chin on my shoulder. "This is nice. Also the fact that my van hasn't been towed or salvaged for saleable items."

"I've been too busy to call a pawn broker in to appraise its contents."

"Too busy... cleaning the roofs?"

"My work is demanding, yes."

"Do you want some help?" Duncan looked toward the pressure washer on the roof. "I could hold your hose."

"That sounds kinky. And I think I'm supposed to offer to hold *your* hose."

"True. Maybe I should simply sit up there, look pretty, and hand you chocolates while you work."

"Now *that* sounds appealing."

THE END

Thank you for reading! If you'd like to continue on with the series, the next adventure is *Kin of the Wolf* (Magnetic Magic, Book 3).

Made in the USA
Las Vegas, NV
08 February 2025